RO
(1+)
4.00

Special thanks to our well-wishers, who have contributed their congratulations and support.

"The best historicals, the best romances. Simply the best!"
—Dallas Schulze

"Bronwyn Williams was born and raised at Harlequin Historicals. We couldn't have asked for a better home or a more supportive family."
—Dixie Browning and Mary Williams, w/a Bronwyn Williams

"I can't believe it's been ten years since *Private Treaty*, my first historical novel, helped launch the Harlequin Historicals line. What a thrill that was! And the beat goes on...with timeless stories about men and women in love."
—Kathleen Eagle

"Nothing satis... ...ng a Harlequin His... ...oricals are the ultimat... ...everyday life."
—Ruth Ryan Langan

"As a writer and reader, I've always felt that Harlequin Historicals celebrate a perfect blend of history and romance, adventure and passion, humor and sheer magic."
—Theresa Michaels

"Thank you, Harlequin Historicals, for opening up a 'window into the past' for so many happy readers."
—Suzanne Barclay

"As a one-time 'slush pile' foundling at Harlequin Historicals, I'll be forever grateful for having been rescued and published as one of the first 'March Madness' authors. Harlequin Historicals has always been *the* place for special stories, ones that blend the magic of the past with the rare miracle of love for books that readers never forget."
—Miranda Jarrett

"A rainy evening. A cup of hot chocolate. A stack of Harlequin Historicals. Absolute bliss! Happy 10th Anniversary and continued success."
—Cheryl Reavis

"Happy birthday, Harlequin Historicals! I'm proud to have been a part of your ten years of exciting historical romance."
—Elaine Barbieri

"Harlequin Historical novels are charming or disarming with dashes and clashes. These past times are fast times, the gems of romances!"
—Karen Harper

HONOR'S BRIDE

GAYLE WILSON

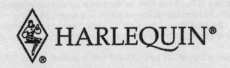

TORONTO • NEW YORK • LONDON
AMSTERDAM • PARIS • SYDNEY • HAMBURG
STOCKHOLM • ATHENS • TOKYO • MILAN • MADRID
PRAGUE • WARSAW • BUDAPEST • AUCKLAND

For Sandra, the very best example of two wonderful relationships in life, being both my dear friend and my kinsman.

ISBN 0-373-29032-2

HONOR'S BRIDE

Printed in U.S.A.

"Are you mocking me, Major?" Judith asked, her lips tilting in amusement.

"I assure you I am not, ma'am. And it won't work, you know," he said, his own teasing grin answering that small smile.

"What won't work?"

"Distracting me. It's been tried before, I promise you. And it's far too late for you to pretend to be missish."

"Missish?" She repeated the word unbelievingly. "How dare you insult me?"

Then she laughed, spoiling the effect of her pretended anger. It was only a breath of sound, almost intimate. Hearing it, Kit realized suddenly that he had no right to be there, no matter the pretense he used.

He had no right to banter with her as if they were at some London party. As he had no right to demand that she take care of herself. No rights at all where Mrs. Haviland was concerned....

Also available from Harlequin Historicals and
GAYLE WILSON

Prologue

London, 1808

"You, sir, are a blackguard and a rogue," the earl of Ryde said softly. "A charming scoundrel, by all accounts, but a scoundrel nonetheless."

Never before had his father subjected him to such a scathing dissection of his character. Of course, never before had he killed a man, Lord St. John acknowledged ruefully. But there were mitigating circumstances behind that death, none of which his father was taking into consideration.

Kit's well-shaped lips tightened, as they had for the last fifteen minutes, over a defense of his actions which he longed to make. Even if he attempted a justification of what he'd done, he knew from bitter experience that nothing would prevent the rest of his father's tirade. Once Ryde reached the point of openly expressing his anger, which happened infrequently, then nothing could deter him. That was a reality Kit had had ample cause to understand through the years.

"More importantly," his father went on, "you continue to bring dishonor to this family. You may enjoy wallowing in the mud of public censure, but I will no longer allow you to drag the Montgomery name there with you. We have endured more than enough of your scandals,'' the earl said softly. "Far more than enough."

Throughout this exchange, in actuality an encounter too one-sided to be classified as exchange, the earl's voice had been filled with contempt and cutting in its sarcasm, but it had never risen. The guiding principle of the earl of Ryde's life had always been control, which was why, of course, his relationship with his younger son was so volatile.

Kit Montgomery, Lord St. John, was almost a throwback, far more attuned to the exploits of his warrior ancestors than to the man before whom he stood today. Yet, ironically, St. John was also the epitome of what was now considered to be the fashionable London gentleman.

Both handsome and confident, Kit was immensely popular with the ladies. The masculine set admired him because he was also a reckless and daring sportsman and a skillful gambler. He frequently wagered stakes whose loss would bankrupt half the businesses in the English capital without the blink of an eye.

Given those accomplishments and his natural physical attributes, St. John had been, since his introduction into society, one of its most popular members. Yet he had become almost too accustomed to winning: at cards, at sporting events, and especially in affairs of the heart. His present boredom with the normal activities of the *ton* had led him to push against the few boundaries that constrained young men of his class.

"Wild" was the epithet most frequently applied to Kit by his parents' contemporaries. His fellow Corinthians considered him simply "Top of the Trees," their highest compliment. The ladies found him to be frustratingly elusive, although undeniably exciting. And his father...

Again Kit tamped down his resentment. Never before had his father called him a blackguard or accused him of dishonoring the Montgomery name. Despite their differing views regarding proper behavior for a gentleman, both Ryde and his son understood family honor. Its principles had been instilled in the younger Montgomerys since their births. The name Kit bore was old and proud, and he had never sought to blacken it.

"You have sullied our name," his father said, almost echoing that thought. "And this time I intend to assure myself that it will never happen again."

The dreaded words had the desired effect, although Kit's classically handsome face did not change. His blue eyes, surrounded by their sweep of long, soot-black lashes met his father's calmly, reflecting only disdain for the threat.

That was not, however, the emotion which seethed beneath the surface. *Disinherited.* He had certainly been warned. His own brother had attempted to explain his father's growing disgust, but despite Roger's cautions, Kit hadn't listened.

He knew there was nothing in his behavior that differed from that of dozens of other young men about town. Except the possibility that he did it all better than anyone else. That was always his goal, and neither he nor his father had ever stopped to evaluate the origin of that particular characteristic.

"Am I to understand you, sir—" Kit began, his voice as dispassionate as the earl's, only to be sharply cut off.

"Understand me?" Ryde questioned derisively. "If you do, St. John, it will certainly be the first time."

"Do you intend to disinherit me, sir?" Kit continued stubbornly.

The earl laughed, the sound scornful. The small flush that had stained the young man's high cheekbones since the beginning of this interview, the only sign of his discomfort, deepened.

"I swear I would," the earl continued, "if I believed that might make you a better man. I'm afraid instead it would simply make you a poorer one."

"I do not fear poverty," Kit said, his eyes now as hard as those of the man seated behind the massive rosewood desk.

"I wonder what you *do* fear," Ryde said. "If I knew that, perhaps I would have some chance of insuring that your worthless life might eventually bear some snatch of honor."

It was Shakespeare, of course, the phrase easily recognized. After all, St. John had been properly educated—at Eton and then Cambridge, and he had done remarkably well at his studies. There was a fine intellect hidden beneath the outward recklessness, but one which had found nothing after university worthy of challenging it.

Kit excelled at calculating the chances that a certain card would fall, at placing wagers in the betting books, and even at figuring to the minute how fast he must push his horses through a particular stage in order to beat the current record along one of the coach roads. Those were not, however, activities which occupied the intellect long enough to provide the type of stimulation Kit had once found in his studies.

Yet a gentleman was not permitted to undertake anything more mentally challenging after the end of his school days. His family's vast estates were managed by professionals, whose activities were competently overseen by his father. At the earl's death the care of those properties would pass into the hands of Kit's older brother, Roger, who had been trained from birth to accept that role.

But for Kit and other younger sons, aristocrats like him,

there was really nothing important to do. Nothing to occupy their brains or their energies, too much of which were expended on activities that called down the disgust of their elders. Ennui had almost certainly played a role in Kit's misadventures, but even had he recognized that fact, there was still nothing society would allow him to do about it.

"Honor, sir?" Kit repeated softly.

"You have now killed a man through your recklessness. And over a woman, of course. I expect the knock of the magistrates on the door of this house at any moment. And may I remind you that is something which has never happened before in its long history. Until now. Until you," his father added.

"It was a duel, sir," Kit reminded him.

His father was certainly aware of the circumstances. Receiving an explanation of the events which had led to that disastrous dawn meeting was not the point of this exercise. The purpose of the earl's diatribe was chastisement. And humiliation. Kit understood that when he had been summoned.

"I never meant to kill Edmonton," Kit went on. "He shouldn't have died from that scratch. I put the ball exactly where I intended. His surgeon did more, I assure you, to cause his death than I. What he had said, however, could not in all honor be ignored. I do not believe that even you, sir—"

"Forgive me, St. John, but I find that I am uninterested in whatever you believe. *If* you truly believe in anything. I must confess I find myself doubtful of that, also."

"Also?" Kit repeated. Despite his efforts to match his father's control, his quick temper was beginning to rise.

"As I am doubtful that you are capable of change."

"I promise you—"

"I am also uninterested in your promises. I believe I

have heard them all before. Frankly, I am becoming uninterested in *you*, St. John. In your endless escapades and
your callous disregard for anything beyond your immediate
pleasures.''

Although it was not a fair assessment of the man he was,
Kit held both his tongue and his temper. It was better to
let his father have his say, to listen in respectful silence,
and then to absent himself from the earl's presence, and
therefore from his attentions, for a few weeks. It had always
worked before.

''So I am going to make you an offer,'' Ryde said. His
eyes swept slowly down the tall, handsome figure of his
son, standing unconsciously at attention before him.

Kit's clothing was the finest London had to offer, and he
wore it to perfection. The coat of navy superfine had been
cut by Weston's master hand, its color chosen to emphasize
the striking contrast between the blue eyes and the curling,
coal-black hair that fell over his forehead. The jacket covered a lawn shirt of dazzling whiteness, an intricately tied
cravat, and a striped silk waistcoat.

Fawn pantaloons stretched over his flat belly and down
the long, muscular legs of a horseman. The tasseled boots,
made of Moroccan leather, were from Toby, and they were
polished daily by his valet with a preparation whose primary ingredient was champagne. The whole ensemble had
cost more than most families in England lived on for a year.

''And I encourage you to think carefully before you turn
it down,'' Ryde added softly.

''An offer, sir?'' St. John said cautiously. This was a
deviation from the familiar format of their previous encounters.

''An opportunity,'' the earl amended. ''An opportunity

to add something which has been missing from your worthless existence for the last twenty-eight years. An opportunity to finally undertake something of real value, to give meaning to what has been, up to this point, an empty and meaningless life.''

Again Kit's lips tightened, but he swallowed the angry rejoinder. That life had not been his choice. As the younger son of a peer his options were extremely limited. There was no question, certainly not among the ladies of the demimonde, that St. John was highly unsuited for the clergy, and the only other career available. . .

''You once asked my permission to enter the navy,'' the earl continued.

''I believe I was sixteen at the time,'' Kit said, fighting a smile, despite the seriousness of the situation, ''and enamored of the uniform.''

''Indeed,'' said his father coldly.

That gibe had been a mistake, St. John realized with regret. One did not offer humor in the midst of Ryde's chastisements.

''But still, an honorable profession, don't you think?'' the earl asked. His thin lips lifted, echoing the inquiring rise of one brow, but there was no matching amusement in the cold eyes.

''Yes, my lord,'' Kit agreed, apprehension at the direction of this conversation stirring in his stomach.

''However, I do not believe the navy would accept the offer of your services. They prefer men from something higher than the criminal classes, or so I have heard.''

Ryde's bitter smile had faded. Apparently he took no joy in the vicious blow with which he had just struck his son. Again, St. John fought for restraint.

"The army, on the other hand," the earl continued, "is, as I understand, somewhat more desperate and therefore less discriminating. I assume even you know that Sir Arthur Wellesley is being sent to Iberia to fight the French."

There was a long silence. It was so prolonged that the sounds of carriage wheels moving on the cobblestones of the city street below drifted between the two men.

"You wish me to join him," Kit said finally.

"*If* they'll take you," Ryde said insultingly. "But, being the army, I imagine they will. And I still have some influence. I'm offering to buy your commission. Not a very lofty one, I'm afraid, my generosity being naturally limited by my disgust. But then it will be better than life as a penniless fugitive on the Continent, I suppose."

"And if I refuse?" Kit asked.

"I don't believe it will be a great loss to this family. Your mother shall miss you, of course. And your brother. For a time," the earl added.

The thin lips pursed, and then Ryde's gaze fell to the correspondence spread across the gleaming surface of his desk. His long white fingers, which had toyed with a gold lorgnette throughout this interview, closed around it with purpose now, directing the glass toward the topmost document.

"I accept," Kit said softly.

His father's eyes lifted and rested briefly on the elegant figure before him. "Perhaps Wellesley and Spain can make a man of you," Ryde said. "It's far more than I have been able to manage."

Again his gaze dropped, and although his son stood before the desk for at least a full minute more, the earl never looked up again. There was no way that Ryde could know it would be almost three years before he would see Kit again. And even had he known that, of course, it would have made not a whit's worth of difference in his behavior.

"I'm sorry, Judith, but there it is. He's within his rights to question why this marriage has not already taken place. And, given the circumstances, why it should be any longer delayed."

Judith McDowell contemplated her father's face, reading far more from the furrowed brow and the unsmiling lips than she had from the gruff words he had just uttered.

This had not been her father's choice, she knew. But he had given his word, and to General Aubrey McDowell his word was more than his bond. It was his honor. If honor demanded the sacrifice of his only daughter to repay a debt, then that was how it must be.

"But surely..." Judith said, seeking only to delay that which she had always known to be inevitable. She had been promised to Michael Haviland since childhood, and the fact that they had not already married was only because of her father's reluctance and Haviland's indifference.

"Wellesley leaves for Spain within the month. Michael's regiment will go with him. Sir Roland wishes you to accompany his son. As his wife."

Judith held her tongue, but the breath she took was deep, lifting the lace fichu that lay over her high breasts. Not Michael's wish, she was aware, but his father's. General Roland Haviland had chosen a wife for his son almost ten years ago, and neither Michael nor she had had any say in the arrangement.

She realized that most people would believe this match to be well made, certainly from her standpoint. She had no

position, no wealth to bring to any union, and her looks
were not those which attracted the attention of gentlemen
who were well-fixed enough to overlook those other det-
riments.

Judith McDowell was tall and slim, with soft brown hair
and dark eyes, which were thoughtful enough never to have
been described as sparkling. Her complexion was most
kindly referred to as olive, and despite the best efforts of
her abigail, none of the popular remedies of the day would
lighten it. Perhaps even more of a handicap than those were
her quick wit and her inability to suffer fools, gladly or
otherwise.

Judith had had her Season, of course. Her father and her
aunt Jane had dutifully seen to that, although it had not
been strictly necessary, given her situation. And it had not
been a singular success, if one judged by the number of
names on her dance card or by the gentlemen waiting each
evening to take her to supper. That didn't make any difference, of course, except as a matter of pride, since she
was already unofficially betrothed.

During Judith's time in London, Michael Haviland had
called when he was in town, but with his duties his presence in society had been a very rare occasion. The round
of parties, routs, and balls her aunt had arranged invitations
to was quickly over, and then, gratefully, Judith had been
allowed to return to the place she loved best—her father's
large, old country house, whose library she had already
devoured by the time she was fifteen.

It was almost ironic that it should be in this very room
that her father chose to deliver this painfully unwelcome
news. Its familiar genteel shabbiness should have been
comforting to her distress perhaps—the low, pleasant fire,

the tea tray, the dearly beloved books and the worn furniture. These were the things she loved best in the world, and she had truly never missed the whirlwind round of London entertainments that she had so briefly been exposed to.

There were always other things to occupy her time in the country—reading, of course; caring for the animals that belonged to the manor; taking long walks across the moors or along shaded country lanes; and chatting with her elderly neighbors, who welcomed her visits and who had taught her so many things from their vast store of country wisdom.

Judith McDowell's life was, to her at least, full and rich. And the prospect of following the drum in a strange country with a man whom she did not particularly admire was not, she was finding, a pleasant one.

"It's a hard life for a woman," her father said. "You know, Ju, that I would never have wished..." His voice faded, the open expression of that wish forbidden by his conscience.

But, of course, she knew it all. The story had been told to her from childhood, and it had never changed. General McDowell owed his life to Roland Haviland because of an act of heroism on some distant battlefield. This was a long-standing debt of honor which led to the agreement the two had made concerning their children's futures.

"I know," she said. From somewhere within the devastation her father had just made of her ordered and orderly life, she found a smile for him. He was worried about her, of course. He knew better than most, far better than she could, what she would face as an officer's wife on campaign in a hostile country.

Her mother had followed her father to his posting in India shortly after their marriage. Judith had been born there, but her mother's health had been permanently broken by the confinement and the climate, and she had died of an unnamed fever within the year. Judith had been sent back to England and placed in her aunt's care until her father's return several years later.

"Haviland's not the man I would have chosen for you, my dear, but there was no way, of course, for either of us to foresee..." Again, her father's words drifted into silence.

Not the man I would have chosen. Not the man Judith would have chosen, either, she knew. In her few encounters with him, she had found Michael Haviland to be arrogant, proud, and brusque to the point of rudeness. His looks were not unpleasant, but his manner during his brief visits had been off-putting to both her father and herself.

They had not discussed that, of course, but they knew one another too well to be in any doubt about the impression Haviland had made on each of them. Not only was Judith not in love with her fiancé, she had found little enough to like about him.

However, since she had not yet met a man who caused her heart to behave at all strangely in her very practical breast, Judith McDowell was beginning to believe, as the world already did, that her match with Michael Haviland was the best she might hope for. And of course, it was the wish of her father and his. More than a wish, she acknowledged. It was to them both a matter of their honor. Of a promise made that must be kept, no matter the circumstances.

If the marriage did not create emotions which matched the romantic fantasies written about in the popular novels of the day or correspond to the giggling revelations of those ethereal blond creatures she had encountered in London, whose dance cards were always full and who knew exactly what to say to gentlemen to make them laugh, then it was just as well. There was probably little place for romance in the ranks of an army on the move.

It would be her duty to become the kind of wife a man who has been sent to fight for his country needed. She could accomplish that, she had no doubt. She was far stronger than her mother had ever been, and she was clever about many things, even if she had never learned to flirt.

She would make her father and her husband proud of her strength and resourcefulness, Judith decided. Never by word or deed would she indicate to either that this was not the path she had wished her life to take.

And after all, she acknowledged practically, it really wasn't as if she had any other choice.

Chapter One

Portugal, 1811

The sound of a whip striking the back of a man who has already endured over eighty strokes is a sound like no other. The sharp crack of the leather thongs against intact skin had at first been accompanied by soft grunts of pain, but both those noises had long ago become something else.

The efforts of the small, trembling man to remain silent before his assembled peers had eventually given way to begging and then to shrieks. Now, after a long time, the leather was sodden, and the skin was certainly no longer intact—not one square inch of it. The watching men had fallen silent, and the flogged trooper's head hung loosely between the tripod of lances to which he had been tied.

Major Lord St. John deliberately raised his eyes from the scene before him to find those of his commander. The blue eyes inquired. Colonel Smythe's head moved once, the arc of movement small enough to be undetected by anyone paying less attention to that order than St. John, but it had undoubtedly been a negative.

One hundred strokes of the lash had been ordered, and

they were to be delivered. Lord Wellington's orders on that point had been unmistakably clear, and they were well-known to the men.

Except in this case it was almost certainly the wrong man who was receiving that punishment, St. John thought bitterly. Involuntarily, his mouth flattened as the whip fell again. Mercifully, the limp body of Private Toby Reynolds didn't even jerk in response. At least he would not feel the last twenty, and when it was finally over...

Kit's eyes again moved, this time meeting those of the only woman among the assembled troops. Who was watching *him,* St. John realized, rather than the punishment being administered. Judith Haviland had chosen to attend this public spectacle of military brutality, and when the trooper was cut down, it would be Mrs. Haviland's competent hands that would attend to what remained of the skin of his back.

Her brown eyes were calm and uncondemning as they met Kit's. After almost three years spent with the English army on the Peninsula, Mrs. Haviland had seen every horror known to man, and she had flinched from none of them.

St. John wondered if she understood why Toby Reynolds was being punished. Not the actual charge, of course. That had been read before the first stroke of the whip descended. The man had been caught stealing from the peasants in the nearby village, and theft was something that an army dependent upon the goodwill of the local populace could not afford.

The French army lived off the land and was hated for it. The British would not, not if Wellington could help it. So far the English general's genius for supply had served them well. His forces had seldom gone hungry, not for bread or for beef, which they carried with them on the hoof.

But St. John's regiment had recently been deployed as

an outpost to guard a vital yet remote road against the arrival of French reinforcements. The duty was not unusual for the highly mobile light dragoons, most adept of any of Wellington's units at scouting, intelligence-gathering, and hit-and-run actions.

This time, however, they been sent so far in advance of Wellington's winter encampment that they had apparently been lost or forgotten. At least, the supply wagons had failed to arrive when expected.

Rations had been cut and then cut again. There were still biscuits, but several of the last barrels of salt beef they had received had been spoiled and inedible. There had been no issue of either rum or wine in more than a month. And no pay.

Kit himself had been sent to negotiate with the locals for whatever provisions were available, for the troopers and perhaps more importantly for the irreplaceable horses. The villagers had little to sell, and in truth the regiment had little with which to buy or trade.

Yet up until now discipline had held through the deprivation. Most of the dragoons, seasoned veterans in this campaign, had been on short rations before. They trusted Wellington, knowing from experience that the supplies would eventually reach them and had simply resigned themselves to waiting out the discomfort. Except, apparently, for Captain Michael Haviland, Kit thought.

There was no doubt in his mind that Haviland had sent his batman to loot in the nearby village, and Kit was certain it had not been the first time. There had been items missing from their own supplies in the past, in all likelihood stolen and then traded to the Portuguese by Haviland and Reynolds. When the regiment's stores which were worth bartering ran out, the two had been forced to resort to stealing what they wanted.

This time the batman had been caught and brought back to the colonel to receive his prescribed punishment, a punishment which every man in this army was well aware of and which most recognized as necessary. As, of course, would Judith Haviland.

He might feel differently about the theft, Kit acknowledged, despite the fact that such a thing endangered them all, had he believed the batman had been sent to procure something which Mrs. Haviland needed, either food or clothing.

Not a man here would begrudge her anything, and most of them, himself included, would willingly have taken those hundred stripes to provide whatever she lacked. But the wine which Haviland's batman had been caught stealing was not for Mrs. Haviland. And everyone watching his punishment today was well aware of that fact.

Haviland's drunkenness was no secret to the regiment. How he continued to procure spirits when there was no official issue had once been mysterious and was now no longer. But if he desired further stimulation from drink, St. John supposed, the captain would have to do his own procuring from now on.

Not that it would make much difference whether he did or not. A sober Michael Haviland in the field was not a particular improvement over a drunken one. That had already been demonstrated on several occasions.

The terrible noise the lash made had stopped, Major St. John realized suddenly. The enormous sergeant who had been chosen to administer the hundred strokes was awaiting his orders.

"Cut him down," he commanded.

The peasants from the village had already been generously compensated by the colonel for their trouble and given an apology. They had been invited to witness the

trooper's punishment, but had chosen, wisely perhaps, not
to.

I damn well wish I had had that option, St. John thought.
No matter how many times he had seen this, it was never
any easier. Not even knowing that it was necessary. And
just.

An army at war maintained discipline. That was only one
of the lessons Kit had learned in the years he had spent on
the Peninsula. He wasn't sure his service had accomplished
what his father had intended, but there were, without any
doubt, lessons he had learned that he would never in his
life forget.

"May I tend him?" Judith Haviland asked softly.

Kit glanced down to meet those remarkable eyes again.
Mrs. Haviland was standing beside his horse, almost at his
knee, her left hand soothing over the neck of the bay. Her
fingers were slender, and they had not lost the summer's
tan. These were not the soft, white hands of a lady, not any
longer, but they had proven more valuable than any others
in the regiment.

"Of course," Kit agreed. Seeing to Reynolds's injuries
was a task he didn't envy her, but one at which she had
experience.

"Thank you," she said simply.

She turned to follow the troopers who were dragging the
unconscious body of her husband's batman to the large tent
which served as the unit's makeshift hospital, and St.
John's gaze unconsciously followed.

The bottom of Mrs. Haviland's gray kersey skirt was
damp and caked along the hem with mud, as were her half
boots. Her soft brown hair had been braided and wound
into a loose chignon, but curling strands of it had escaped
and drifted around the back of her neck and shoulders as
she struggled over the rough, snow-covered ground.

The heavy skirt was not full enough to completely camouflage the contours of the body it covered. Her hips were slim, yet womanly, below a narrow waist that led upward to high, firm breasts.

Conscious suddenly that he was taking an inventory, part of it from memory, of the body of a fellow officer's wife, Kit forced his eyes down to his gloved hands, to the reins threaded loosely between his fingers. And he wondered again at his undeniable attraction to Judith Haviland.

There was nothing in her appearance or her demeanor that would have attracted him three years ago. Nothing that would have warranted a second look from the man he had been then. But, of course, he was no longer that man.

And he *was* attracted to Judith Haviland. It was not a temptation he would ever do anything about, though. In all honor, she was for him the most forbidden of women. However, after fighting against it for three years, the attraction he felt was one he no longer bothered to deny. Not to himself at least.

When Kit reentered his tent, Michael Haviland was waiting for him. The confrontation shouldn't have been unexpected, he supposed, but it was. Somehow he had thought Haviland would have the decency to stay out of sight until the remembrance of this morning's exercise in military discipline had faded. But of course, decency was not something that meant a great deal to Captain Haviland.

"I suppose you took some satisfaction over that," Haviland said angrily. "Beating half to death a man who couldn't defend himself."

He had been drinking. It was obvious by the slight slurring of the word "satisfaction." He was also unshaven and his uniform was stained, but neither of those things was unusual enough to occasion comment. War made men or it broke them. And despite his family's long and distinguished military tradition, it was obvious which effect it had had on this one.

"You're a fool," Kit said coldly. He stripped off his gloves and threw them on the narrow cot, which with his folding campaign desk and his small chest made up the entire furnishings of the tent, and the entirety of his belongings. "You must have known he'd be caught eventually."

"Are you accusing me of *sending* Reynolds to that village?"

"Here?" St. John asked. "Between the two of us? Then yes, of course, I am. And you may thank Smythe's respect for your father that that same accusation was not made in front of the regiment or in the dispatches."

"If it had been, I would have called him out. He knows that. So should you," Michael said. His eyes were bloodshot, and his cheeks were gaunt, almost gray beneath the surface tan.

"You may do so now, you know," Kit offered. He found himself wishing the bastard would.

"So you can kill me, too?" Haviland mocked. "Save your threats and your chivalry for the French, St. John. Everyone knows why you're here, relegated to this bloody backwater unit. Your own father couldn't stand having you in England any longer. You're not fit to sit in judgment on anyone. Certainly not on me."

Kit's fingers trembled over the button he had been pushing through its opening. By a conscious act of will, he controlled them and his automatic response to the contempt he heard in Haviland's voice.

"I may have been responsible for a man's death," he said softly, the blue eyes hard, "but I've never let another man suffer for my crimes. And I have never in my life mistreated a woman.''

Haviland laughed. "That's what this is, isn't it? This isn't about Reynolds or the wine or Wellington's prissing Methodist orders. This is all about Judith.''

"One has nothing to do with the other,'' St. John denied.

"And you're a bloody liar, my lord. One has *everything* to do with the other. But she is *my* wife, you know. I'll damn well do with her what I will. And there is nothing you or Smythe or anyone else can do about it.''

Suddenly Kit was very still, exerting a rigid self-control that would have made his father proud. What he wanted to do with the hand that he forced to move calmly to the next gold button was to drive it into the nose of the drunken coward who stood before him.

Haviland was right. There was nothing he could do. Especially when Mrs. Haviland herself claimed that the bruise which had marred the smooth, fragile line of her jaw this past week was the result of an accident.

There was not a man in the regiment who believed that. And not one who was willing to add to Mrs. Haviland's shame by openly questioning her explanation. Though several of them had come to him privately, however, to express their concerns.

They were not gentlemen, not even by the lowly standards of the army, but they had enough of what Haviland mockingly called chivalry to know that if ever a woman was undeserving of a blow from her husband's fist, it was Judith Haviland.

"An angel is what she is, Major St. John,'' one of the troopers had said. "You know that, and we know it. And it's not right that that bastard should abuse her.''

Judith would have been the first to laugh at that complimentary sobriquet, but it was not far from the truth. Not to the men of this regiment, depleted by illness and battle losses to less than half its original strength. Theirs had been one of the units left in Portugal after Sir John Moore's army departed after Corunna, so they had been in continual service since the beginning of this campaign. And had suffered for it.

There were three other married women in camp, wives of enlisted men chosen by lot to accompany their husbands onto the transports. They and the camp followers handled the cooking and laundry, what little there was of either.

But Judith was the only officer's wife, and as such, in a class by herself. And although it was not a fitting task for a lady, with her knowledge of herbs and their effects, it was Mrs. Haviland who saw to their wounds when they were away from the surgeons that accompanied the main force.

She also wrote countless letters for the men, most of whom were illiterate, and in the case of a trooper's death, her letter of condolence always went home to the family, along with the colonel's. She had suffered with them, without a single complaint, all the endless deprivations of war, which no English gentlewoman should have had to endure.

Angel, St. John thought, remembering the earnest, wind-burned face of the Yorkshireman who had called her that. He was right, of course. She should never have to suffer this bastard's abuse again.

"Be warned, Haviland," St. John said in immediate, unthinking response to that realization. "If you ever strike your wife again, I *will* kill you. And you're wise to remind us both that you won't be the first man I've shot. There is not a man in this regiment who would bring charges against me or who would feel compelled to testify at my court-martial even if I did it openly, with the regiment drawn up in square to watch. You might want to remember that."

"Are you threatening me, you noble popinjay?" Haviland asked, his mouth arranged in the smirk Kit had grown to hate.

"If you like," Kit agreed softly. "I prefer to think of it as a promise, maybe simply a word to the wise, but you are certainly free to take it any way you wish."

He shrugged out of his coat and turned away from his visitor. Despite the pervasive winter dampness, his shirt had become soaked with sweat while he supervised the flogging. "Now if you'll excuse me, Captain Haviland," he suggested, "I must remind you that I have other things to do. I'm sure you have duties to attend to as well."

"She won't have you, you know," Haviland said, ignoring the obvious dismissal. "She might like to. You know more about that than I, I suppose. They say you're very…experienced with women. But even if she fancies you, St. John, Judith won't do anything about it. It would go against everything that old prig taught her, against everything she believes."

Kit didn't turn around, afraid that something in his features, no matter how carefully he schooled them, would reveal his disgust. Or more importantly would let Haviland know that his jeering comments had struck home.

"That's a pity for you, of course," Haviland went on, despite the determined lack of response from his victim. "For such a brown mouse, she's really *quite* entertaining. Especially on a cold night like this one is going to be. I'll be sure to think about you while I'm topping her," he promised, his voice full of vindictive amusement. "And who knows? Maybe she will think about you, too."

Only when Kit heard the flap of the tent fall, the movement of the stiff canvas audible even above the rush of blood pounding through his temples, did he allow himself to react. He closed his eyes, thinking about what Haviland had said.

She won't have you, you know. The bastard was right about that. Kit understood Judith Haviland's concept of honor as well as her husband did. As well as he understood his own. He had never believed otherwise.

But it had been the last of Haviland's words which would live in his imagination. And tonight, as he lay on the hard mattress of his cot, alone in this small tent, he would certainly remember them. Along with the dark bruise that was still visible on Judith's clear olive skin.

"How is he?" St. John asked, his voice kept very low out of consideration for the injured man.

Judith Haviland looked up at him, laying the book she had been reading by the light of the brazier down in her lap. It was one he had loaned her from his small collection, a volume of obscure Latin poets she confessed she hadn't seen.

She smiled at him, but shook her head slightly. "I have nothing else to give him," she whispered, her eyes troubled. "I administered the last of the laudanum. When he wakes up…" She shrugged, slender shoulders lifting under the thick woolen shawl. "If I only had something else, *anything* else. I've worried about the effect of spirits on the wounded, but at least with that, as with the drug, there is some blessed oblivion."

She turned to consider the man lying prone on the cot on the far side of the tent. A coarse blanket had been pulled up to his waist, and his ruined back was mercifully covered by a poultice which Mrs. Haviland had almost certainly brewed with her own hands and placed there.

Judith's profile was briefly limned against the low glow of the fire, and St. John wondered suddenly how he could have once thought her to be ordinary. The line of brow, nose and chin the light revealed was classic, pure and incredibly beautiful.

And she is another man's wife. A man who had justly accused Kit of coveting her. A man Kit had threatened to kill if he touched her again. *Touched* reverberated within his head, and the image he had fought since his confrontation with Haviland was all at once there as well, as clear in his mind's eye as the profile outlined against the flames.

Judith Haviland slowly turned back to face him, questioning his silence perhaps. "What's wrong?" she asked, her voice soft.

"Do you have a cup?" St. John asked instead of answering.

Her brow furrowed slightly at the request, but she didn't question it. "Of course," she said.

She brought him the cup, a tin one, battered through its travels, and held it out to him enclosed in the slender fingers he had admired. He produced from behind his back, almost like a conjurer, the canteen he'd brought. He took the cup she offered and, after pouring a small measure of dark liquid into it, held it out to her. When he looked up from that task, her eyes met his, full of wonder.

"Rum." She had identified his offering by its pungent aroma. "Where in the world did you get this?"

"A private store. I've been saving it for an emergency," Kit confessed, unable to resist the urge to smile at her.

"And you're willing to let me have it for Private Reynolds?"

"This is for you—what's in the cup. The rest you may do with as you see fit. I'm only sorry I hadn't thought to give it to you before now."

"It's very generous of you, Major St. John, but I think, if you don't mind, that he needs it more than I."

"But I *do* mind. It's cold, and despite your fortitude, it can't have been easy watching what was done today. Or easy doing that," he said, gesturing toward the figure on the cot.

She shook her head, her eyes falling again to the cup. "I promise you—" she began.

"Drink it, or I shall keep the rest. You can do none of us any good if you fall ill from exhaustion. We've come to depend too much on your strength."

Her eyes lifted again, surprisingly luminous in the dimness of the tent. "My strength?" she repeated, her voice filled with the same quiet humor that so often answered the hardships she had faced for the last three years. "Are you mocking me, Major St. John?" she asked, her lips tilting in amusement.

"I assure you I am not, ma'am. And it won't work, you know," he said, his own teasing grin answering that small smile.

"What won't work?"

"Distracting me. It's been tried before, I promise you. And it's far too late for you to pretend to be missish."

"Missish?" she repeated the word unbelievingly. "How dare you insult me?"

Then she laughed, spoiling the effect of her pretended anger. It was only a breath of sound, almost intimate. Hearing it, Kit realized suddenly that he had no right to be here, no matter the pretense he used.

He had no right to banter with her as if they were at some London party. As he had no right to demand that she take care of herself. No rights at all where Mrs. Haviland was concerned.

Even as he thought it, her hand closed around the tin mug, her fingers brushing against his. An unintentional contact. Kit understood that, but the hot jolt of reaction which flared through his body was no less powerful for that knowledge.

Judith raised the cup and, tilting her head back bravely, drank down the draught as if it were a dose of medicine.

"Good girl," he complimented lightly when she had finished.

She raised her hand, using her knuckle to wipe a trickle of the spirits from the corner of her mouth, and he noticed that the skin on the back of her hand was chapped and reddened from the cold.

"Purely for medicinal purposes, I assure you," she said, a spark of mischief in the dark eyes.

"We are agreed as to that," St. John said, handing her the canteen.

"But I promise you the rest of this shall be devoted to my patients. I assure you, Major, I am not yet a secret tippler."

"I never believed you were, ma'am. Pray send me word if there is anything else you need to care for Reynolds."

He had already turned, preparing to retreat from a situation that was far too dangerous, when her question stopped him.

"You believe Michael sent him there, don't you?"

St. John turned back, his blue eyes carefully guileless. "I beg your pardon?" he said.

For a heartbeat there was silence in the tent. Kit forced his eyes to meet the searching ones of Michael Haviland's wife.

"But you must know that it was Reynolds—" she continued, despite the fact that Kit hadn't answered her question.

"Someone had to be held responsible," Kit said. "Whatever the reason he went to the village, Reynolds knew the penalty."

"I don't understand why you would believe that Michael—"

"Good night, Mrs. Haviland." St. John again deliberately cut off whatever else she intended to say.

"Thank you for the rum," she said softly as he raised the flap of the tent, but St. John did not look back.

When she was alone, Judith turned to look at the man on the cot, but the even rise and fall of Toby Reynolds's mutilated back indicated that he was still asleep. She sat down again in the chair by the brazier, but didn't take up her reading.

Instead she held in her hands the battered tin cup St. John had filled for her. Unconsciously, her thumb moved over the dented metal, as she thought about the man who had just left.

She remembered St. John from London, of course. It would be difficult to forget such a striking figure, especially one who caused a clamor of excitement whenever he attended an event at which the young ladies in town for their Season were present.

Judith knew that St. John was almost certainly unaware they had met before. His eyes had skimmed over her face with patent disinterest then. Sally Jamison's brother had made the introduction, and there had been whispers aplenty after St. John had moved on, without bothering, of course, to lead any of their small party onto the dance floor.

That's simply St. John's way, Bob Jamison had assured them when he disappeared into the crowd. *He don't mean anything by it, you understand, but you're all too young.* An involuntary grin had accompanied that pronouncement.

He means we're far too inexperienced to be interesting, Sally had whispered behind her fan. Judith had joined in the laughter, but she hadn't really understood why they laughed. She did now, of course. Because after all, she was neither young nor inexperienced any more.

Despite the fact that St. John's hair was now cropped close for campaigning, and that the evening dress he had worn that night had been replaced by his now less-than-spotless regimentals, the earl of Ryde's younger son would still have set feminine hearts aflutter in any London ballroom.

The unmistakable aura of danger he had carried with him then had not lessened. If anything it had been intensified through the crucible of war, through his exposure to real hazards. Judith knew his record, his undeniable bravery in battle.

She had never been called upon to treat him, thank heavens. The minor scrapes St. John received in the last three years had all been attended to by the army surgeons. She wondered if her hands would have trembled if forced to touch his body, as they had trembled tonight when she took the mug from his fingers.

They were long and brown, she remembered, the nails short and very clean, despite the primitive conditions in which they all lived. They were the strong hands of a strong man, and yet they had been as gentle as a woman's the day he had touched the bruise on her jaw.

That had been the only time in the three years she had known him that he had touched her, and that had been in shocked reaction to the evidence of the blow Michael had struck her. St. John's eyes had questioned, and she had answered them with a lie.

He hadn't believed her explanation, of course. It was obvious to everyone, she imagined, what had caused that bruise. She usually was more skillful in avoiding Michael when he was drinking, but she had been tired and cold that night, and there really had been nowhere else to go. There was no privacy in the camp, not even inside the tent they shared.

Until that time Michael had been more careful about where he hit her, not wanting his mistreatment of her revealed to his commander or his fellow officers any more than she did. But every day those inhibitions were weakened by drink, by indifference, by anger over his situation.

Her husband had come to the Peninsula to follow his father's grand plan for his career. The general intended for Michael to use this campaign to rise quickly in rank and then return to London and a favored position in the Horse Guards. Instead, this war had slogged drearily along, and Michael's shortcomings as an officer and a man became more evident with its increasing pressures. When he was sober enough to indulge in self-examination, he worried, as she did, that his father's dreams of glory for him were more likely to end in disgrace.

And that was all the more terrifying after the last letter they had received from home. Michael's father had suffered a stroke and was in very ill health. They both understood he must be protected from the knowledge of his son's failings at any cost. At least Michael still understood that, she thought.

She had been so afraid that this last episode would be reported to the colonel. Not by St. John, of course. She knew instinctively that he would protect her from that humiliation. According to his reputation, he was more likely to call Michael out or to thrash him soundly than to be tempted to report his actions to his commanding officer.

The latter would be no protection against the next time her husband hit her in a fit of drunken anger and frustration. There *was* no protection from that. Michael was her husband, and it was his legal right to treat her as he wished.

Judith found that her fingers had whitened over the small

cup, their grip reflecting her growing realization that this was a situation about which she could do nothing. She was Michael Haviland's wife, and however he treated her, she felt she had to protect both his reputation and the life of his aged father.

But sometimes...she thought, her dark eyes again falling to the tin mug she had taken from St. John's long, brown fingers, it must surely be permissible *sometimes* to wish that her life might have taken a different turn.

Chapter Two

"I thought I would find you here," Michael said. Unheard, he had pushed aside the flap of the medical tent and was standing in its opening, watching her.

Judith knew it must be after midnight. Through Mrs. McQueen, her very efficient helper and the wife of one of the enlisted men, she had sent word to her husband that she would be staying in the medical tent throughout the night. She had assumed Michael would, as he did most of the time, fall asleep as soon as his body hit his cot and never give her whereabouts another thought. Instead...

Judith laid down her book, but with a reluctance that made her ashamed. Michael was her husband, and she felt no joy in his presence. There was no leap of pleasure as she had felt seeing St. John standing in this same place. Assaulted by guilt, she forced her lips into a welcoming smile.

"He seems still to be sleeping from the laudanum," she said. She was beginning to worry about Reynolds's prolonged slumber. There had only been a few drops left in the small brown bottle, but perhaps in his weakened condition, she had given him too much. It was so difficult to tell about the proper dosage.

She stood up and laid aside the book, intending to check on her patient. She presumed her husband had come out of concern for his orderly, but his gaze did not even flicker in the direction of Toby Reynolds. Instead it was focused on her face with an intensity which she suddenly recognized.

She fought any revelation of the revulsion that was her automatic response to his look. She knew what it portended. It was not an expression which she had seen in a long time, but she had not forgotten what it meant.

"I understand St. John visited you earlier. Overcome by a paroxysm of guilt and duty, no doubt?" Michael asked mockingly.

"I think he was sorry for Reynolds. Sorry, perhaps, that it fell to him to see to the punishment."

She knew why St. John had been chosen for that role. He was the most popular by far of the officers. That his popularity was deserved by virtue of his courage was a certainty, but it also owed something to the mantle of leadership which had been bestowed on him at birth. The men were willing to follow him unquestioningly where they might have grumbled about the same orders from another officer. The attitude of common British soldiers toward the aristocrats in their ranks was a paradox, perhaps, but it was well-documented.

"Are you pitying St. John, my dear?" Michael asked. He stepped into the tent, allowing the flap to drop behind him, affording them some privacy.

"Not...pity, of course," she said. It would be hard to pity a man who has everything, she thought. "But I do believe he is not as inured to that sort of duty as one would think."

She turned to look again at her patient, the "victim" of St. John's duty. Before she was even aware that he had moved, her husband's hand caught her chin, holding it tightly. He turned her head, at the same time forcing her face up to his in order to put his mouth over her lips. They opened in a gasp of shock at his unexpected tactic, and his tongue invaded quickly, hot and hard, almost suffocating in its demand.

Judith fought not to recoil. She stood motionless, stoically resolved to endure his unwanted embrace. His head lifted suddenly. When her eyes opened at that miraculous respite, she found him looking into her face, his brow furrowed.

"Where the hell did you get drink?" he asked.

"Major St. John brought rum for Reynolds. He made me drink a measure against the cold."

"Made you?" Haviland repeated, his voice full of amusement. "And have you already administered St. John's medicinal draught to your patient?"

"I—" she began, and then she stopped. She had intended to explain that Reynolds was still sleeping off the effects of the laudanum or had simply lapsed again into unconsciousness after she had applied the new poultice. The words faltered, because suddenly she knew exactly where this was leading.

"Transparent as glass, Judith," her husband said, laughing. "I always know whether or not you are telling the truth. Your face reveals your every emotion."

He still held her chin, her face tilted up to his. "And you might do well to remember that, my dear, when St. John is about. *I* may be understanding of your weakness for our gallant major, but I doubt those who believe you to be a candidate for sainthood would welcome the knowledge that their idol has feet of clay. Especially where her marriage vows are concerned," he added.

"How dare you," Judith whispered. She resisted the urge to jerk her head away or to wipe off her lips the moisture his mouth had left on them. Nausea at what he suggested rose into her throat. She had believed that her unspoken and unacknowledged attraction to St. John was unknown to anyone, including Michael.

Her admiration of the major was only an innocent fantasy, a harmless daydream which she never had any intention of acting upon, of course. But Michael's accusation made her realize how those idle thoughts, if they became known, might be misinterpreted by the malicious. "You have *no* right to—"

"I have *every* right," Michael interrupted, his voice still soft and yet menacing somehow. "I have every right in the world where you are concerned. You would do well not to forget that."

He was right, of course, but her dark eyes remained locked on his in a battle of wills which she was determined not to lose.

He laughed suddenly, contemptuous of her small show of courage. "Tell me where you've hidden it, Ju."

"I don't know what you mean," she said almost defiantly.

His hand lifted, away from her chin and threatening. Instinctively she put her arm up, palm outward to ward off the blow. "I swear, Michael, if you strike me, I'll appeal to Colonel Smythe," she said.

"And shame your father and mine before their old comrade in arms? I don't think that would be wise, my dear. And so cruelly unnecessary. My father's health is precarious now, as you know," he reminded her, smiling.

The seconds drifted by in silence, but their positions did not change. Slowly, Judith's arm fell, and she took a breath. This was the choice she faced. Resistance or humiliation for them all, her father and his. And into that familiar equation was now thrown the reality of what Michael had just threatened.

Given the very small world of the English army, any scandal begun here would surely follow them back to England. By protesting Michael's treatment of her, she would hurt two old men who had lived their lives in such a fashion that neither deserved to endure gossip about the actions of their children.

"It's in the medicine chest," she said.

Michael's mouth relaxed into a wider smile at her capitulation. With the hand he had raised to threaten her, he suddenly caught the braid at the back of her neck and pulled it downward, forcing her chin to lift again. Tears sprang into her eyes. He lowered his mouth to hers with deliberate slowness, holding her moisture-washed eyes. His breath, hot and almost fetid, stirred sickeningly against her nostrils.

His lips closed over hers as his left hand found the softness of her breast. His fingers gripped hard and then he squeezed, deliberately causing pain. She fought not to give him the satisfaction of struggling against his hold, and she did not try to escape his covering mouth to cry out. After all, there might be someone near enough to hear.

Finally, it was over—as she had known it would be. There was something else in this tent that Michael wanted far more than he wanted her. She had been aware of that for a long time.

"That's my sweetling," he said softly, when he had lifted his head. He watched the deep shuddering breath she took, and his lips moved again into a smile, apparently in genuine amusement this time.

He released her and strode quickly to the chest she'd indicated. He rummaged through her meager supply of simples before finding the canteen of rum. He tossed it lightly in his right hand to test its weight and fullness. Again smiling, Michael sketched her a quick salute as he left, allowing the tent flap to drop closed behind him, mercifully leaving her alone.

The attack the following dawn struck the English outpost with lightning swiftness. It came out of the semidarkness almost without warning. Despite the placement of the pickets on the high ground above the road, there had been too little time between the single shot fired by one of the British sentries and the arrival of the first of the French cavalry patrol within the circle of the tents.

They had swept unhampered down the defile and breached the outer ring of security to overrun the camp before the officers could muster any sort of defense. Although seasoned soldiers, most of the English dragoons had been awakened from a sound sleep, stumbling out of their blankets to face cavalry sabers wielded by equally seasoned Frenchmen.

Colonel Smythe and the other officers attempted to impose order. Kit shouted himself hoarse, rallying men to him in the darkness. His efforts had some effect, for although they didn't have time to mount to meet the charge, within a couple of minutes he had gotten them drawn up and firing at the enemy.

The effect of the carbines in the hands of men who knew how to use them was the same on foot or on horseback, and eventually the French began a slow and very professional retreat, melting back into the morning mist along the route they had taken into the valley.

"St. John?" Smythe's voice rang clear in the confusion.

"Here, sir," Kit shouted, moving toward it.

"An advance patrol?" Smythe questioned when they were close enough for conversation, despite the noise of the scattered individual conflicts that surrounded them. Smythe was holding his handkerchief against a bloody cut on his forehead.

"They were as surprised as we were," Kit agreed. "They weren't expecting to find an English outpost this far north of the French lines. I don't think they came to do battle."

"Possibly reinforcements for Massena?" Smythe questioned.

The French commander had given Wellington's army considerable difficulty the previous fall. Rather than risk another encounter after the autumn rains began and yet determined not to abandon Portugal, Massena had dug in, apparently in a desperate attempt to survive the winter and await the promised reinforcements from France.

Intelligence suggested that Napoleon intended to strengthen Massena before the arrival of the English army's own reinforcements, expected some time in March. Colonel Smythe's dragoons had been stationed along this road to notify Wellington of the arrival of any French reinforcements and to delay them until the English commander could move his troops into position.

It seemed too early in the year for any massive troop movements, but the French were hard-pressed for supplies. It was possible Napoleon was sending both soldiers and provisions for his faltering army, which would allow Massena to renew his attack on Wellington instead of retreating back into Spain as the English had hoped. Whatever the situation, Smythe's primary job was to notify Wellington of what was happening in this district, and for that he needed better information about the purpose of the enemy patrol.

"Someone will have to follow them," Smythe said. "I need hard intelligence before I send word to Wellington."

Kit nodded agreement. Although the sky was beginning to lighten, the smoke from the guns was still thick around them, adding to the nightmare quality of the encounter. "And if they *are* the advance guard of a larger force?" he questioned.

"Then get that word back to me as quickly as possible. I need to know the strength of whatever Napoleon has sent."

"Shall we engage them, sir?"

"Not unless you have no other choice. We are ordered to defend this route until Wellington can get us some help, and I need every man we have. We can't afford any more losses simply to give chase to a French patrol. Observe and report, St. John, but avoid a clash. I'll send Haviland's troop with you in case you run into anything unexpected."

"I understand," Kit said.

"St. John and Haviland," Smythe shouted, his voice raised over the confusion, "mount your men."

As soon as Kit had given his own orders, his dragoons rushed to saddle their horses, throwing on their equipment as they ran. Amid the chaos, Kit saw that the men of Haviland's troop were mounting also, according to the colonel's orders, but Haviland wasn't with them. St. John realized that he hadn't seen Haviland since the attack had begun, but given the conditions in the encampment at the time, that was perhaps not too surprising.

"Where's your captain?" he asked Haviland's sergeant.

"I don't know, sir. Haven't seen him. Maybe he's fallen," Sergeant Cochran replied.

There were more than a few dead and wounded men on the ground. In the growing light of day, those who had not been ordered to follow the fleeing French patrol were already beginning to find and give succor to their fallen comrades.

It was possible that Haviland was among the wounded, Kit supposed, but he wondered if it were not more likely that he was hiding in his tent, avoiding the encounter. Then he wondered with self-disgust how much of his suspicion about his fellow officer was colored by Haviland's treatment of his wife. Or by his own admiration for Judith.

"Find him and then follow us," Kit ordered. "Tell him that we are ordered to observe the size of any forces we encounter, but not to engage them. We can't wait on you. We may lose the French if we delay until Captain Haviland has been located."

"Yes, sir, Major St. John," the sergeant said.

His eyes met Kit's in perfect understanding. Haviland's men knew his failings as well as Kit and his colonel did. After all, they were the ones required to follow him into battle. But Kit trusted Haviland's Sergeant Cochran. He was an old India hand. He would do as he was told. And he would make sure Haviland understood his orders. As Kit swung into the saddle, the man was already hurrying to do as he'd been instructed.

St. John knew that as wild and rugged as this country was, if the French got any jump at all on the pursuit, it would be almost impossible to follow them. He really couldn't afford to wait, whatever the cause of Haviland's absence, legitimate or otherwise.

"Taking a break," Lieutenant Scarborough whispered.

He and Kit were stretched out on their bellies, looking down on the beginnings of the valley that stretched north from the opposite end of the pass they'd just traversed. The French patrol had stopped to give their horses a rest and tend to their casualties, apparently unaware that they had been followed.

Kit realized that his squad was heavily outnumbered.

Even with the addition of Haviland's troop, they would not have been a match for the French. They had lost too many men during last summer's campaign and to the winter's illnesses, and then additional casualties had been added in this morning's action.

Smythe hadn't realized how large the French detachment was, of course. Apparently, their attack on the camp had been caused by the undisciplined excitement of the outriders. At finding the English camp asleep, they had rushed into the assault in a headlong pursuit of glory. It was a failing that the English cavalry had often been accused of.

And one I don't intend to be guilty of, Kit thought grimly. His job was to follow this detachment to whatever force they belonged to and then report back on the size of the French reinforcements. Smythe would then be able to provide the hard numbers that Wellington would need to counter any spring push the French made.

It was at that moment that Haviland's squad came riding out of the rocky defile and into the flat, suddenly face-to-face with the French, who reacted quickly. They were remounting and offering defensive fire before the English reached them.

"Bloody hell," Kit said under his breath. "What does that fool think he's doing?" It was already a rhetorical question, given what was happening below, but Scarborough answered it.

"He appears to be attacking them, sir," his young lieutenant said calmly enough. "And they're going to cut him to ribbons."

He was right, of course. The English dragoons had almost staggered backwards, faced with the withering French fire. Now Haviland's men and horses were milling purposelessly, with, it seemed, no one to give them direction.

"Rally your troop, damn it," Kit urged under his breath.

He could pick Haviland out. He wasn't giving orders. He
seemed almost… The thought was incredible, but watching
what was taking place below, Kit was forced to give it
credence. The captain appeared to be drunk. He was almost
reeling in the saddle. And if that were the case…

"Come on," Kit ordered, scrambling up.

He ran, Scarborough following, over the same rocks they
had noiselessly picked their way across only a few minutes
before. Despite Smythe's orders, the enemy had been engaged, and Kit didn't feel he had a choice. He couldn't
leave Haviland's men to suffer that counterattack, heavily
outnumbered and under the command of a drunkard. It
would be little less than a slaughter.

He and the lieutenant swung into their saddles at the
same time and rode as quickly as the rugged terrain would
allow across the ridge, guiding their horses down the steep
slope to where their troop waited below.

"Haviland's squad have run into the French," Kit
shouted to his men.

He owed them no explanation for the charge he was
about to lead, of course. He would offer none that was
critical of his fellow officer. However, he was so infuriated
by Haviland's actions that he no longer felt a great con-
straint to protect his reputation. Haviland was not only disobeying the orders of his commander, he was costing the
lives of his own men.

As they rode to join the battle, it became obvious that
Scarborough had been right in his first appraisal. Haviland's
force was being cut to ribbons. Kit assessed the situation
as his troop poured down the ridge behind him. Instead of
joining the battle surrounding Haviland's scattered command, he led his men direct as an arrow against the French
flank.

The shock was enough to drive them back. It wouldn't

take long, however, for them to realize that they still outnumbered the English. Kit and Scarborough began shouting encouragement to Haviland's dragoons, who, given some direction, began to rally and fight with renewed determination.

This was the kind of fighting that the cavalry of both armies was notorious for—close, brutal and incredibly bloody. The dragoons were laying about with their heavy sabers now, and despite the close-packed horses, far too many of those blows struck their targets, slicing through flesh and cleaving bone.

Fighting with single-minded determination, Kit was almost unaware of the passage of time or of the number of men he engaged. His arm was already beginning to tire, however, from the mechanical rise and fall of his saber, when he was hit. He felt the glancing blow on his left arm, but there was no pain.

Just no pain yet, he acknowledged. The impact had been numbing in its force, almost as if he had been struck with a club instead of a blade. Intellectually, he knew that wasn't true. It was a saber wound, and it was probably deep.

He ignored that knowledge and dispatched the man who had struck him. Using his knees, he urged his charger forward to the next target, a captain who seemed to be in command of the patrol.

The Frenchman's eyes were black, and they glittered beneath the visor of his tall helmet, his face grim with determination. Kit raised his sword and slashed hard at the bobbing target of the hat. His blade clashed against the chin strap, just under the Frenchman's ear, and was briefly deflected. Then it slipped off the metal and sliced into the hussar's throat. The Frenchman fell, and the sorrel he'd been riding careened away from the fighting.

As suddenly as it had begun, it was over. There was no

order, perhaps because there was no one left to issue it, but the French turned tail and, deserting the wounded who had been unhorsed, streamed off across the empty plain, pinions flying.

Kit looked for someone else to engage, but there was no one left. There was a slight ringing in his ears, and the pain in his arm had begun, making up in its viciousness now for the small respite the numbness immediately after the blow had given him.

"You're bleeding, sir," Scarborough said. His face was chalk-like beneath the freckles, but his voice was still amazingly calm. Kit's horse suddenly sidestepped the approach of the gray the boy was riding, and Scarborough reached out to catch his major's reins, recognizing how rare that lack of control over his mount was for St. John.

"I have him," Kit said, too sharply.

He felt light-headed, and despite the number of times he'd been in combat, the scene around him had an almost surreal quality. There was a screaming horse he should order someone to kill. A man was lying at his feet, the front of his uniform soaked with blood which still spurted upward like a small fountain with every beat of his dying heart.

Kit's left glove was also crimson, he realized, almost sodden with blood, and it took a long minute of thought to realize that it was his own, which was running down his forearm under his uniform sleeve.

"We need to get that tied up," Scarborough said calmly. "You get down now, sir, and I'll tend to it. It's bleeding bad."

Kit nodded, but the ground appeared a great distance away. Trusting his years of experience and not his strangely distorted vision, he lifted his right leg over the saddle and was pleased to find that it was still able to maintain his weight as he took the left out of its stirrup to join the other on the ground. But he was forced to lean against his horse, his eyes closed against the sudden vertigo.

"Should we go after them?" a voice asked at his shoulder.

Kit lifted his head to find who had asked that reasonable question. The face of Sergeant Cochran swam into focus before him. He nodded, trying to think. At the same time he was aware that Scarborough was touching the left sleeve of his uniform.

Wellington would still need the intelligence about the size of the reinforcements Napoleon had sent. That's what they had been sent to find out. And that reminded him...

"Did you convey my orders to your captain?" Kit asked softly, his language deliberately formal.

The sergeant's mouth twisted. He glanced at Scarborough, who was standing at St. John's other shoulder, working to push the tip of his knife into the seam of the sleeve in order to split it.

Cochran's voice was low when he answered, but there was no doubt about what he said. "I told him right enough, sir. Just what you and the colonel said. But...the truth of the matter is he was drunk, Major. Drunk as a lord."

The sergeant's eyes widened suddenly as he realized what he had said and to whom he had said it. Despite the dead and dying men around them, despite the disaster they had barely escaped, Cochran grinned suddenly, obviously remembering St. John's title. "Begging the major's pardon."

Kit laughed. "That's all right, Sergeant Cochran," he said. "No offense taken. Drunk as a lord," he repeated softly.

It was only what he himself had surmised watching Haviland in action. Or in *inaction,* he thought bitterly.

"I should'a left him in bed, Major," Cochran went on. "I should have known he was going to get somebody killed. But I thought of Mrs. Haviland, and the disgrace, so...I just drug him out. I swear to you I told him just what you told me to, and he understood me. Then when he saw those damn Frenchies... He ordered that charge like he had the whole division behind him. Looking for promotion, no doubt. Stupid drunken bastard," Cochran added under his breath, but not softly enough that it wasn't audible.

Kit nodded. "I didn't hear that last, Sergeant."

He turned to his left to find Scarborough trying to tie his neck cloth around his major's upper arm. Kit gasped a little at the last strong tug on the two ends, and the lieutenant's eyes came up to his.

"I don't suppose you could put your finger over the knot, sir," Scarborough said, smiling at him. "Damned hard to get it tight enough to stop the bleeding using only two hands."

The freckles were pronounced against the drained skin of his boyish face and his fingers were covered with Kit's blood, but Kit would give the boy credit. He had guts and coolness. A little more experience and he would make an excellent officer.

"'ere, sir," Cochran said. "You let me do that."

He stepped around St. John to lay a thick, grubby finger over the knot. Still holding his major's eyes, the young lieutenant pulled again. This time Kit controlled any response as the bandage tightened agonizingly over the wound.

"Where's Haviland now?" he questioned instead of letting himself react to that pain.

"You didn't see?" Sergeant Cochran asked, his voice rich with contempt. "One of His Majesty's bad bargains is that one."

"See what?" Kit wondered if the drunken captain had been cut down in the fighting. And he deliberately destroyed the hope which had leaped into his mind at that possibility.

"He ran, sir," Scarborough said.

"Retreated," Kit corrected.

"That weren't no retreat, begging the major's pardon," Cochran explained. "He didn't order the troop off. When he realized how outnumbered we was, I guess he got scared. Next thing I know, he's heading back through that pass—all alone. I was about to get the men out of there when you hit them on the flank. I knew you'd come to help us, and I wasn't about to leave you to fight the bastards alone."

"Thank you, Sergeant Cochran. I appreciate your courage."

"Not courage, sir. Just..." The sergeant paused and shook his head. "I ain't never run from a battle in my life, and I didn't intend to start now. I've retreated when I've been ordered to, and I'm not ashamed of those times. Live to fight again, I always say. But I ain't never run."

Kit could hear the strong disgust in the veteran's voice, and he had to work to keep it out of his own. Michael Haviland had sealed his own disgrace, and there wasn't much anyone could do about it now. Kit turned his attention to the young lieutenant still standing at his elbow.

"Take what men are fit to travel, Scarborough, and follow the patrol. Not close enough that they know you're there," Kit ordered, trying not to think about the growing pain in his arm or about what her husband's actions today would mean for the rest of Judith Haviland's life. Trying not to think about anything but what he'd been ordered to accomplish. "Bring back an estimate of the size of the force they're attached to as soon as you can. Cochran will go with you."

Scarborough nodded. "And you, sir?"

"I don't think I can ride fast enough to keep up," Kit said. He knew damn well he couldn't. He was reduced to wondering if he were going to be able to get back to camp. "I'll go back and report what happened to Colonel Smythe."

"What about Captain Haviland?" Cochran asked.

"Haviland can go to the devil," Kit said softly. "I intend to report him as drunk on duty. You'll testify to that, won't you, Sergeant?"

"I'll testify to everything I saw today. You make no doubt about that. But sir, what about…" The dark eyes were questioning, filled with compassion.

"We do her no good in protecting him. You saw the bruise on her face this week. And you know well enough how it got there," Kit said. "We all knew."

The man nodded, but he was still concerned, and Kit didn't blame him. These charges meant sure disgrace for Haviland. And that dishonor would touch Judith's life forever, of course.

"You watch your back, sir," Cochran said softly. "He'll know what you intend."

A good warning, Kit realized. If he didn't make it back to camp, then no one would bring charges against Haviland. Not the enlisted men. They wouldn't be believed if they did. That was simply the way the army worked.

"Thank you, Cochran. You two do the same."

"You need a hand up?" the sergeant asked.

Kit wanted to refuse, but he knew he couldn't afford to. His job now was to get the wounded back to camp and to inform Smythe about what had happened out here. Scarborough would see to the French. And Cochran would take care of the young lieutenant.

"Forgive me, Sergeant," St. John said simply. "But I'm afraid that I might."

Gayle Wilson

tomorrow would see to the burial. And Cochran would take care of the young lieutenant.

"Forgive me, Sergeant," St. John said simply. "But I'm afraid not I might

Chapter Three

"What happened?" Judith Haviland had asked when Kit arrived back in camp with the wounded.

One of the men had died on the way, and St. John could only hope that none of the other injuries would prove fatal. They would need every man they could muster if Wellington ordered them to slow down Massena's reinforcements rather than to fall back before the French advance. If the patrol they'd encountered this morning *was* part of a larger force, then this severely depleted light cavalry regiment would be caught between two much larger French armies.

In view of the situation, Kit simply shook his head in answer to Judith's question. There seemed no point in trying to explain the events of the morning. He wasn't sure he was enough in control of his own emotions to contain his disgust with Haviland's action.

She held his eyes a moment before she turned away to assess the casualties the men were bringing in. Those who had been injured in the dawn attack on the camp had already been attended to, and most of the cots in the tent were occupied.

Toby Reynolds had recovered enough to be displaced by the wounded apparently. Haviland's batman was sitting on top of an overturned box in the corner of the tent. He met Kit's eyes, undisguised hatred in the depths of his, and then he spat into the dirt before he looked away, deliberately turning his gaze from the major who had been ordered to carry out his punishment.

St. John ignored the insult. He couldn't blame the private for his bitterness, but he wondered if it extended to Haviland, the rightful target of his anger.

Kit had stopped in the opening of the tent, leaning against the support pole as he supervised the troopers who were helping the last of the casualties inside. He shook his head when Judith returned to offer him one of the remaining cots. "There are others who need you more," he said. "This has stopped bleeding."

Her eyes studied his features a moment, and she put her fingers lightly against the bandage Scarborough had devised. The neck cloth was stiff with gore, as was the damaged sleeve of Kit's uniform, but there seemed to be no fresh blood on it or on the material of his coat.

It was obvious that he was right about the needs of the other casualties, so she nodded and returned to a corporal who was the victim of a saber cut that had cost him most of his ear. He was still unconscious and had been brought back to camp over the back of his horse.

St. John closed his eyes. He was still leaning against the pole, and he let the sounds of the women who were working on the other side of the tent drift around him. He tried not to think about what had happened, but, against his will, his mind went back again and again to Haviland's charge and its results.

Only when he felt Mrs. Haviland's hand on his arm did he realize that he seemed to have lost track of the passage of time as he had in the heat of the skirmish. He glanced around the tent. Everyone had been treated. The troopers he'd brought in were either resting in the cots or had been released.

"It's your turn," Mrs. Haviland assured him, her fingers working at the knot the young lieutenant had pulled so tightly.

"My men have—"

"Everyone else has been attended to, Major, I promise you," she interrupted. "I've sent Reynolds to Colonel Smythe to report on the injuries. I'm sure he'll want a report on yours as well."

"It's nothing so bad as what you've been dealing with," Kit said, watching her fingers work at the cloth.

"Perhaps I'm better qualified to make that assessment than you," she advised him softly. "A saber cut," she said, when she had loosened and gently pulled the makeshift bandage away from the wound. "And a nasty one, I'm afraid."

Kit glanced down. His was typical of the kind of injury that resulted from a cavalry clash. A flap of flesh and muscle had been sliced away from the bone, the edge of the blade cutting diagonally into his arm just above the elbow. Clotted blood was now holding the raw edges of the wound together, preventing further bleeding. Apparently Scarborough had known what he was doing with his makeshift tourniquet.

"Wiggle your fingers," Judith ordered, her voice sharper than it had been before. She watched intently as he obeyed. "Now move the arm below the elbow."

When Kit had successfully accomplished both, she took a small, but audible breath, and he realized she was relieved.

"I don't believe the bone is broken," she said. "Although, given the location, there may be some permanent damage to the muscle, even after it heals. It may atrophy or shorten. I'm afraid that only time will tell us about that. However," she said, "you would appear to be a very lucky man, Major St. John."

"So I have always been reputed to be, ma'am."

Her eyes lifted from the wound to find his, certainly reading in them the small amusement her comment had caused. His cronies in London had called him the luckiest bastard alive, and apparently his luck still held, even in this godforsaken war.

"You know what the surgeons would do for such a wound?" she asked, destroying his pleasant diversion into the past.

"Amputate the arm," he said evenly.

Kit was relieved that his voice was so steady, but there was a sudden coldness in the pit of his stomach. It was not the horror of the surgery he feared. Other men had endured that and much worse, but he didn't relish the idea of living out his life with only one arm, not if he could help it.

"At a point well above the injury," she agreed.

Near his shoulder, she meant. They both knew that's where the surgeons would make their brutal incision.

"Is that what you advise, ma'am?" Kit asked, working to keep his voice as emotionless as hers had been.

"It would really be the wisest course, you know," she said, truthfully, "given the odds of infection in this climate and with this type of wound. Unfortunately, however, I don't feel that I have the experience to attempt such an operation on my own. So I suppose we must try other, less drastic methods." She paused, but her calm, dark eyes held to his steadfastly.

"I must confess that I much prefer your second option, ma'am. Do your best for it, please."

She nodded, and her gaze returned to examine the injury again. Her fingers touched gently along the edge of the gash. "I only wish that I had—" The sentence she had begun stopped abruptly, the soft words cut off as if she had suddenly realized that thought should not be spoken aloud.

"Had what?" he questioned her sudden silence.

She looked up into his eyes again, hers clearly troubled. "Another, more professional opinion," she finished softly.

Judith Haviland had just lied to him, Kit realized, as she had lied about the bruise on her cheek, and he couldn't imagine why, unless the wound was more serious than she'd indicated.

"First, I'm going to try to clean the blood away," she went on, "and then try to make sure that the wound is free of debris. That won't be very pleasant, I'm afraid, but I've found that an injury heals better if there is nothing closed up within it that doesn't belong to the body. No loose threads from your uniform or dirt from the field."

"I'm completely in your hands, Mrs. Haviland," Kit said.

"Indeed you are, Major St. John," she agreed, smiling at him for the first time. "And I promise I shall do my very best for you. You would be better on the table, I believe."

Kit obediently followed her across the tent, his stride only the slightest bit unsteady. It was a little more difficult maneuvering himself, one-handed, onto the edge of the trestle table she had had the men set up as a makeshift examination area.

Suddenly it seemed very warm in the tent, despite the chill of the morning. He raised his right hand to unfasten the top button of his uniform and was surprised to find his fingers trembling weakly over that simple task.

"I do have some experience, you know," Judith assured him.

Kit realized she had been watching the small vibration

of his hand. "I trust you implicitly, ma'am. Much more than the sawbones, I promise you."

"Well, I shouldn't go that far," she said lightly. She smiled at him again. "Shall I help you with your coat, Major?"

Getting him out of the ruined jacket wasn't easily accomplished, even with her help, and Kit's face was covered with a dew of perspiration by the time they had managed it. The white lawn shirt he wore underneath was also badly stained with blood and damp with sweat. He tried to watch as she cut the sleeve of that garment away, but his head was swimming with blood loss.

"Why don't you lie down?" she suggested when she had finished and glanced up at his blanched features.

"Will that make it easier for your work?" he asked.

"My suggestion was intended to make it easier for *you*, Major St. John," she said. Her soft laughter was again intimate.

"Then I believe I shall continue to sit up, ma'am."

"But you trust me implicitly, remember?" she reminded him, the laughter still caught in her dark eyes.

"As long as I can see exactly what you're doing," he countered, smiling at her.

Despite his determination to play the stoic, Kit found that the rest was an ordeal. With each involuntary flinch of muscle, Judith Haviland's eyes lifted to his face, still assessing.

"I'm not going to faint on you," he assured her finally.

"Actually, I was rather hoping that you might," she said. This time her eyes didn't lift, but the corners of her mouth tilted.

"I wouldn't, however, turn down a swallow of the rum I gave you yesterday," Kit suggested after a few more minutes of her painstaking and extremely painful cleansing of the gash. "Strictly for medicinal purposes, you understand."

It took a moment for her to respond. She handed the basin of bloody water and the sponge she had been using to Mrs. McQueen, before she looked up. "I'm sorry, Major, but I'm afraid that's impossible."

"Blood loss?" he asked. She had said she worried about the effect of spirits on the wounded. Maybe...

"*Rum* loss," she corrected, taking from Mrs. McQueen the needle and thread that the motherly, gray-haired woman was holding out. "Are you ready for this?" she asked softly.

"Of course," Kit said, setting his teeth into his bottom lip. The sewing surely couldn't be much worse than what had gone before. It wasn't, he found, but still it was several heartbeats before he trusted his voice enough to ask for an explanation.

"Rum loss? You've already used it?"

"No," she answered calmly, "but I assure you it's gone."

Suddenly he understood. This was where Haviland had gotten drink last night. Judith had given it to him. Voluntarily or otherwise? he wondered. "Your husband?" he asked.

Her eyes lifted again, holding his for a long moment. In them was regret and embarrassment. As he watched, a small flush spread across her cheekbones. Finally she nodded, and then her gaze returned to the needle which she pushed into the torn muscle of his arm, carefully placing the next stitch.

"There's something I feel I must tell you, ma'am," Kit said softly, wondering if hearing what had occurred this morning wouldn't come better from him than from the colonel or from regimental gossip. No matter who told her, he knew it would not be easy for Judith Haviland to learn the truth.

"Something about Michael?" she asked, her concentration now apparently fully on the neat line of stitches she was setting.

"Yes, ma'am."

"Then I'm afraid that I really don't wish to hear it, Major. Whatever criticism of my husband you intend to make, I hope you will not make it to me. I assure you I am not unaware…"

She hesitated, and then she went on, her eyes still resolutely on her work. "I am aware that Michael is not as…strong as you, but he is my husband, Major St. John. I'm sure you'll forgive me if I say that it would be best that you *not* tell me whatever you feel constrained to say about Michael's actions. Much better for us both."

She looked up, her eyes very calm and very sure. *He is my husband.* No matter what Haviland had done, Kit realized, there was nothing she could do to change that relationship.

Nothing anyone could do, Kit thought with real regret. Judith Haviland was bound to suffer for her husband's disgrace. But he realized thankfully her words had freed him from what he had felt was his duty to tell her.

"Fourteen men are dead, Haviland, through your actions this morning," Smythe said, his voice cold. "Fourteen men who didn't deserve to die, whom this regiment could ill afford to lose."

"Colonel Smythe, I hope that you will—"

"What I will do, I assure you," Smythe went on, overriding the protest, "is report this sorry episode to Lord Wellington. The story of this morning's action will go out in the next dispatches. And those shall be sent as soon as

Lieutenant Scarborough returns from the mission I asked *you* to carry out.''

''Major St. John—'' Haviland began again, only to be once more interrupted.

''I have St. John's report. Which he assures me will be corroborated by Lieutenant Scarborough and Sergeant Cochran upon their return. The charges against you include disobeying an order, being drunk on duty, and the worse by far, desertion in the face of the enemy.''

''None of those are entirely true,'' Haviland said. ''There were circumstances, sir, that—''

''This is not a court-martial, Captain Haviland. I'm not asking for an explanation of your actions. I assure you that will be required later. I simply wished to inform you that this is the report I shall send to Lord Wellington.''

''Colonel Smythe, I must protest—''

''Protest and be damned,'' Smythe said, his anger allowed for the first time to break through the carefully detached recitation. ''It took Captain Scott more than two hours to sober you up and to get you in a condition to listen to the charges which I intend to lodge. I assure you that after that, whatever you can say will have little bearing on my actions.''

For the first time since he had known him, Kit realized, Haviland looked frightened. His skin was pale and his hands shook, but of course those might be put down to drink as well.

His eyes had met St. John's when he had entered the tent, escorted there by Captain Scott. In them had been the same cold hatred Kit had seen in the eyes of Haviland's batman. It seemed he had acquired two enemies.

''My father's health is precarious,'' Haviland said. His tone had changed. It was softer and less aggressive, and apparently it or his words had the desired effect. For once

Smythe didn't interrupt. "You must know this will kill him, sir."

The older man's eyes reflected his regret, and his mouth pursed slightly before he answered. "That is something you should have considered earlier, Captain Haviland. I'm afraid there is nothing I can do to prevent whatever will happen as a result of your actions this morning."

Haviland's eyes were bleak. It seemed that finally the realization that his "mistakes" were not going to be ignored or forgiven this time was beginning to sink in. The men all knew what lay ahead. Professional condemnation, certainly, but that was the least of it. That would swiftly be followed by personal disgrace, especially given the Haviland family's strong military traditions.

For some reason his father's face was in Kit's head, exactly the way it had looked the last time he had seen the earl. He had never forgotten his words that morning: *You continue to bring dishonor to this family. You may enjoy wallowing in the mud of public censure, but I will no longer allow you to drag the Montgomery name there with you.*

Haviland faced the same kind of public and private humiliation Ryde had described. For the first time Kit felt some fellow feeling for Michael Haviland. Undoubtedly he, too, loved his father and might be forced to live the rest of his life, Kit thought, knowing he was responsible for his death...

"I'm begging you for a chance to redeem myself, sir," Haviland said softly, his eyes focused intently on his colonel, who was, as they all were aware, an old friend and a former comrade-in-arms of General Roland Haviland.

"Surely whatever mistakes I've made, my father doesn't deserve to suffer for them. Please don't send that dispatch, sir. Instead..." Haviland hesitated before he went on. "Give me some mission. I don't care how desperate, how unlikely its chance of success. I'm begging you for an opportunity, Colonel Smythe, to redeem myself. A chance to save my father's life."

Kit found himself hoping that his commander would relent, and was surprised to feel those stirrings of sympathy.

"The men who died under your command this morning will have no second chance, Captain Haviland," Smythe said coldly. "Why do you believe I should give you one? Your father, I know, would be the first to agree. General Haviland was a fine and courageous officer, and I find that I must live up to his standards. However unpleasant that may be for me personally."

There was a long silence in the tent. Finally, Colonel Smythe's gaze fell, and his hand idly moved a paper on his desk. It was obvious that the painful interview was at an end.

"If you'll escort Captain Haviland back to his tent and place him under guard, Major," he ordered softly, but he didn't look again at the disgraced son of his friend.

St. John had been cradling the elbow of his aching left arm in his right palm as he listened. Mrs. Haviland had devised a sling, which gave some relief, but he knew it would be a long time before he'd be back to full strength and able to help in whatever action Wellington directed this ravaged regiment to take. He supposed that setting a guard over a prisoner would be the extent of the duties given him for the next few days.

As he led the way outside the command tent, holding the flap open for Haviland to follow him, the captain spoke to him.

"You could talk to him, you know," Judith Haviland's husband said softly.

Kit turned in surprise, realizing that his prisoner was appealing to him for his help. "Talk to Smythe?" he repeated. "What good do you suppose I might do?"

"He likes you, admires you. Your *nobility,* perhaps." The emphasized word was almost an insult. "And besides, you're the one responsible for bringing those charges."

"Your actions this morning were witnessed by over fifty men. Do you suppose you can convince each of *them* to lie for you?"

"I wouldn't have to. Not if you told Smythe you were mistaken. The men wouldn't go against your word."

"You know I can't do that," Kit said. He had already turned away, heading toward Haviland's tent, when the captain's next words came from directly behind him.

"Not even for Judith's sake?" he asked, his voice still very low, almost a whisper. "Not even to save Judith and her father from disgrace? And to save my father's life?"

The soft words stopped Kit's advance. He turned back, his eyes tracing over the face of the man who made that request. Despite all that had happened, there was in Haviland's features that small hint of arrogance which seemed to indicate that he still, somehow, expected to be able to talk his way out of this.

"I'm sorry for your family," Kit said truthfully, "but you're a danger to everyone here. I won't lie for you, not even to protect your father from learning what you've done. To leave you in your present position would eventually cost other men their lives. I know you, Haviland. I know you too well."

"Not even in exchange for Judith's...undying gratitude?" Haviland asked, his question soft enough that Scott, who had just walked out of the tent behind them, couldn't possibly have heard what he'd just suggested. "I can arrange that, you know," he added. "Judith is very fond of my father. And of her own, of course."

St. John knew exactly what Haviland was offering, knew and was sickened by the idea that he would try to trade his wife's body for his own reputation. Kit held the dark, almost smiling eyes a moment. To his shame, he had felt the smallest breath of temptation. There had been within him a quick, yet undeniable, physical response to that obscene suggestion.

And then he remembered Judith Haviland's hands, workworn and reddened with cold, moving with kindness over the injuries she had treated today. His and all the others. He remembered her voice, comforting and reassuring to the men she tended, and reacting to his own unspoken fears with amused tenderness.

Slowly, Kit shook his head, rejecting a despicable offer made by a man he despised. Haviland's eyes fell, finally, before St. John turned away and, holding his injured arm protectively against his body, continued across the muddy field of the encampment to the tent where he would make Haviland a prisoner.

"At least five regiments, sir," Scarborough said breathlessly. "All of them looking fresh as daisies."

"You're sure they didn't spot you?" Smythe asked.

"We never got close enough, sir. But they're not more than four hours away, and coming on fast."

"Along this road?" the colonel asked.

"Straight as a die," the lieutenant agreed. "They'll be here well before sundown."

"Two thousand men," Smythe said under his breath. They all knew that he was thinking about his options, which were limited.

There was no time, of course, to send to Wellington for further orders. A messenger would carry the information that Napoleon had finally come through with the promised replacements for his army in Portugal. But as to their own role...

"Thanks to Haviland, we now have wounded who are unable to fight," Kit reminded him.

"And there are the women, of course," Smythe agreed, raising his eyes to meet those of his second-in-command. "We could send them west toward the coast by wagon. I believe that Trant and the militia are still in control there."

Kit nodded agreement. It seemed the best plan. Even if the unit retreated in front of the oncoming forces instead of offering resistance, the wounded would slow them down. And Massena's main army still lay between them and Wellington.

Whatever happened in the next few days, they all knew that this small band of dragoons would be caught between the two larger French forces. Caught and probably crushed.

"In case my own courier doesn't get through, you'll have to see to it that Trant sends word to Wellington of what's happened here as soon as you make contact."

"I, sir?" Kit questioned in surprise.

"You're not in any shape to fight, St. John, even if you're willing to hold your reins in your teeth," Smythe said, humor touching his voice for the first time since the lieutenant's grim assessment of their position. "I need someone I can trust to see to the safety of the wounded."

"We could all move to the west," Kit suggested, reluctant to leave his men, despite the fact that he knew Smythe was right. One-handed, he wouldn't be very effective in a cavalry fight, and the women and the wounded had to be protected. It was not a duty he had anticipated being given. Nor one he wanted.

"The last order I received from headquarters was to guard this route until we were reinforced or removed," Smythe reminded him. "And I have not yet received any instructions from Wellington to the contrary, Major St. John. Given that situation, I can't simply surrender this road to the French."

"You can't hope to stand against them, sir," Kit warned.

"We can stand," Smythe said softly. "Whether or not we can hold them will be another story."

Scarborough had been chosen to carry the dispatches to Wellington. Kit made it a point to see him off. The boy's pleasant, freckled face was calm and determined, but he was no fool, of course. He knew the difficulties of eluding the French army which stretched across the land before him like a net.

"Take care," St. John advised, handing him the packet he'd brought from Smythe's tent.

"Don't you worry about me, Major," the young lieutenant said. "You see to the lads. And to Mrs. Haviland and the others. You get them safe away, sir. I'll do just fine."

"Of course you will," Kit said. Their eyes held a moment. Both of them knew the enormous odds that they would ever see one another again, and then, fighting emotion, Kit slapped the gray sharply on the rump. He watched until horse and rider had disappeared into the mist of the winter afternoon.

When he turned, Judith Haviland was standing outside the medical tent, her eyes on him rather than in the direction the messenger had gone. "We're almost packed, Major St. John," she said. "In reality, other than the wounded, there wasn't that much to put into the wagons."

"Probably just as well," Kit said. "With the terrain we'll be crossing, the less baggage we're hampered by, the better."

"Baggage or baggages?" she asked, reminding him of the army's slang for the women who followed them, but she was smiling at him. "I know that this particular duty isn't your choice."

"There aren't many choices where duty is concerned, ma'am."

"And all of them are sometimes hard," she said softly.

She had heard then. She knew about his role in the charges that had been brought against her husband, and probably better than anyone else, she would be aware of the impact of those charges on the life of Michael's father. And on her own.

Still, he could read no condemnation in her eyes. They met his with the same steady regard and friendship they had always held. Unlike her husband, Judith Haviland understood duty.

"Colonel Smythe's messenger?" she asked, her gaze shifting in the direction the young lieutenant had taken.

"Carrying the dispatches to Wellington," Kit admitted.

Her eyes came back to his. Despite her knowledge of the import of those messages, they hadn't changed. "We'll be ready to leave in fifteen minutes," she said. Turning, she disappeared into the medical tent.

St. John looked again into the distance where Scarborough had vanished. He could only wish the boy Godspeed, but he knew that if Smythe's packet reached the headquarters of His Majesty's army in Portugal, Haviland's military career was at an end.

As was any semblance of a normal life for the members of his family. Judith Haviland knew that as well as he, and yet, as always, she had made no protest over the blow fate had dealt her. Or any outcry against the unfairness of it all.

That was the same courage with which she had met every hardship of the last three years. And if there was any single virtue Kit had come to admire and to value above all others, since the day his father had sent him into this hell, it was courage. It seemed a shame that only one of the Havilands possessed that precious commodity.

Chapter Four

"Bloody hell," Kit said, the expletive uttered under his breath, too quietly, he hoped, for anyone else to hear.

"What do we do now, Major?" Cochran asked.

Kit realized that the sergeant was standing at his elbow, his gaze following St. John's over the expanse of churning water they were supposed to cross to reach the coast road.

What St. John had discovered when he arrived at the river's edge were only the remnants of the medieval stone bridge which had once spanned the broad, swift-running current, its destruction almost certainly carried out by engineers acting under orders from Wellington.

It was a highly effective way to direct the enemy's progress and one the English commander had used successfully in the past. Roads that would support the movement of artillery were few in this country, and access to them depended on bridges such as these. Only in this case...

"We go back the way we came," Kit said.

He had already considered his options and had been forced to admit he was left with little choice. There was no way he could take these lumbering carts across the mountains to another bridge, and there were too many wounded who were not yet ambulatory to allow him to abandon that means of transport.

"Whatever happened back there..." Kit paused, further expression of yesterday's merciless reality almost blocked by emotion. "It's certain to be finished by now," he concluded.

In the distance behind them, as they wound their way up the first of the ridges that now lay between them and the road they had guarded throughout the winter, they had heard the noise of their regiment's resistance to the French advance. They had already been some distance away from that fighting, of course, but the sounds of it traveled to them, pushed upward by the land's topography from the valley below.

Kit knew that the men in the wagons, even those most severely wounded, had reacted to that noise just as he had. With guilt, primarily, and with despair that they were not below, struggling beside comrades with whom they had shared every hardship of these last three years.

In the faces of the women had been a resigned sadness. Most of them had lost husbands before in this war. That was the way in the army. By necessity, widows remarried quickly and went on with their lives.

Only one of the women St. John was assigned to protect had not left her husband behind. For Mrs. Haviland it might have been better if she had. It would have been a reprieve for his family if Michael had been killed in yesterday's action. If Kit had been in the captain's situation, death in battle would have been his fervent wish. However, given what he knew about Haviland, it would probably not be his.

St. John had been given three able-bodied men. He had requested Sergeant Cochran and been grateful when Smythe agreed. Two corporals had been sent along to guard the prisoner, who was allowed to ride his own horse at the back of the caravan.

St. John had already decided there was nothing he could have done differently in bringing the charges against Haviland. His first obligation was to the men of this regiment. And it did no good thinking about the consequences of his action. Besides, they now had more immediate problems.

"Turn the wagons, Sergeant," Kit ordered.

As Cochran rode off to put that command into effect, Kit looked down again into the current, dreading a return to the encampment they had left yesterday afternoon. It was possible there were survivors of that battle, men who had somehow escaped being killed or taken prisoner, and their addition would strengthen his party. And if there were other wounded, then they, too, would become St. John's responsibility.

Whatever the situation behind them, Kit knew he had no choice but to retrace the journey they had made. Since they were cut off by the river, the road they had followed here led back to the only route over which he could now move these wagons south. There was nowhere else for his small detachment to go.

The bodies they found had been stripped. The peasants in the surrounding countryside were too poor for that not to have happened, especially at the end of a long, hard winter. Kit ordered his men to bury the dead in graves they dug near the site. Colonel Smythe's body had been among them.

It had been little more than forty-eight hours since they'd set out, and yet so much had changed. The regiment to which they belonged had been virtually eliminated, its members either killed or, if they were lucky, taken prisoner by the swift-moving enemy. However, judging by the number of friends they buried, the French had not bothered to take prisoners.

The fact that they had swept through the regiment's resistance so quickly was almost an advantage to their own position Kit realized. At least they were well to the rear of whatever fighting would take place within the next few days.

He had to admit to some relief that the enemy was by now miles ahead of them. Without supplies or resources, he bore the responsibility of taking four wagonloads of wounded men and the women through those same miles of hostile territory.

More frightening than the thought of that was the growing realization that, despite Mrs. Haviland's treatment, his wound was becoming inflamed. He had felt the effects of the fever in his body throughout the afternoon.

He had also been aware that Sergeant Cochran's eyes had focused questioningly on his face from time to time. They had been filled with speculation, although the enlisted man had as yet said nothing. But if Cochran realized he was ill, then Judith Haviland would almost certainly notice.

"Now what?" The sergeant stood again at his elbow, questioning as he had at the bridge yesterday. St. John realized that Cochran had seen to most of the work of the burial, and he blessed his colonel once more for assigning him to this unit.

"South," Kit answered simply. Despite what hostilities they might face, without medicine or supplies, they had no choice but to travel toward Wellington and the main British force still encamped, as far as he knew, at Vedras Torres.

"Shouldn't we spend the night here, Major?" Cochran suggested. His eyes were again considering. "There's water."

"The road parallels the river for the next ten or twelve

miles. We'll do better to find a more secluded spot to set up camp, away from the possibility of encountering more looters."

Cochran nodded his agreement. They were watching a couple of the women, under the direction of Judith Haviland, bring water to those wounded who were unable to leave their beds in the wagons. Mrs. Haviland had not watched the hurried burials, but had spent the time attending to the needs of the living.

"How are you at poaching, Sergeant Cochran?" Kit asked, thinking of his own responsibilities. "We're going to need something to feed these people tonight."

"Try my hand at hunting, sir?"

"I thought you might range ahead and see if you could scare up some game." In late winter, that would be difficult, but the sergeant didn't question the order.

"I'll do my best, Major. Allowed to use my firearm?"

There was always the possibility that shots might attract the attention of someone, either one of the bandit groups that inhabited these mountains or, perhaps even more dangerous, a band of French deserters. But given the condition of some of the wounded and the journey they faced, there was probably more risk in their going any longer without food.

"If you have to," Kit agreed reluctantly. "Just make sure that we'll have something nourishing to feed them tonight."

Cochran was a good shot, and everyone in the regiment knew it. Kit himself was better, of course, but in this situation he would have to trust in the sergeant's skills.

"I'll bring home the bacon, sir," Cochran said with a grin. "Don't you worry none about that."

"Can you find the ruins of the old mill where we surprised the French outpost last year?"

"Maybe six or seven miles south of here?"

"About that. We'll set up camp near there for the night."

"I'll meet you. You take care of yourself, Major. I'll see to supper, providing the French ain't devoured all the game like they've devoured everything else in this blasted country."

"I'm counting on you, Sergeant," Kit said.

For the first time, he put his right hand on Cochran's arm, the touch of his fingers quick and light as he squeezed the solid muscle, an unspoken expression of his gratitude. Surprisingly, the sergeant's eyes were suddenly full of emotion.

"I won't let you down, sir," he promised softly. "Or them," he added. "You can count on that. There'll be food tonight, Major. I promise you that."

Cochran's vow had been easily made, Kit supposed, but now the sun was setting and the soft sounds of twilight were beginning to infiltrate the glen where Kit had ordered the wagons circled. The location he'd chosen was sheltered from the eyes of anyone passing by on the road they'd been following and near enough to the river to make hauling water convenient.

Kit was beginning to worry less about food and more about the sergeant himself when Cochran finally guided his mount into the circle of the campfires. He was leading a gray gelding, and tied across the saddle of that animal, St. John was infinitely relieved to see, was a brace of rabbits and a few birds.

The women would have to make the game into stew in order to have enough to go around. However, with the hard tack they had been given from the regiment's meager stores, at least no one would go hungry tonight. Kit felt a weight lift from his spirits at the sight of the sergeant's round, honest face.

It wasn't until he had walked over to welcome him, near enough to read Cochran's eyes, that St. John knew something was wrong. The sergeant slid out of the saddle and handed the string of game to one of the women. Then he met his commander's gaze, tilting his head toward the woods that lay between their bivouac and the river. Unquestioning, Kit followed him a short way into the surrounding trees.

"Bad news, Major," Cochran said as soon as they were out of earshot.

Kit couldn't imagine what could be worse than what they had already encountered today, but he braced himself for whatever news was bad enough that the optimistic Cochran had decided no one else should hear it.

"I found a body in the woods."

"A body?" Kit repeated.

"Scavengers had already been at it. Pointed it out to me or I'd never have seen it. About five miles from the old camp."

Cochran's eyes shifted to where the women were working. The birds he'd brought in were being spitted, and they had already skinned the hares in preparation for putting them into the pot. The sergeant watched a moment, apparently reluctant to finish what he'd begun. Finally his gaze returned to Kit's.

"Scarborough," the sergeant said softly. "The boy didn't get very far, Major. Not to Wellington, in any case."

Despite the fact that he thought he had been prepared, Kit felt that blow. He had lost men before, of course, and some of them had been good friends. But even with Cochran's warning and his obvious reluctance to reveal what he'd found, St. John had not been prepared for the boy's death.

He forced himself to ask the more important question, despite his heartsickness. "What about the dispatches?"

"The packet wasn't there. I looked. But the thing is, sir, his horse *was*. That's what don't make sense. French regulars would have taken both. The Portuguese would have taken the horse, to eat if nothing else, and left the pouch. And..." Cochran hesitated before he added the rest. "Not only had he been shot, Major, but the boy's throat had been cut as well."

"Good God," Kit said, feeling a chill of horror. "Why would anyone..." He shook his head in disgust, despite his familiarity with the brutalities of this war.

"Making sure, I guess. Just in case the bullet didn't finish him off. But Wellington won't have had word about what happened to the regiment, Major. Or about us. Whoever took those dispatches, you can be sure they ain't going to frank 'em off to headquarters."

"No, of course not," Kit said, again forced to reevaluate their situation. That was the other thing he'd been ordered to do—the last order Smythe had given him, the last he would ever give anyone. Make sure Wellington got word that Napoleon had finally sent the long-promised reinforcements.

Their number didn't represent enough men to make a difference to any major battle, but still, getting that intelligence through had been Smythe's job. His duty. And now it was Kit's.

"Thank you, Sergeant," he said finally, knowing that no matter how much he had come to depend on Cochran's good sense, this particular problem was his and his alone. "Go on and get your supper. You've more than earned it. And Cochran..."

The sergeant, who had already turned toward the camp, halted at the soft admonition. "Well done," Kit added and again saw the unspoken response to his praise reflected in the man's face.

After Cochran left, St. John stood alone in the darkness under the trees, trying to think. The logical thing would be to send the sergeant south with a message detailing the size of the advance, what had happened to the regiment, and requesting help for the wounded he guarded.

But with his own condition worsening, that was a move Kit was reluctant to make. If anything happened to him, if he became unable to command, then Cochran would be the one he would trust to look after this vulnerable party.

Haviland outranked the sergeant, of course, but officially the captain was a prisoner, which made Cochran Kit's second-in-command. The two corporals, relative Johnny Raws, were not familiar with the country that stretched between their position and the main British force in the south.

"I thought I might check on your arm," Judith Haviland said.

Kit looked up, surprised that she had followed him here. Cochran had sent her, he supposed. Despite the calmness of her voice, he could read concern in Mrs. Haviland's brown eyes. Of course, he warned himself, given the gravity of their situation, that concern didn't have to be personal or even for him.

"My arm's fine. You made a good job of it," he said. "Just as you promised."

Sounds of laughter from the camp came to them on a gust of cold wind. It was the women, probably celebrating the unexpected bounty the sergeant had brought in. Neither of them commented on that, but listening to it, Judith said nothing else for a moment.

"That's not really your reputation, you know," she offered finally.

Her voice was so soft, Kit could not read her tone. And for the first time since he had known her, he was forced to wonder what Mrs. Haviland had heard about him.

The narrow world of London society had seemed so distant that Kit sometimes forgot his notoriety there would almost certainly cause comment here. But the infamous Lord St. John was a very different man from Major St. John, and he found it disturbing that she would refer now to his scandalous past.

"My...reputation?" Kit repeated reluctantly.

"You were never reputed to be a flatterer," she said. "Or a liar," she added. "Will you let me look at your arm, Major?"

"It's inflamed," he admitted.

"And you're fevered, just as Sergeant Cochran suggested."

"I have a score of wounded men and four women to look after. I'm afraid, ma'am, that I really can't afford to be fevered."

He smiled at her, trying to tell her without words that he understood the ridiculousness of the claim he had just made. And the undeniable truth of it as well.

"I see," she said. Her voice was almost amused.

And this time there was something else there, he realized. Some other emotion that had lain, not quite hidden, under that covering amusement. In surprise, Kit realized that in her tone was something which the notorious Lord St. John had certainly heard before.

Had that emotion been in the voice of any other woman he had ever known, any woman other than this, Kit would have been sure what its subtle undercurrent conveyed. But that emotion was alien to their relationship, and so he discarded the incredible idea it had fostered in his heart.

"And you believe that because of the seriousness of your duties, you can deny the functioning of your own body?" she asked reasonably.

"I certainly hope so, Mrs. Haviland," he said, smiling at her again. "At least, until we are well out of this."

"How long do you think it will take for help to reach us?" she asked. "Considering the fact that the French are between Wellington and ourselves."

It was a legitimate question. She had seen Scarborough leave camp more than two days ago and had been aware of the purpose of his mission. Apparently, despite his betrayal of Kit's condition, Cochran had not seen fit to inform her that the young lieutenant would never arrive at English headquarters.

"I suppose," Kit said carefully, "that will depend on the conditions Colonel Smythe's messenger encounters."

"You *do* realize, Major, that if your wound goes septic..."

Her voice faltered suddenly over that horror, but they both knew well enough what she intended to warn him about. If gangrene set in, he would die. His only hope would be the amputation they had discussed before, and that might then be too late.

"I understand," Kit said calmly.

Her eyes were on his face. In the growing darkness he could still read worry in their depths and an undeniable fear.

"Days," she warned. "It will be only a matter of days."

"Perhaps by then we'll be with the surgeons."

"Perhaps?" she repeated.

He fought against the urge to tell her the truth. Not that

it would do any good, but as with Cochran, he trusted her common sense and would value her advice.

"Major St. John, are you afraid that—"

"Of course," he said, breaking in deliberately before she could finish the question. "Of course, I'm afraid," he confessed, forcing amusement into his voice. "I'm not a fool, Mrs. Haviland. Whatever you may have heard in London."

She laughed. "No, I assure you *that* wasn't your reputation either," she said, but her tone had lightened, just as he intended. "Did you even remember that we once met there?" she asked. The smile that was the lingering residue of her laughter still played about her lips.

He didn't, of course. Kit had no idea that he had ever seen Judith Haviland before his arrival in Spain.

"Of course," he lied easily. "How should I ever forget having met someone like you, ma'am?" He was rewarded again with her laughter, as soft and as intimate as it had been within the medical tent that night.

"*That*, sir, is a blatant untruth. A gallant one, perhaps, but certainly a whisker. You have no memory whatsoever of our meeting," she chided, laughing again. "At least be honest, sir."

"I was befuddled with drink?" he suggested, his tone matching the teasing quality of hers.

Her laughter suddenly disappeared, fading more slowly from her eyes.

"I'm sorry, Mrs. Haviland," he said softly. "That wasn't intended—"

"I know," she whispered. "I'm just so afraid of what will happen."

"I assure you, ma'am, Wellington will not abandon us to—"

"Not of this," she broke in quickly. "It's not…" She took a breath, deep and calming apparently, for when she continued there was none of that previous agitation in her words. There was only regret. "It almost seems that here, until we reach the English lines…"

She didn't finish, but Kit understood instinctively what she meant. Here there were other problems, concerns more pressing even than the charges that had been brought against her husband. Here her worries focused on the lives that she guarded. And in the scope of those duties, she could forget for a time that which loomed like a storm above the future of her family.

"I'm grateful, ma'am, for all you're doing." In his own concerns, Kit realized that he had failed to thank her for her care of his men. That was something he had learned early in his brief military career, what a word of thanks or encouragement might mean to someone under his command. Not, of course, that Judith Haviland was. "No one could do more for them than you have done. Not even the surgeons."

"John Penny died today. They buried him with the others."

Penny was the trooper who had received the head injury in Haviland's fatal charge, Kit remembered. He had been one of the most severely wounded, of course. Still, even if he should have been, Kit had not been prepared for that either. Especially not on top of the news about Scarborough.

"I have almost nothing left to treat these men with," Judith went on softly. "No herbs, no drugs. Even the rum you…"

Her voice faltered, remembering her husband's disgrace perhaps. Or his own role in it.

"Do you realize," she said, "if I had had those spirits to cleanse your injury, then…it might all be different?"

"And it might not." Kit found himself comforting her.

"Whatever happened, it was not your fault. Surely you understand that."

She nodded, seeming to agree with his words, but her eyes had fallen, and her hands played restlessly with the fringe of her shawl. He waited, aware of her distress over the incident, but when she went on, lifting her eyes again to his face, it was something different.

"The surgeons feel that in order to heal, a wound must first suppurate. Perhaps that's all that's happening with your arm. Perhaps it doesn't mean—"

"Mrs. Haviland, you must realize that I don't want anyone else to know about this," he said. "I would have preferred that Cochran kept his suspicions about the fever to himself."

"He was worried about you. I understand that you feel it best that news of your illness not become general knowledge. If you'll come to me tonight…"

Her voice faded, but her eyes remained on his face. That soft suggestion had inadvertently been phrased as the age-old lover's invitation. Kit's body reacted, and the reaction was swiftly denied.

That was not something that had ever been within the well-established bounds of their relationship. Friendship, certainly. Mutual respect. But never anything between them that went beyond those two acceptable emotions.

"When everyone else is asleep," she added, apparently trying to induce him to agree. "No one else will know you're there."

Kit's heart responded to the appeal inherent in those words. Their intent was very different from what they seemed to imply, he knew, but still, with her whispered invitation, an unthinkable image had been engendered. And must, in honor, be fought.

St. John nodded, and then he brushed past her in the

darkness, making his way through the shadows cast by the trees toward the safety of the light of the campfires. In his head, unwanted and unsought, echoed again the simple words that Judith Haviland had just said to him.

The bandage was stained, and not with blood. Judith had taken great care in peeling the cloth away from the wound. And when she had, she realized that the fears she had fought since Sergeant Cochran had come to her were not unfounded.

"You were right," she said, fighting to keep her voice even in the face of this setback.

She looked up from the angry, swollen arm to find St. John's gaze. The blue eyes did not reflect the fear that had suddenly tightened her breathing at the sight of what lay under that bandage. His courage was not from ignorance, she knew. St. John had probably seen as many wounds go septic in the last three years as she had. As this one almost certainly had.

The wound and the stitches she had set had almost disappeared, swallowed up by the poisons building under the swelling of proud flesh. Streaks of red had begun to creep upward toward his shoulder. Judith tried to think of anything that was left in her small store of medicines with which she could treat this. Of any plant which grew here that might have some effect on the spreading infection.

That was the problem, of course. She was still too unfamiliar with the flora that were indigenous to the region, despite her determined questioning of the natives she'd encountered during the last three years. Someone's life might depend on her knowledge, she had told herself. And now her worst fears had come true.

"A poultice," she suggested aloud, feeling compelled by the major's trust to offer him some remedy, even if her

brain seemed incapable of identifying one. "Something that
will draw out the poisons. Or perhaps…a blister," she suggested, hesitating to mention a procedure that seemed to
her little more than medieval torture. The surgeons, however, swore by that method as they did by swift amputation.
And if she had had the courage to take his arm at first, she
thought, then none of this would be happening.

Their voices had been kept so low they were almost
whispering, although the camp was asleep. And if not, no
one would think it strange that the major had visited Mrs.
Haviland's tent for treatment. However, it would be better,
they both understood, if the men didn't know about the
potentially serious consequences of what she had discovered under that bandage.

"Do you believe those might help?" St. John asked.

"Perhaps," Judith hedged. She preferred the poultice, of
course, if only she had access to the right ingredients. "But
I must tell you—" she began before St. John interrupted
calmly.

"That in all likelihood, nothing will help."

"Yes," she admitted. He deserved to be told the truth.
It was his life they were discussing. His life that she held
now in her hands, with too few weapons to fight against
the unseen, yet terrifying enemy with whom she had become all too familiar.

Would it be better for her, who was not a surgeon and
who had never before performed an amputation, to try to
take off the arm before the infection could climb higher?
She had watched more of those operations than she wished
to remember. She knew the procedure, but to actually carry
out that ghastly surgery, without the proper instruments and
on this particular man… Suddenly her eyes lifted again to
his.

St. John's face was dispassionate. She could read nothing

there beyond a genuine need for information. He was in command of this unit and, as he had reminded her, the lives of the people Smythe had placed under his care were his first responsibility.

She had seen men with courage such as St. John's endure a great deal and then go about their duties as if determined to ignore the pain and weakness of their bodies. *I can't afford to be fevered,* he had told her. How could he afford then the other?

"How long?" he asked quietly.

She understood what information he was seeking, because she knew his character. *How long could he continue to command before his body betrayed him, refusing to respond to the demands of his iron will?*

"Five or six days. A week," she guessed. "Perhaps more if we can slow the spread of the poison through the body."

"Can you do that?"

"I still have some dried willow, I believe. But Major, you must understand—"

"I understand perfectly," he interrupted again. "You've been very forthright." There was surprisingly a thread of amusement in his voice. And still no fear.

"Surely Sergeant Cochran can manage whatever needs to be done," she said.

He didn't reply for a moment, and briefly his eyes tried to avoid the question in hers. "Sergeant Cochran will have other responsibilities," he said finally.

"*Other* responsibilities?"

"I'm sending Cochran south in the morning."

"But why?" she whispered. She was aware of how much St. John depended on the bluff sergeant. And when the major became truly ill...

"Because I have no choice," he said simply. "Scarborough was ambushed. Cochran found his body while he was hunting.''

Judith's first thought was for the boy, of course. A quick, burning sorrow that his young life had been so brutally snuffed out before he had a chance to live it. Only gradually did she realize all the implications of that death.

"Then... Wellington won't know what happened," she realized. "Or about us."

"I need a messenger I can trust to get through. None of the others are familiar enough with the country to find a way to circle the French and reach Vedras Torres. We need help for the wounded. I can't take them through the French lines. The best we can hope for—"

"Michael knows the country," she broke into his explanation. She didn't know where that thought had come from, but once it had been voiced, she very quickly realized it was the solution to so many problems. Almost the perfect solution for them all. "He knows it as well as you. As well as Cochran," she argued.

It was only after she had made her suggestion aloud that she thought to question her motives. Had she proposed this to offer her husband a chance to redeem his life? Or had there been some other reason, something less rational? Something dark that grew within her own soul and whose existence she had never before acknowledged.

"Captain Haviland is a prisoner," St. John reminded her.

"But it's a chance," she argued. "Don't you see? It's an opportunity for him to make up for what happened. These men were wounded because of Michael's actions. Who better than he to go for help for them?"

"Do you realize..." St. John began, and then he hesitated.

"How dangerous that will be?" she asked. "Is there less danger in this situation? At least..." She hesitated as he had, examining her motives again even as she tried to convince him. "At least, it's a chance," she whispered finally.

"Forgive me, Mrs. Haviland, but perhaps it's a chance your husband doesn't deserve."

His assessment hurt. She knew Michael's weaknesses, but he was her husband. And when she pictured his father, and her own, she could not be sorry that she had thought to suggest this to St. John, no matter what the major's answer might eventually be.

"Do you love your father, Major St. John?" she asked softly.

The sudden pain in the depths of his blue eyes was unexpected, but she went on, knowing that this man represented her only chance to change the fate of two brave old soldiers. They had played no role in that dawn battle, but they would certainly become casualties of her husband's disgrace.

"Of course," he said. For the first time tonight, despite the terrible truth of the diagnosis that she had given him, there was an echo of emotion in St. John's voice.

"As he loves you. Very much, I'm sure," she went on. "And no matter what..." She paused again, remembering what this man faced. A soldier's fate he had accepted with equanimity, and so she went on, trusting his strength to hear this.

"No matter what happens to you here, even if..." Her voice faltered, but she strengthened it and continued. "Even if your father loses you, he will be able to look back on your life with pride. To glory in your accomplishments, in your unquestioned valor. He will always be so *proud* you were his son. But...for Michael's father, unlike your own—"

"Don't," St. John ordered suddenly.

The shock she felt at the harshness of the single word

must have been reflected in her face, because when he spoke again, the major's tone had softened and was once more controlled.

"Believe me, Mrs. Haviland," he said, "I understand the price of disgrace. And of dishonor. Even of disappointing your father's expectations. You don't have to remind me of that."

"Major," she protested softly, but he had already turned away, picking his jacket up from the table where she had placed it before she'd begun to examine his arm.

She called to him again, softly, from the door of the tent, but St. John didn't stop. Instead, he continued across the center of the encampment and disappeared into the darkness of the woods on the other side.

Chapter Five

"What makes you think St. John will be willing to listen to anything I say?" Michael asked. "I can assure you he never has listened before."

"Because his options are extremely limited," Judith said truthfully.

This was betrayal, and she recognized that, but the more she thought about those options during the long, sleepless night, the more certain she was that only in this way might everyone win. It was so simple a solution. Cochran would be free to assume command if she were forced to carry out the horror of the amputation which was probably St. John's best hope for survival. And with the sergeant in charge, Kit might be willing to agree to that. And for Michael and his father...

"You're not trying to get rid of me, are you?" Michael asked. "Leaving the field open for our gallant major, perhaps?"

And of course, Michael in his shrewdness had hit upon the other question she had considered throughout the night. Why, really, had she suggested this?

"It's up to you," she said. "I'm simply telling you the situation. I'm not urging you to volunteer. I know..." Her voice faded suddenly, but then she forced herself to go on. "I know how dangerous this is. Lieutenant Scarborough had made it only a few miles from the encampment before he was killed. But I thought that you might *want* to do something…" Again her voice faltered before the cynical gleam in her husband's eyes.

"Something so valiantly right and honorable that it would make up for all the wrongs I've ever done before?" he asked.

There was no mockery in his voice, however, and she wondered if he were really considering volunteering to be the courier.

"That's just what St. John's father intended when he sent him to Wellington," he said. "Did you know that, my dear?"

She shook her head. "I don't know anything about Major St. John," she said.

It was not the absolute truth, of course, but she knew nothing about whatever Michael was suggesting. She remembered, however, St. John's reaction last night to her simple comments about his father's pride in his military record. So she wondered exactly what Michael knew about the earl's relationship to his son and how he knew it.

"You think he's such an honorable knight," he said. "But do you know, Judith, we are more alike than you think. He, too, was a constant disappointment to his noble sire. And it's possible, I suppose, that I can use that to my advantage."

"I don't understand," she said, feeling a frisson of unease.

St. John had asked her not to tell anyone about his condition. And of course, the news of Scarborough's death was not something he would want the others to know. Although he had not put her under any restrictions about that, Judith had fully understood that his disclosure was intended to be confidential.

Yet at dawn she had come to her husband in order to betray St. John's trust. For Michael's sake. For the sake of his father and her own. Now her husband was talking about using the knowledge she had given him to his own advantage, and she was sickened again by the way his mind worked.

"Don't worry," he said. "I'll be able to make St. John see it our way. As you said, he really doesn't have many choices left, does he?"

"Michael," she whispered, realizing suddenly that there was no guarantee that if he were given this mission, he would carry it out. If St. John released him, there was nothing to stop him from traveling in the opposite direction, away from the English lines. "You wouldn't..."

For some reason, she hesitated even to suggest such a contemptible action. If he hadn't thought about the possibility, then she shouldn't bring it up.

"I wouldn't what?" he questioned. "Run away and leave you surrounded by the enemy?"

Her fear of his cowardice must have been in her eyes, or her feelings were as transparent to him as he had once claimed. He laughed before he went on. "Leaving you here with our noble major? No, my darling, that I would *never* do."

She wanted to be reassured by that promise, but then he added, "That bastard has had more than enough of life's riches, far more than his share. I promise you I don't intend to give him something which belongs to me. But be warned, Judith, against whatever...temptation you may feel while I'm gone."

His eyes moved slowly down and then back up her figure, obviously taking in the worn, almost shapeless gar-

ments that covered her slender curves, even pausing to assess the work-roughened hands and her unbecoming
hairstyle. He smiled when he saw the slight blush of reaction creep into her cheeks.

"You really *aren't* up to St. John's standards, you know.
If he ever looks your way, my darling, try not to make a
fool of yourself. Just remember that it's only the result of
his isolation from his own kind. And the lack of
more…acceptable women. Only here, Judith, could someone like you possibly be interesting to a man like St. John."

It was a cruel taunt, especially if he believed what he'd
said to her before about her attraction to the major. She
was a married woman, and she had been faithful to those
vows, in deed and, except for her admiration for the kind
of man she believed St. John to be, even in her thoughts.

She had always known that men like the earl of Ryde's
son were far above her reach. She had clearly read St.
John's disinterest when they met in London. She had never
entertained the notion that the handsome aristocrat considered her to be in any way appealing.

St. John had offered her his friendship, and she valued
it. They respected each other, she believed, and she would
never do anything to destroy that respect. Except, she remembered with regret, in revealing the major's situation to
Michael, perhaps she already had.

She swallowed the impulse to reply to her husband's
warning, fighting the urge to defend herself from Michael's
caustic tongue. She had learned long ago the futility of that.
But with his reaction to the information she'd given him,
she wondered again if she had done the right thing in coming to him. Had it been the right thing for any of them?
Her gaze fell, her guilt over what she had done a burden
almost too strong to bear.

She heard Michael's soft laughter, and he put the crook

of his forefinger under her chin, lifting it so that her eyes were forced to meet his. He studied them a long time before he spoke.

"Thank you, my dear, for telling me," he said simply. He lowered his mouth to hers, and for the first time in months, his breath was free of the stench of alcohol. There was no brutality in the kiss he gave her. And no passion.

When he released her, their eyes met again, but they said nothing else. And Judith realized that she now had no control over what she had just put into effect.

"Because you have no choice. And you're certainly smart enough to know it," Michael Haviland said. The same arrogance, the same cold mockery that had always been there, was in his eyes and in his voice, despite his situation.

Kit had not expected to be confronted by this when he'd been asked to speak to the prisoner. St. John had told no one but Judith about Scarborough's death. Cochran had known, of course, but the sergeant could be counted on to keep that secret. He had believed that Mrs. Haviland might be counted on as well, Kit thought bitterly.

"I'll get through to Wellington," Haviland vowed, his normal confidence apparently restored by the possibility this mission offered. "But in exchange, St. John, I want your promise."

"*My* promise?" Kit repeated, although he had known this was the crux of the offer. It was, in reality, the same one Haviland had made to Smythe. Only he had made it to the colonel in terms of respect. And now...

"Your sacred promise. Made on your bloody, precious honor," Michael demanded. "I want your solemn oath that if I go for help, if I carry the news of the French reinforcement and your situation here, that you'll never repeat to anyone the charges you made against me. That you'll never by word or deed divulge what happened that morning."

"You know I can't agree to that," Kit said.

"Why not? The regiment's destroyed. Smythe's dead. There are only a handful of people left who know anything about what happened that day. And without your pressing them to testify, those few can be trusted to keep their mouths shut. Even if they don't..." One of Michael's brows arched, and he shrugged.

He was right, of course. No one would care what people such as Cochran or the few remaining men of Haviland's troop would say. Too many enlisted men disparaged their officers. They would simply be ignored. They both understood that.

"You can't send Cochran," Haviland argued. "You need him to feed your charges. The other two would be less than worthless for that. They'll end up spitted on some Portuguese bandit's dagger before they stumble across anything fit to fill the cooking pots. I'm your best hope to get these people through this country, and you know it."

"When Cochran leaves, I'll see to the provisions."

Michael laughed and then seeing the quick reaction to his mockery in Kit's eyes, he wiped the amusement from his face. "Perhaps you can. For a while. *But* that will then leave this detachment without a commander. Cochran will be gone, and you propose to be out foraging all day," he said, his derision for the plan still clear, somehow, in his voice. "And when you are no longer able to function?" he added softly. "When you're no longer competent to command? What then, St. John?"

"I'll consider that possibility only if I have to," Kit said stubbornly.

"Possibility?" Haviland repeated in mockery. "If Judith

says you'll not be fit to give orders, then I can assure you it's not simply a *possibility*.''

"Did she tell you that?" Kit asked sharply, feeling both anger and fear at her appraisal of his condition.

"You won't even recognize when you have reached that point," Haviland said. "Your mind will begin to play tricks on you. What is irrational will seem supremely rational. Fever does that to a man. You know it as well as I."

Kit couldn't deny that truth. They had both seen the sequence: the rising fever, the trembling physical weakness and the near stupor it produced, followed almost inevitably by wild ravings and the unnatural strength of true delirium. Thinking of that progression, St. John said nothing, until Michael asked the crucial question.

"Who will be responsible for these people then, St. John? Will you trust me to lead them?"

"Perhaps," Kit said.

"But I won't, you know." Deliberately, Haviland belittled that unwilling agreement. "Because then there will be nothing in it for me. I don't care if you *or* they live to reach Wellington's surgeons. It's to my advantage that none of you do. Why should I take any of these men to a place where I'll face disgrace and dishonor? A place where I'll again be made a prisoner. No, my friend. You have one deal left for the game. One hand to play. Or we'll probably *all* die."

Kit expected death. He had already begun to prepare himself for it. And he would willingly die if he could keep the others safe. But that willingness was only in exchange for the lives of the others. Judith's face was suddenly before him. He had seen women caught before between the opposing armies of this war. And the thought of that happening to her was unbearable.

"How do I know you'll keep your word?" Kit asked.

Haviland was right about so much of what he said, despite
the immoral premise behind the suggestion.

"Because..." Haviland hesitated. Suddenly, for the first
time since Kit had known him, the captain seemed unsure.
He looked younger, less cynical, and what Kit read in his
eyes was a pain that had never been revealed there before.

"Do you love your father, St. John?" Haviland asked
finally, instead of finishing whatever easy explanation of
his motives he had begun. "Did you seek his approval?
Have you sought his approval your whole bloody life and
known that you never quite lived up to his expectations?"
Michael's voice was caustic and yet somehow filled with
longing. "Do you have any idea what it's like never to
measure up? No matter how hard you try?"

Again, as they had in Smythe's tent, his own father's
words echoed in Kit's head. *You continue to bring dishonor
to this family. You may enjoy wallowing in the mud of public censure, but I will no longer allow you to drag the
Montgomery name there with you.*

But, despite that bond which they undoubtedly shared,
could he trust Michael Haviland? And did he really have a
choice? St. John wondered bitterly.

"Your wife is here," Kit reminded him. However despicable Haviland was, surely he would not desert Judith to
face starvation or capture in order to save his own hide.

"Of course," Michael said softly. "The thought of that
will travel with me every mile of the way, I promise you."

Again Kit heard an undercurrent, but he couldn't identify
it. He wondered suddenly if what Judith had predicted
about the ultimate failure of his faculties was already beginning. But that, too, was a chance he would have to take.

"All right," Kit agreed reluctantly. "You have my
word."

"I want your oath, St. John. Whether or not I succeed,"

Haviland demanded. "We both know what lies between here and Vedras Torres. I may not make it through. I don't want my father to suffer because of that...failure. I want your word," he said again, "that the story of what happened the morning of the French attack will never pass your lips. Or any other disparagement of my conduct. I want your solemn oath made on your own noble honor." And there was mockery in that, too.

"Then in exchange," Kit demanded, his own temper flaring, "I want *your* oath that you'll do everything in your power to get through. No stratagems, Haviland. No hiding. No cowardice. The lives of these people depend on your faithfulness to this bargain."

"I'm not a coward. No matter what you think."

"On your honor," Kit ordered again, ignoring that claim.

Their eyes held, weighing one another. They were not friends. They had no respect for each other, but they had both been raised according to a code, taught to them by men who had adhered to its rules all their lives.

Slowly, Michael Haviland held out his hand. Kit hesitated, still considering all that was on the table, still trying to assess the man who stood before him and the situation. Finally he allowed his own right hand to close firmly around the other. Only then did the familiar smile appear on Haviland's lips.

"Poor St. John," he said softly. "Forced by fate to make a bargain with the devil."

"And if you don't keep to it, you bastard, I swear I'll hunt you down in hell," Kit promised, his voice as low as the other man's had been, "and I'll bloody well make you wish you had."

But even as he watched, the small, cynical smile widened.

* * *

"Is he gone?" Judith Haviland asked.

Kit wondered if her husband had not bothered to say goodbye, but that was not a question he could ask her. The beautiful oval face was as colorless as poor Scarborough's had been the morning of the battle.

"Almost an hour ago," he admitted.

She released the breath she'd been holding, and the strength of its passage through her slim body was visible. Relief, he thought, identifying the emotion that showed briefly in her eyes, which were then quickly veiled from his assessment by the fall of long, dark lashes.

"Thank you," she said.

"As you pointed out to your husband, Mrs. Haviland, I really had very little choice."

Hearing the bitterness, her eyes flashed up to his. "I'm sorry. Truly I am, Major St. John. I did what I thought was for the best. For *all* of us."

Kit said nothing, still hurt by her betrayal. He deliberately shifted his gaze from her face to watch Cochran supervising the reloading of the wagons.

As soon as they were on their way, the sergeant would ride ahead, not only scouting the territory they must cross for signs of the enemy, but seeking something for the cooking pots tonight. They had made do with only the hard biscuits and water this morning, but their store of those was running dangerously low.

"I'd like to look at your arm again, Major St. John. I think it might help to wrap the rest of the willow I infused under a new bandage. Eventually, you know—"

"You made all the eventualities extremely clear last night," he interrupted. "To me and apparently also to your husband."

She glanced down at his elbow, his left arm bent and held protectively against his body. The crimson uniform sleeve was stretched tightly over the swelling, and that must be excruciating. He hadn't given her a chance last night to replace the bandage she had removed. And she knew the wool would chafe the tender flesh all day as he rode.

"Do you believe I lied to you, Major?"

When she looked up from his arm, the blue eyes were again on her face. She had nothing to hide, and so she let him examine it, meeting his appraisal without fear.

"I believe you used your knowledge of things I should never have told you to your husband's advantage," he said finally.

"And to yours. To the advantage of *all* these people. Surely you can understand that," she argued. "I meant you no harm. I only wanted to help. To..."

Her rationale faded in the face of the coldness in his eyes. Within them was an indifference to her explanation that was as chilling as the aristocratic boredom which had been there the night they met. He hadn't known her then. Surely by now he knew her better than this, she thought. His gaze finally moved away from her face, again checking Cochran's progress.

"You need Sergeant Cochran to hunt," she said, her eyes following his, "and to scout. *You* are needed to lead, so you must stay physically strong as long as possible. No matter what you think of my motives, Major, you know I'm the only one who can help you to do that. Please let me treat your arm."

The cold eyes came back to her, again assessing.

"For their sakes," she added softly.

And for your own, her heart pled, but that was an argument she didn't dare offer because she knew him well enough now to know it would have perhaps the opposite effect of what she sought. Finally, after a long time, he nodded.

She resisted the urge to draw in a breath in relief. Instead she led the way to her small tent and the concoction she had begun brewing some time before dawn, knowing full well that perhaps neither it nor her prayers would make any difference in the progress of the creeping infection.

And if it didn't, she knew also that she would have to try something more radical. *The best hope for survival,* she had told him before. And although she didn't remind him of that this morning, they both knew it was still true.

He had tied a neck cloth around the wound, and when she removed it, she realized that even in these short hours the redness and swelling around the saber gash had grown more pronounced.

"I need you to remove your shirt," she whispered.

He had replaced the shirt she had cut up with a fresh one from his campaign chest. When she had tried to roll up the sleeve to allow her to work, it wouldn't now go far enough above the swelling for her to evaluate how rapidly the corruption was spreading, but she hesitated to destroy another garment of his limited wardrobe.

"I can help you," she offered, seeing the hesitation in his eyes.

Abruptly, St. John shook his head. He reached behind his neck with his right hand and pulled the loose shirt off over his head and then more slowly off the swollen arm.

Judith had cared for innumerable injured men. She had seen them in all stages of undress and had performed services that no gentlewoman, not even a married one, should have to carry out. There was little that was any longer mysterious to her about the masculine body.

But at the sight of St. John's, her breath caught in her throat and even her stomach reacted. And somewhere below. Something roiled within her body, hot and immensely disturbing.

St. John's shoulders were broad, his skin as dark as her own. Despite his coloring, his chest was smoothly bronze, the small brown nubs of his nipples pebbled now with the chill of the morning.

Judith simply stood a moment, almost mesmerized, staring at the expanse of graceful muscle and the perfection of bone structure he'd revealed. The only thing that marred the smooth expanse was a thin line of dark hair that ran down the center of his ridged stomach to disappear into the top of the white knit pantaloons.

"Is it very far advanced?" he asked.

Only with his question did Judith realize that she had forgotten the purpose behind this disrobing.

"No," she said softly, thankful to realize that that was reality. The streaks were there, climbing upward under the dark skin that stretched over the long, firm muscle of his upper arm, but they seemed no farther advanced than they had been last night.

"Perhaps if I blister the wound itself..." she began and realized what an impossibility that would be, given the swelling.

"Try the other first," he suggested softly.

Her eyes lifted, questioning. She had forgotten the infusion she'd prepared. Forgotten almost everything in the sheer physical reaction to his body. She didn't understand what had happened. There had never been anything about Michael's body... *Michael,* she remembered suddenly. *Michael, who was her husband.*

"You said there would be some time..." His eyes met hers unflinchingly, despite what he knew he faced.

"Especially if we're successful in slowing this," she

said, grateful for the reprieve from her tangled emotions that his calm question offered her.

She moved to the other side of the tent for the infusion she'd begun last night, using the last of the dried willow leaves she'd brought with her from England. They wouldn't be as potent as fresh, she knew, but perhaps this would have some effect.

Time, she thought. Only a little time. Enough for Michael to bring help. Enough for them to get the wounded through. To get St. John to the surgeons. *Please, dear God,* she prayed, *just enough time.*

When she had dipped the cloth into the amber liquid, making sure it was thoroughly soaked, she brought it back to where St. John was sitting. She carefully placed the steaming rag over the swelling and heard the inward hiss of the breath he drew.

"I should have warned you," she apologized.

His face was averted, and he didn't turn at her words. He was still angry with her about what she'd done, she supposed. Losing his trust was the price she would pay for trying to find some solution for all that had happened.

There was nothing she could do about that, she thought, as she wound a new bandage over the still steaming cloth. She had done what she thought was best for the people she cared about. For all of them, but she was unwilling to enumerate exactly who *they* were. If her action resulted in the loss of St. John's respect, it was a small enough price to pay for his life.

"Shall I help you with your shirt?" she asked when she had finished tying the ends of the cloth over the poultice.

"I can manage, thank you, Mrs. Haviland."

He stood up again to pull the shirt awkwardly over his head, and she watched him struggle unsuccessfully to get the sleeve down over the swelling in his left arm, but she didn't repeat her offer. He still hadn't looked at her.

"He will do his best," she said softly. At that the black lashes lifted, revealing clear, fever-bright eyes. "He won't betray you," she promised, believing that because she must.

"Or you," he suggested.

But she had no guarantee of that. She was aware that her marriage was not what her father's and mother's had been. It had never been a love match, of course.

There was nothing in her heart of what she should feel for a husband. Nothing of desire. Or of affection, even. She had blamed herself for that lack, and for the shivering revulsion she had come to feel when Michael's hands moved against her body.

That guilt was hers. Innate still. But now she knew that the familiar coldness was not.

"Honor," she said softly.

St. John's blue eyes narrowed slightly, but he didn't question her use of the word in this context. Or the thought which had produced it.

"Thank you, Mrs. Haviland," he said again. And again, he picked up his jacket and walked out, leaving her once more alone.

the above cloth over the swelling to his left arm, but the thigh ...

Chapter Six

They made frustratingly slow progress over the course of the next four days, and two more of the wounded died. The jolting carts were agonizing for broken bones and damaged bodies, of course, and there was little food, a subsistence level only, although Sergeant Cochran did his best to provide fresh meat each night. They had run out of biscuits the day before yesterday and now were wholly dependent on Cochran's skill, or more importantly, St. John thought, on his luck.

Kit shifted his swollen left arm, trying to find a more comfortable position for it, although intellectually he had already acknowledged there wasn't one. His eyes were burning with the growing fever, and more than once this afternoon he had found himself swaying in the saddle. He had also fought the ridiculous urge to discard the wool jacket in hopes that the cold rain would ease the almost unbearable heat of his body.

Mrs. Haviland patiently placed steaming cloths over his wound each night, replacing them with fresh ones as soon as they cooled. She was trying to draw out the poison and reduce the swelling, and she had had some small success with that. But the nightly fomentations had given him little relief from the pain or the building fever.

She had not been able to stop the spreading infection, but still he was grateful, because she had given him four days, and they were now four days closer to the English lines and to help. And if Haviland had reached Wellington...

Kit's wandering attention was suddenly attracted by a horseman, approaching out of the gray curtain of mist and rain. The red coat marked him as English, and seeing it, Kit's sudden anxiety abated. However, the rider was trying to push his tired mount too fast through the sucking mire the roadway had become.

The wagons had fought their way through the mud all day, every slogging step an effort. They had been forced to stop twice this afternoon to free the wheels of the heaviest cart. Unloading and then reloading the wounded had not helped their condition, and the rain had continued all day, slowing this already endless journey, adding hours they couldn't afford.

The approaching rider was Cochran, Kit realized. The sergeant pulled his exhausted mount up beside Kit's.

"The French," he gasped, his beefy face red with exertion.

"How large a patrol?" Kit asked. He had already turned in the saddle, preparing to order the wagons that stretched behind him to move off the road.

"No patrol." Cochran's breathing had eased somewhat, allowing him to get out more words. "Whole bloody French army."

"Massena?"

"Every French bastard in Portugal."

"What the hell..." Kit breathed.

"Starving. Just like we are. Apparently the emperor sent

two thousand more men and no provisions. And Major, there ain't a chicken left alive between us and Wellington. Not after this winter. You can't feed an army on promises. Not even Massena can do that, so he's taking his army home.''

"And they're coming this way."

"There's not any other. The Beau's blown the bridges on the Targus. Eventually the French will turn east, but not before they reach us.''

"Do you have a suggestion, Sergeant?" Kit asked.

He was aware that his capacity to think clearly, to make appropriate decisions, had been diminishing, swallowed up by his illness. The warning Michael Haviland had given was still in the back of his head, as it had been throughout the endless hours of these last four days.

You won't even know when you've reached that point, the captain had taunted him. What action the caravan should take was Kit's decision, and his responsibility, but he would value the sergeant's advice. At least he wasn't too far gone in the throes of fever or too big a fool to know he should ask for it.

"Won't do no good to turn around. We can't travel fast enough to outrun them," Cochran observed. "Not in this mud.''

"Then we find a place to hide until they've gone past us.''

The enlisted man's eyes rested on his commander's face a moment before he nodded agreement. "There are caves in the hills,'' Cochran offered. "I ran across one not too far from here, but you can't get the wagons up to it.''

"Thompson can't ride," Kit reminded him.

"Leave him somewhere off the road in the woods,'' Cochran advised bluntly. "You got no choice, Major. He'd be the first to tell you that.''

"The French won't take prisoners. Not if this is the full-blown retreat you believe it to be."

The sergeant nodded. "Then leave him a gun."

It was the usual procedure in this sort of circumstance. The welfare of the unit was more important than the life of one man. Every British soldier understood that reality and most accepted it. But, whether influenced by the effects of the growing fever or not, Kit rejected that logical option. It wasn't an order he would ever give about one of these men. Their British stubbornness and will to survive had gotten them this far. He wouldn't abandon them now.

"Put him up in the saddle in front of you," Kit ordered.

"He won't survive the ride, Major," Cochran warned softly. "You know that as well as I."

"Then at least he won't die alone," Kit said.

Except for Thompson, they made it to the shelter of the cave Cochran had found, but it had been another nightmare journey. The women and the remaining wounded had been placed on the backs of the cart horses and Judith was mounted on Scarborough's gray.

In the end, they had to climb the last half mile, walking beside the struggling animals to encourage them. Only those too debilitated by illness or by their wounds were allowed to ride on that final leg. Kit did not choose to be one of them, and he was exhausted when they finally arrived.

The sanctuary the cave represented was only a temporary reprieve, he knew. They could kill one of the horses for food, and they found water in the back of the cave, a cold trickle that slid down the rock wall to collect in the shallow basin it had worn over the years in the stone floor.

But with the countryside overrun with the retreating French and the ever-present threat of Portuguese bandits and cutthroat bands of deserters, Kit knew that the smoke from even a single fire might give away their location. At least for now, however, thanks to Sergeant Cochran, they were relatively safe.

Kit was standing outside the entrance of the cave into which the two corporals had already carried the wounded. One of the soldiers from Haviland's troop had a badly broken leg, and throughout the jolting ride up the rocky slope to the cave, his pain-filled eyes had clearly expressed his suffering, but he had sketched the major a cocky salute as he was being taken inside the shelter.

Kit had already sent Cochran out to scout, hoping that by some miracle the sergeant might stumble across a living, breathing creature in this war-devastated landscape where the French had survived by scavenging for food all winter. And if he did not...

Kit's eyes shifted unwillingly to the thin, rack-ribbed draft horses. One of them would have to be sacrificed, and he supposed then they'd be forced to take their chances with a fire. His stomach roiled with nausea at the alternative.

Again he pushed the unpleasant possibility from his mind, not even questioning why he hadn't already given the order. They had all eaten horse meat at some time during the last three years. That should no longer be as unthinkable to him as it had been when he'd first arrived in this country. But somehow he hadn't been able to make up his mind to order the slaughter.

He would ask Cochran, he thought, closing his eyes against the deep ache behind them and leaning his head against the cool dampness of the rocks. And as soon as the sergeant returned, he would ask him to post sentries for the night.

Kit knew there must be other things he should attend to,

but the ideas seemed to slip out of his brain before he could grasp them. He could almost watch them drifting away from him to disappear into the mist. And he was no longer certain whether that mist was reality or was a growing fog within his own mind.

"I need to see to your arm," someone said softly. "Before nightfall. Before it gets so dark that I can't."

Kit opened his eyes, pushing the heavy lids upward against their determined resistance. He turned his head, which was still resting against the dampness of the rocks, and found Judith Haviland standing beside him in the gathering twilight. He had not even been aware of her approach.

Apparently, as it had during the long horror of the afternoon, his mind had retreated from the worries of the present into more pleasant memories of the past. He had been thinking of England. Of the vast estate where he had grown up. Of summer rains that caressed instead of battered. Of horses grazing in lush meadows instead of being butchered and eaten by those whom they had so faithfully served.

See to his arm? At least he thought that's what she had said, but he couldn't remember why she would want to do that. She had said *something* about his arm.

She lifted her hand to put the back of it against his brow, but he jerked his head away, recoiling from that contact.

He couldn't allow her to touch him. He remembered that, all right. It was too dangerous. That was one of the things he knew he must hold on to. Mrs. Haviland was married. Out of his reach. Forbidden. Any caress of his hand was forbidden. Or hers, he supposed. Even the thought of allowing her to touch him must be fought. And instead...

At his reaction, Judith had hesitated, her hand still raised between them. He wasn't looking any longer at that, however. His eyes found her face instead, tracing over the clear, rain-touched beauty of her skin. Examining the fragile bone structure, too clearly revealed by the deprivations she had suffered. Too exposed. Exposed to his eyes.

He blinked, suddenly reminded that this, too, was not allowed. He was forbidden even to look at her. Forbidden. All of it. All of what he wanted.

"What is it?" she asked softly. "What's wrong?"

He shook his head, unable to find the words he needed to frame an answer to that. The ones that clamored for expression were those he had no right to say. Could not in honor ever say to this woman. And if he died without telling her what he felt, then that was only as it should be. No right, he thought again.

"Major St. John?" Judith whispered, her wide, dark eyes examining his face.

He was frightening her, Kit realized. She wouldn't understand why his lips had flattened into the taut line that was necessary to prevent the escape of those words. Forbidden words. Forbidden thoughts.

But still he *had* thought them. They had drifted through his brain in increasingly vivid images. He was no better than his father had accused him of being, he thought in disgust. Without honor. Even about this.

"Your arm?" she said again.

"Of course," he managed. He tried to straighten his elbow, to move it away from the protected position against his body in which he had held it all day. And he couldn't prevent the involuntary gasp of response to the agony of that movement.

"We'll have to get your jacket off," she said.

Kit tried not to think about that. He couldn't bear to move his arm, and she was suggesting that they pull the woolen sleeve off over that grotesquely swollen flesh. But of course, he knew that was the only way she could treat it. He couldn't understand why he had forgotten that necessity.

"I think tonight we might need to cut the coat away," she suggested. "I can split the seam up the back of the arm."

"They'll hang me," he said with conviction. And if they did, his father would be ashamed of him again, he reasoned.

His argument against cutting up his coat made perfect sense to him. Everything he owned had been left with the wagons they'd deserted. If she destroyed this coat, he would be in enemy-held territory without a uniform. But for some reason, Judith Haviland was smiling at him. She put her hand gently on his arm, thankfully his good one.

"Well, I promise they won't hang you tonight," she assured him softly. "Uniform or not. They'd have to find you first, Major, and we won't allow them to do that. I think you'd better come inside with me. Don't you think that would be better than standing out here in the rain?" she asked gently.

She was speaking to him as if he were a child, but then Kit hadn't realized it was raining. He closed his eyes, lifting his face to the fine mist, and took a deep breath, pulling the cold, damp air deep into his lungs. He liked the feel of the moisture on his skin. It was almost soothing.

There was something he knew he was supposed to be doing. Some duty he was responsible for. So he opened his eyes again, and found that Mrs. Haviland was still smiling at him, her hand still resting on his arm.

He looked down at it. He could almost feel its warmth through the wool of his uniform. Despite the heat of his body, her fingers were burning against his skin. Long slender fingers, always reddened from the cold and the endless hard work she did for everyone. For him and the others.

But they shouldn't be work-worn, he thought. It wasn't right. They should be the soft pampered hands of a lady.

His lady? he wondered. She would be if she married him. And then he remembered, of course, and the sudden, terrible loss created by that remembrance was cold and bitter in his chest. The woman he loved was already married. Married to someone else.

The woman he loved. He examined the phrase which had appeared in his head, knowing that it, too, was forbidden. Still he didn't destroy the words. He found that he couldn't, now that they had finally been allowed expression in his consciousness.

"What are you doing out here?" Judith asked.

"Waiting for Cochran," he said. He had forgotten why he was waiting, but at least with her question, he had remembered that's why he was here. Part of his duty, and he knew that whatever he was waiting to tell the sergeant must therefore be important.

"I'll ask Corporal Timmons to wait for him. Will that be all right?"

She had taken Kit's arm and was guiding him toward the dark entrance of the cave. He followed because it seemed easier to let her do what she wanted than to marshall an argument against it. It was hard to think of the words he wanted to say. There was something else, he knew. Something that…

"Sentries," he said suddenly. The word had popped into his fevered brain like a miracle.

"I'll see to them," she promised him.

And she would. This was Mrs. Haviland. He could trust her. But at the back of his mind was a warning. Something that he should remember. Something his father wanted him to remember, he thought. Maybe when he was inside, in the cool darkness of the cave and out of this terrible heat, it would come back to him.

Maybe.

"How is he?" Cochran whispered. The question echoed slightly because they were at the very back of the cave. Everyone else was asleep, exhausted by the exertions of the day and weakened by the lack of food.

Tonight the sergeant had brought nothing back from his brief scouting trip in the fading light, and perhaps that was just as well. They all understood the risk of building a fire, but it would have been hard to resist the urge to cook if they had had anything to put into the pot.

As it was, sleep was the only escape from hunger and the cold. So they huddled together, still in their drenched garments, drawing what warmth they could from one another.

Judith shook her head in answer to the sergeant's question, and then wondered if Cochran saw the movement in the darkness. There was some shifting moonlight, despite the clouds, and the lighter darkness of the sky outlined the entrance of the cave.

She had watched Cochran come in from the outside, from sentry duty, and make his careful way past the sleepers to the back of the cave. His first concern had been for the major.

"He's burning up," Judith said truthfully. "Everything he said earlier…" She paused, hesitant to reveal Kit's confusion, even to Cochran.

"Delirious," the sergeant suggested.

"Just…wandering. He doesn't seem to have a very clear understanding of what's happening."

"You did all you could, Mrs. Haviland. The sawbones couldn't 'a done no more for him. The major knew it, too.

Don't you go blaming yourself, now. Whatever happens," he added.

"You talk as if—" There had been sharp protest in the sentence she began, and then she wondered what she was protesting. Cochran sounded resigned. But she was not. Not yet, at least. "They would have taken the arm. It's what I should have done," she said.

She had known that would be the safest way. That's why there were so many amputations when an extremity was injured. No one could argue about the success of that common practice.

"Could you do that? Can you do it now?" the sergeant asked.

"Here?" she whispered, her doubt clear despite the softness of her tone.

"There's not likely to be a better place. We'll probably be holed up here for a while," he said.

"Where no one can find us," she suggested bitterly. "Not even Wellington."

"The general can't send men into that French exodus, ma'am. Much as he might want to if…when he finds out about us."

Judith understood the sergeant's doubt. He had found Scarborough's body. He knew the odds against Michael getting through. Or perhaps he feared, as she had, that her husband might not even try.

"It would be a suicide mission," Cochran continued, and he wasn't talking about Michael's, she realized. "One with little chance of success, and the Beau will know that full well."

"So no one will come. Even if my husband gets through."

The sergeant said nothing in response. There was, in reality, nothing to say.

"What will we do?" she asked finally.

"Tomorrow we'll kill one of the horses. There's water. We can survive here for a few days."

She looked down in the darkness at the pale oval of St. John's face. *We can survive,* Cochran had said, and if no one stumbled across their hiding place, that might be true. For the rest of them perhaps, but for the major...

"Can you do it, Mrs. Haviland?" Cochran asked again. "Will it help if you do it now?"

She had almost forgotten what he had asked her before. Or had managed to block from her mind once again the thought of the operation she had been thinking about for the last week.

"I don't know," she whispered into the surrounding darkness, and even as she said it, she wasn't sure which of those questions she was answering.

The morning brought a weak, watery sunshine. The two corporals cheerfully helped Judith move the wounded out of the dampness of the cave and into the clearing in front of it. Relishing the small warmth of the winter sun on her back, as she knew the men would be after yesterday's cold rain, Judith cleaned and rebandaged their wounds and, with the help of Mrs. McQueen, saw to their most pressing needs.

All but the major, she thought, who was still on the bed they had made for him at the farthest reaches of the cave. St. John had begun to talk. There were only whispered words and phrases, but some of them were clearly articulated enough to be understandable.

And most of them had been references to his father. Remembering the major's reaction to what she had said about the earl's natural pride in him, Judith had also realized that some of those muttered expressions might be very personal in nature.

Whatever his relationship to his father, it shouldn't be so cruelly exposed to the others. And for some reason, she was still reluctant to reveal the extent of his illness to them as well.

While she had seen to the other wounded, Cochran had killed the weakest of the draft animals, and the women had been set to work preparing the meat for the cooking pot. At least there would be food today, and hot, nourishing broth for the major, Mrs. McQueen had promised her that, and Judith was determined to get some of it down him.

The sergeant had posted sentries on the rocks above the entrance to the cave. Their position here was probably as secure as any they were likely to find, but he had cautioned them all about unnecessary noise. So in contrast to their usual chatter and laughter, the women were subdued as they worked. Under no illusions about what would happen to them if they were captured, they understood the situation as well as the soldiers.

Cochran had agreed to build a small fire, but he had devised a thick screen of interwoven branches that could be placed across the narrow entrance to the cave. The sergeant had laid the wood in preparation for the fire just inside. The opening would draw the smoke outward and the leaves of the screen he'd made would help to break it up. Which should make it less noticeable, he had explained, to anyone who might be looking.

Cochran had followed Judith when she went back inside to check on St. John. The soft, broken monologue the major had carried on throughout much of the night was continuing.

The sergeant watched as Judith knelt to touch Kit's forehead. There was no reaction to the coolness of her fingers against his brow today. No recoil from her touch, as there had been yesterday.

"Maybe the fire will help to keep him warm," Cochran offered.

Judith had been concerned about the coldness of the cave last night. She had known that she shouldn't allow St. John to sleep in his wet clothing, but, against her medical judgment, she had not removed anything but the jacket she'd had to cut away.

At some time in the coldest, darkest hour of the night, she had even thought about lying down beside him to keep him warm, but, of course, she had not done that either. Instead, she had tried to make sure that the blanket stayed tucked about his shoulders. He had thrown it off again and again, fighting against the rising heat of his fever.

She looked up at the sergeant, no longer attempting to hide the worry in her eyes, infinitely glad that she had someone she trusted to share this burden with. "I don't think the cold is bothering him," she said softly.

"You're going to have to try to take that arm off, Mrs. Haviland," he said.

Cochran was trying to help. He understood, as she did, that there was probably only one thing that might make a difference in St. John's condition now.

"I don't know that I can, Sergeant," she said truthfully. "I've never done an amputation before. I have no instruments. And in his condition..."

"He ain't going to get any stronger, ma'am. You know what fever does to a man. Just burns up his strength."

"I know," she said.

He was right. This was a decision that would have to be made today. And it was her decision to make. Perhaps with Cochran's help, she could succeed. At least, she thought, the delirium of the fever would provide its own escape from the pain.

"I'll be outside if you need me," Cochran said. "The women just about have the meat ready to go into the pot. I'm going to start the fire, and then we'll put the branches over the entrance. Will you be needing the light to see to the major, Mrs. Haviland? If you do, we can wait."

"Of course you must not wait. The sooner those men are fed, the better, Sergeant Cochran. The fire will provide what light I need," she said. "I'm going to try to get some water down the major's throat. We'll be fine."

Turning, she stooped to dip her handkerchief in the shallow basin at the foot of the rock wall and then knelt beside St. John. She allowed the water to drip off the cloth onto his parched lips. She had hoped that he would lick it off, an automatic reaction to its coolness. But he didn't.

She rubbed her thumb gently over the fullness of his bottom lip, and it opened slightly. She squeezed the handkerchief, and two or three drops of icy water fell into his mouth. This time there was a reaction. His tongue moved slowly over his bottom lip, touching her finger as well as the moisture.

She smiled at her success or perhaps at that small contact with his tongue, and then she continued the slow process. It wasn't until she stood up to make another trip to the basin that held the water, that she realized Cochran was standing near the entrance watching her.

"That's a good sign, ain't it, ma'am? Taking the water?"

Unwilling to deny the hope she could clearly hear in the sergeant's voice, she nodded agreement. She knew full well, however, that her small success with this would make little difference in the larger battle she fought.

Her eyes were still directed toward the opening, where the sergeant was silhouetted against the morning light, when she heard the first shot. And then another, rapidly following.

Cochran whirled, looking out through the entrance even as he pulled his pistol from its holster. Judith had no idea what he saw, but before he stepped outside, he turned back to face her, laying his finger over his mouth and shaking his head.

Judith nodded to indicate that she understood what he wanted her to do, but since she was hidden in the darkness at the back of the cave, she wasn't sure he had even seen her agreement. Her own fingers closed over St. John's pistol, which she had laid on top of the uniform coat last night.

When she turned back, the gun in her hand was pointed at the entrance to the cave. She saw that Cochran was now on the outside putting the screen of branches over the opening, hiding the entrance to the cave from whoever was out there.

She wouldn't know what was happening outside, not until someone removed those branches and entered the darkness of the cave. But in obedience to Cochran's unspoken command, Judith crouched beside the major, his pistol gripped in her trembling fingers, and almost without daring to breathe, she listened.

There were other shots which seemed nearer than the first two had been. The English soldiers were apparently returning fire. There was an occasional outcry, guttural and sharply cut off. It was the sound a man makes when he's been hit by a ball or by a saber's slash. Judith had heard that noise often enough to know she was not mistaken.

When the firing diminished, a small hope began to grow within her heart. It lasted until the screaming began. The women, she thought. The women. Judith closed her eyes, but it didn't help. Her brain conjured up the images of what was occurring only a few feet from where she hid.

She should help them, Mrs. McQueen and the others. She had a pistol. Perhaps she could...

But if she went to help the women, she realized, then she would reveal St. John to whoever was out there. Even as that thought formed, another sound distracted her. The fever-induced mutterings of the man who lay behind her had begun again.

They were very soft, but if they followed the pattern they had taken last night, they would grow in volume as his agitation increased. And when the screaming outside stopped...

Cochran had told her to be quiet. In this situation that was an order. Here in the back of the cave, hidden from sight, they might escape detection. That had been Cochran's intent, she knew. To provide the best protection he could for the two people he had left hidden in the cave.

The low murmur of St. John's voice was increasing in volume. She turned, leaning over him. She laid her left hand lightly over his mouth, the pistol still gripped in her right, her eyes focused on the screened entrance.

She could hear someone talking out there. Giving orders? The tone was right, but the words were too rapid and still too far away for her to decipher. Not French, she realized, but Portuguese. She had picked up a smattering of the language in the last three years, but not enough to know what was being said.

St. John turned his head restlessly, and her hand slipped off his mouth. She looked down, distracted from whatever was happening outside. The major's eyes were open. She could see them, the whites shining in the darkness of the cave.

Maybe she could make him understand that he must be very quiet. She leaned closer, pressing her own body over his, almost lying on top of him. She put her palm over his mouth again.

"Shhh," she whispered, her lips against his face. She could tell by his sudden stillness that he was listening.

She lifted her head, trying to see his eyes, to read them. He was still motionless, and she couldn't know if he had understood what she was trying to tell him. From outside the cave, she could hear the sound of horses milling around the small clearing where she had tended to the wounded this morning, their morale buoyed by the promise of the sunshine. And where now...

Again, St. John turned his head, escaping the confinement of her palm in order to say something. She couldn't distinguish anything that made sense in the words, and realizing that he was probably too far gone in delirium to heed her warning, her heart began to pound in her throat. Whoever was out there would surely hear him, and then they would come in here and...

Suddenly St. John's right hand reached upward to cup the back of her head. His fingers stirred in the loose chignon, and then his thumb trailed down the side of her neck. Down and back up. Slowly. Caressing the shivering chill of her skin with its fevered heat. Touching her.

Despite what was happening outside, despite the real terror of their situation, a matching heat began to grow inside Judith's body, moving upward, in a warm, honeyed wave of sensation, into her stomach. Her lips parted slightly with the shock of that feeling, breath sighing out in reaction.

What she felt was totally unfamiliar. And it was frightening. Not terrifying in the same way that whoever was outside was terrifying, of course, but still it filled her with fear. Because it was stirring sensations that she had not realized she was capable of feeling, that she should *not* feel.

But she didn't resist when the gentle pressure of St.

John's hand increased, urging her face down to his. His lips opened beneath hers, and his tongue touched her mouth, drifting sensuously across the fullness of her bottom lip. It moved as slowly as his thumb had, when it had glided against the sensitive skin of her neck. This movement too was unhurried. Undemanding.

And then his tongue pushed between her lips, opening them. Seeking admittance. Trying to enter and find hers. His lips were firm, and his mouth had automatically aligned itself into position under hers.

This, then, is what it should be, she thought. This was how a man's mouth should feel against her own. Inside hers. Caressing. And it was nothing like Michael's kiss had ever been.

With that thought came the realization of what she was doing, and she tried to lift her head, attempting to pull her lips away from that heated contact with his. St. John's hand refused to release her.

He said something, the tone of the whispered words seductive somehow, but loud enough that she was afraid whoever was out there must surely be able to hear them. In her terror and confusion, his voice seemed to echo within the cave. Or maybe the whispered words echoed only within her head.

She was frozen, held motionless, because she couldn't decide. And because she was listening. Listening to see if whoever was beyond the screen of branches, all that separated them from certain death, might have heard him.

And then, while she was still listening, she felt the heat of St. John's breath flutter against the corner of her mouth. The warmth of his tongue followed it, touching her lips again with that practiced expertise.

When his head lifted slightly, bringing his mouth to fit again under hers, she didn't resist. He had no idea what was going on outside. And probably, she acknowledged with an uncharacteristic bitterness, no idea even of who she was. But when he was kissing her, he was quiet. That was the reality. The very important reality.

She could hear clearly now footsteps just beyond the opening of the cave. As they came ever nearer, Judith Haviland deliberately lowered her mouth over St. John's. Hers was open, as he had taught her, and it was, against her will perhaps, and certainly against her lifelong values and the precepts of her religion, this time receptive to his tongue.

Her eyes closed and, knowing that this might well be the last voluntary action of her life, Judith Haviland gave in, letting the notoriously experienced Lord St. John demonstrate exactly how a man's mouth should move against a woman's.

Chapter Seven

The kiss went on for an eternity, it seemed, his lips and tongue moving against hers. Demanding now. His mouth ravaged her senses. His long fingers touched her hair, gently tangling themselves in the curling tendrils that had escaped their confinement. Or they caressed the small arch of her neck as she bent above him or moved again over the skin of her throat, trailing a shimmering heat in their aimless path.

It was a long time before the sounds of men and horses faded away outside. And then, for a long time after that, Judith still waited. Her mind occasionally examined the silence in the clearing, but more often it drifted, anchored to reality only by the touch of St. John's lips.

This was sin, and she knew it. On some conscious level she still understood that. It was a betrayal of her marriage vows. She might rationalize that she had given in to this temptation in order to save his life—and her own. But she would always wonder within her own heart if that were the real reason.

Her husband was attempting even now to bring them help, to effect their rescue, while she... *While she lay against St. John's body and covered his hot, seeking mouth with hers.*

Finally, after it had been quiet a long time in the clearing, she lifted her head. Her moist lips had clung a moment to the parched heat of his, as if her very skin was reluctant to break the contact that had flared between them.

"Don't go," St. John whispered.

Those were the first words she had clearly understood, and yet she knew that even they were meaningless. To him she was only a woman, a woman who had pressed the softness of her body against his. And he had instinctively responded.

Despite his whispered protest, St. John released her. Again she listened to the stillness that surrounded them. It was unnatural. The same terrible brooding quiet that lingered like a pall of smoke over a battlefield when the fighting is done. That terrible, eerie silence of death.

She pushed away from St. John, and his hand fell bonelessly, to lie limp and relaxed against his chest. His eyes were closed, and she knew that he was again asleep, wandering once more through that fevered world of nightmare dreams and hallucinations from which she had briefly roused him.

But that meant she might have a few moments before the soft murmur of his voice began again. A few moments to tiptoe to the screen of branches that had saved them and determine the fate of those who had been their friends and companions. Sergeant Cochran and Mrs. McQueen and all the others.

She hurried across the stone floor, knees shaking, and peered through the tangled branches. What she saw in the small clearing was as eerie as the silence.

Bodies were sprawled in unnatural positions, too awkwardly arranged to be mistaken for anything except death.

Her gaze briefly touched each before it sought the next. She picked out the sergeant's bulk, lying protectively in front of the cave. Then those of the other men. She couldn't see any of the women, and suddenly she realized why.

They had been taken. They would be kept alive and would travel with the bandits as long as it was convenient, as long as they were useful. Or cooperative.

She might have been one of them, had it not been for an accident of fate. And for Sergeant Cochran. She shivered, rejecting the horror of that thought as she remembered their screams. That was almost more obscene to her than the thought of death, especially after the gentle warmth of St. John's mouth.

She closed her eyes against the sting of tears. Crying would serve no purpose. With his final silent admonition, Cochran had given her a job. It was her responsibility now. To take care of his beloved major.

Judith stood a long time behind the screen of branches, watching the shadows stretch across the clearing with the slow movement of the sun and listening to the low murmur behind her. She didn't react to St. John's whispers now, knowing the sound of them no longer mattered. Because now they were truly alone.

It had been shock that held her motionless, she would later decide, looking back on the events of this morning. Perhaps her mind needed that time to deal with what had happened. Eventually, however, she gathered her courage and shifted the framework of branches far enough away from the entrance to allow her to slip out behind it.

She pressed her body against the rocks, again holding her breath, again listening. There was nothing. No movement. There was no living creature in the clearing.

Whoever had been here, bandits she believed, had taken

the horses, except for the one the sergeant had killed. That was still there, its corpse as bizarrely lifeless as all the others.

Moving slowly, like a very old woman, she made herself examine them all. Desperately hoping for a miracle, she checked by putting her cold, trembling fingers against the place in the neck where the reassuring pulse of blood should be.

And was not. Not in any of them. Their bodies, too, had been stripped of everything of value, anything that might be useful in this war-scorched nation.

When she had verified that all the others were dead, she walked back toward the entrance to the cave, to where Sergeant Cochran lay facedown in the mud. His big body had already begun to stiffen, and it took all her strength to roll it over.

She wondered why she wanted to. It was obvious he was dead, just like the others. But for some reason it was important to her that she see his face. His eyes were open, glazed and unseeing now, and again she fought the sharp, demanding sting behind her eyes. She needed Sergeant Cochran to tell her what to do. She needed *someone*.

The sob caught in the back of her throat, and she lifted both hands to push her fingers hard against her mouth, trying to stop the sound. But that noise didn't matter either. There was no one left to hear her cry. No one at all in the terrible, empty silence of the clearing.

The scavengers would come eventually. Both animal and human. That was inevitable, she knew. And they might not be so lucky the next time.

Her almost undeniable need was to go back into the cave and return to the mindless, unthinking escape of St. John's lips moving under hers. Of his fingers tangling in her hair. The warmth of his body lying beneath her own.

She could make endless arguments, some of them even logical, as to why they should stay here. But they could not. They needed to find someone to help them. Even if it were the French, even if they were taken prisoner, it would be better than what had happened here. She would find an officer, demand to be taken to one, demand to be taken to *someone* who would listen to her.

St. John was an English aristocrat, the son of a rich and very powerful nobleman. Someone would understand the importance of seeing that he got medical treatment. She would make them understand. But if she didn't find them some help soon, St. John would die, and then so would she.

She held to that thought as she did the things she had to do. She could not bury the dead. That was a physical impossibility, but she searched the bodies and the impromptu camp for anything that might have been left behind by the bandits.

And she coldly closed her mind to the fact that these were men she had succored, who had talked with her about their families, about the wives and children they had left in England. Now they were dead, she reminded herself, and her responsibility was to the living. They would understand her need.

When she went back inside the cave, she wet her handkerchief again. This time she used the icy water to bathe the major's face. At the first touch, his eyes opened, almost as unfocused and unseeing as the empty, glazed ones of Sergeant Cochran.

"We have to go," she said urgently.

There was no change in the blue depths, and no understanding. His right hand lifted, as it had before, shaping the side of her face. She could feel the calluses, rough against the smoothness of her cheek.

She didn't bother to resist the small comfort his touch gave her. His thumb moved to trail across her mouth, pulling slightly against the dampness of her bottom lip, and she wondered if he remembered what had happened between them.

"We have to go now," she said again, deliberately blocking her own remembrance. "The enemy will find us if we stay here. You have to get up."

She took his right wrist in her hand and began to rise, thinking that if she pulled upward, he might understand what she wanted him to do. Instead, his hand found the fullness of her breast as she rose.

She could not know if his touch were accidental, but it was shattering. Her body recoiled as his had yesterday, jerking away from that contact. Trembling, she released his hand and stood there, looking down on him.

His gaze had followed her, rising as she did. His hand hesitated in midair a moment and then began to fall. It dropped against the heavy wool of her skirt, and his fingers caught a fold, holding on to it as his eyes held hers. Holding her prisoner? Or perhaps…

He was too sick to know what he was doing. In returning his kiss, she had introduced into his fever-disordered brain the idea that she was the kind of woman who would welcome his embrace. And in brutal self-honesty, she wondered what woman would not.

One who is married, her conscience answered. *One whose husband is even now risking his life to save hers.*

She reached down and, using both hands, she pried St. John's long fingers away from her skirt. When she had succeeded, she didn't release his hand, but pulled upward on it again, trying to convince him that he must make the effort to rise.

"We have to go, Major St. John. You have to get up."

The unblinking blue stare did not change. There was no reaction to the growing urgency of her demands. And then, suddenly, she remembered. Something she didn't fully understand, but an idea that had been gleaned from both his actions and from Michael's words. Something that might, just might...

"Your father believes you aren't man enough to do this," she said softly. "He thinks you haven't the courage to stand up and come with me."

Whatever the relationship between the earl of Ryde and his son, it was despicable, she knew, to use his guilt against a man who was too ill to understand this situation. Despicable to taunt him with his father's disappointment.

But watching his eyes, she knew that he had understood something in those words and that they had had an effect. His face began to change, the muscles tightening even as she watched, the handsome lines shifting into hardness. He swallowed, and his tongue reached out to moisten the dryness of his lips.

"My father?" he whispered. "My father thinks..."

When his voice faded, she waited. But as his lids began to drift over the glassy blue eyes again, she cruelly, desperately, added, "He thinks you don't have the courage to get up and come with me. He thinks you are hiding here, Major St. John. Hiding from the enemy. And he is ashamed of you."

His eyes opened again. There had been almost no color before in his face. Only the parchment gray of sickness lying beneath the sun-darkened skin. And that had been stretched too tightly over his high cheekbones, made more prominent by the ravishment of fever. But even so, she could see the effect of what she had said in the quick loss of blood from his cheeks.

He nodded once, and finally he began to move. Slowly. Painfully. Laboriously lifting his injured body in obedience to her demand. In obedience to his father's words.

As soon as she realized what he was trying to do, she bent and put her shoulder beneath his right arm. She could feel his legs trembling as he tried to push up off the stone floor, but with her help, eventually he stood swaying beside her.

"Coat," he said, so low that she didn't hear it clearly.

"What is it?" she whispered.

"My coat," he said again. The request was still soft, but this time she understood. He had told her before, and she had laughed at him, but now... Now that threat, too, was reality. Especially if she were forced to seek assistance from the French.

She helped him lean against the wall. As he had yesterday, he put his head back, turning his cheek against the coolness of the stone. She stooped and gathered up his possessions. The pistol and canteen and the blanket that she quickly folded were pushed into the pack she'd found outside. It had been lying empty in the clearing, but it was still useful for this.

Finally she picked up the uniform coat and helped St. John slip his right arm into its sleeve. When she pulled on his wrist, he leaned toward her cooperatively, and she draped the other side of the mutilated coat over his shoulder.

Then she slipped his good arm around her shoulders and together they made their slow, staggering way out of the cave and across the clearing, leaving behind them the lifeless bodies and the terrible silence.

* * *

"Only a little farther," she pled, as she had begged several times before. Encouragement now, where before she had used the scourge of his past to make him move. She was sorry for that, but it had accomplished the goal of getting him up and out of the cave, which she could not regret.

"No more," he had whispered once, but again she had ignored the exhaustion in his voice to drive him on.

It was not until she estimated they had come almost a mile from the clearing that she felt she could let St. John rest. As she had in the cave, she helped him to lean against the rock wall that rose steeply to the right of the path they were following. She was afraid to let him sit down because she knew if he did, she might never get him up again.

She gave him water from his own canteen and left him while she walked a few feet farther down the path, trying to see beyond the next rise. They had stumbled across this narrow, winding trail only a few yards from the clearing and, knowing that all paths lead somewhere, even in this seemingly empty terrain, she had followed it, thanking St. John's infamous luck. This smooth track alone had made their staggering progress this far possible.

But even with her support and the worn path, it had been a terrible exertion for St. John. She could feel through his clothing the heat from his body, burning against her own.

When she reached the top of the incline, she traced the farther progress of the trail with her eyes. It dipped downward and then rose to disappear over the next ridge. She wasn't sure what she had hoped for. A village, perhaps, some sign of civilization. At least some evidence that she was pursuing a reachable goal. Instead, there was only more of the same rocky, inhospitable terrain they had already crossed.

Judith walked back to where she had left St. John, moving more slowly than before because she was trying to decide what to do. Perhaps they were far enough from last night's camp to take an hour's rest. Then they could—

She looked up and realized that St. John was no longer where she'd left him. Could she have been mistaken about the location? Frantically she looked around. The canteen and pack were lying beside the rock the major had been leaning against. Only, St. John was no longer there.

Her eyes scanned her surroundings. Could he have gone back the way they had come, back toward the clearing? She ran a few steps in that direction before she heard the noise. Something was moving through the bushes to her right, moving away from the trail and down a decline that led to the mountain stream which had been weaving in and then out of sight as they walked.

It was St. John. She could see him now, staggering through the wind-gnarled shrubs and misshapen trees that dotted the side of the mountain. He had already discarded the crimson uniform coat she had draped over his back, dropping it on the ground.

When he reached the edge of the water, he sat down purposefully on a rock, tugging with one hand at the back of his boot. When he had succeeded somehow in getting the right one off, he began to struggle with the left.

He was going into the stream, she realized suddenly. And considering the heat that had radiated from his body, she could even understand his fever-induced madness. She had seen delirious men do things this strange before, their capacity to think burned up by the sickness of their bodies. But the icy water would be an incredible shock to his system, already dangerously weakened by the wound and infection.

She should never have left him alone, she thought, hurrying down the slope he had somehow managed to suc-

cessfully navigate, even in his condition. She never thought
to call out to him. It was too great a risk. A handful of
tumbling pebbles, dislodged by her passage, went rocketing
down the hill before her. One of them rolled to the water's
edge and then splashed into the cold torrent.

St. John stood up and followed it, using the rocks of the
streambed as stepping stones, moving across them in his
stocking feet with reckless disregard for their slickness. He
teetered dangerously once, throwing out his right arm for
balance. The left was still held closely against his body.
Not even seeming to be aware of its cold, he continued to
move out into the current until the icy water was well above
his waist.

Then, as she watched, the major sank beneath the cas-
cade of the foaming stream, totally disappearing. Heart
thudding, Judith increased her speed, clambering down the
shifting rocks as recklessly as he had moved over the stones
of the streambed.

She kept her eyes on the spot where he'd vanished, only
occasionally allowing them to scan the treacherous ground
she was traversing. *Too long,* she thought. *He's been under
too long.*

Then he broke the surface, moisture sheeting off his body
like silver foil. His head was thrown back, almost in ec-
stasy. The black hair was plastered to his skull, and the fine
lawn of his shirt was transparent, molding to the firm muscles of his chest like a second skin.

His head straightened and the blue eyes opened, somehow finding her face. Judith was standing on the edge of
the catapulting stream now, hesitant to plunge into its cold
depths after him, again trying desperately to decide what
to do.

"Major," she said softly. Unbelievingly, she watched
him smile at her. He stretched out his right hand, water

dripping from his fingers. He held it out before him in unspoken invitation. In involuntary response to that eloquent and touching gesture, she returned the smile.

But her mind was racing. It was late February, and the man she was supposed to be caring for was already terribly ill. She had let him wander into the middle of an icy mountain stream and now he seemed to be urging her to join him.

"If you'll come out of the water," she said softly, "we'll build a fire. It will warm you."

For some reason that seemed to amuse him. The smile widened slightly, revealing an unexpected flash of even white teeth, their contrast startling in the gaunt, bewhiskered cheeks. And there had been a dimple, Judith realized. She had never noticed that intriguing indentation before. Or perhaps she had never seen him smile. Not this broadly. Not this particular smile.

She took a deep breath and tried again. "Please come out of the water, Major St. John," she said, holding out her hand, as he had done. "It's too cold. It's dangerous in your condition."

Smiling still, he shook his head, moving it slowly from side to side like a mischievous little boy who knew very well he was doing wrong. As if he were almost daring her to do something about his disobedience.

"Your father wants you to—" she began in desperation.

"To hell with my father," he said softly, but each word was distinct and very clear. "To hell with what my father wants. *You* come in."

She took a deep, unsteady breath at the seductive tone of that command. But despite the smile and the outstretched hand, his body was vibrating like a tuning fork. The pervasive shivering was visible even from where she stood.

The skin of his face had been gray; now his lips were

changing to blue with the cold. This would kill him if she didn't get him warm soon. Suddenly there was no doubt in her mind about that.

Not bothering to remove her half boots, she gathered up her skirt in one hand and stepped out into the icy stream. Its cold was so shocking that her breath sucked inward. Without pausing, however, she stepped across to the next rock. And then realized that there was nothing visible on which to put her foot in order to take the next step.

Bravely, she extended her foot into the ankle-deep water and felt around until she found a submerged rock. She shifted her weight forward, and then repeated the process, feeling carefully for the next step. Painstakingly, she made her way into the stream, being careful not to let the swiftness of its current unbalance her.

The water inched upward as she worked her way across. Each step took her deeper into the liquid ice which seemed to pull the air from her lungs in gasping exhalations. Soon she, too, was trembling uncontrollably, and *she* wasn't suffering from a fever. The icy water covered her lower body completely now and was beginning to push around her breasts.

When she looked up again to judge the distance she had to go, St. John's hand was right before her. It looked strong and brown, as competent as always, except for its trembling.

The next step would take her to him, she realized, so she took it. Suddenly, just as she began to transfer her weight to the new stone, her foot slipped off it, and she started to fall.

Her outstretched hand flailed wildly for a second and then was caught. Caught and held firmly by the long fingers of St. John. She fought to regain her balance, body swaying precariously, and finally with the support of his strong, unwavering grasp, she succeeded.

She looked up, breath sawing in and out of her lungs from fear and exertion. And then her heartbeat hesitated. Her breath caught and held, her body seemingly unable to draw in another inhalation. And her sudden paralysis was not in reaction to the cold water swirling about her body.

St. John was no longer smiling. His face was fixed in lines that might have been chiseled from the granite outcroppings that surrounded the stream. Set and still, its darkness framed his eyes, brilliantly luminous with illness and surrounded by the wet, black spikes of his lashes. As Judith watched, the sun touched the moisture that beaded them, which glittered suddenly like a band of diamonds placed around sapphires.

Still holding her hand, he pulled her toward him. His head began to lower to hers, his lips parted in anticipation. Another invitation, one whose intent was as expressive as his outstretched fingers had been. And as compelling. But for totally different reasons.

This time, however, his life did not depend on her kissing him. There was no danger if she didn't put her lips against his, not as there had been in the cave. There was no one to fear. No need to use her mouth to keep him quiet and safe. No legitimate reason at all to respond to this unspoken entreaty.

And yet, somehow, she couldn't make herself move away. She stood, the water rushing around them, as his mouth slowly lowered to hers. It seemed she was suddenly incapable of movement. Incapable of thought. Incapable of protest.

His head tilted, subtly aligning his lips to meld with hers. It was not until the black lashes drifted closed that the spell released, freeing her from her enthrallment. She retreated, stepping away from him. She was still holding his hand, and at the increased pressure on his fingers, his eyes opened again, looking down into hers.

"No," she said. It was all she could think of to say to him. The blue eyes rested questioningly on her face. "Come with me," she urged softly, taking another step backward. And was infinitely relieved when he obeyed.

He didn't look down, but began moving with the same dangerous disregard for the placement of his feet as he had when he had entered the stream. His eyes never left hers as they moved together out of the center of the stream.

She had made it safely to the edge when her foot slid off the slime-covered rock that was barely visible under the shining surface of the water. She had been hurrying, feeling prematurely that they were safe. She had not been thinking about her footing, but about getting the warmth of the wool uniform coat around his shoulders until she had time to start a fire.

When her boot slipped, she struggled to regain her balance. However, her other foot had been no more firmly planted, and St. John had been in the act of stepping across to the same rock. Instead of offering the firm support that had saved her in midstream, he was unbalanced by the pull of her body, so that as she tumbled backwards onto the bank, he fell with her.

Instinctively, he had pulled his hand from hers. His body turned and he used his right arm to break the fall rather than landing solidly on top of her. His long legs had become entangled in the heavy wet wool of her skirt, his lower body stretched out over hers. His chest was propped above her breasts, his weight resting awkwardly on his right forearm.

Judith had landed hard, her head banging against one of the stones that edged the stream. The air thinned and shimmered around her, her vision seeming to darken with the force of the blow, and she fought to stay conscious. In the center of her blurring vision was St. John's face.

As her world shifted slowly back into focus, the blue eyes looked down into hers. His mouth was taut, almost stern. Again, as it had in the cave and in the middle of the rushing stream, Judith's awareness of her surroundings faded into nothingness, everything lost in what was happening between them.

She could feel his growing arousal even through the cold, wet fabric of her skirt. The woolen material was twisted around her legs and his, almost holding them prisoner, locked together by its icy grasp. She was pinned beneath the solid weight of his body. And he seemed to have no inclination to move away. The fever had apparently destroyed his natural inhibitions in this situation, as it usually did in all others.

"Please," she begged softly, beginning to be afraid.

His eyes softened at her tone, the hot blue flame that had been in them smoldering into tenderness. His fingers lowered to the delicate curls at her temple, touching them almost in wonder.

"I won't hurt you," he whispered. "I would never hurt you."

Mutely, she shook her head. She wasn't afraid of pain in this situation. That was the known, the familiar. It was the other that terrified her. The stern, burning need that was etched so clearly in the austere lines of his face, open for her to read. That incredible want—his and, she knew to the endangerment of her immortal soul, hers.

"My lady," he whispered. "My beautiful lady."

With those heartbreaking words, she also knew that she had been right about her original surmise. He had no idea who she was. In his near-delirium, he might have reacted this way to any woman. She might *be* any woman, and it wouldn't matter to him.

Only here, Judith, could someone like you possibly be interesting to a man like St. John. Michael had told her that. And of course he, too, had been right.

"Please," she whispered again. This time she put her hand on St. John's chest, pushing against the hard muscle.

His eyes held hers, trying to interpret whatever was in them. And when he had, his face lowered instead, lips parted, preparing to cover hers.

She did not resist again. Like the poor, mad opium eaters of India that her father had once told her about, her body craved this. Her intellect might deny that need and reject her own desire, reject it for all the right and virtuous reasons, but her body wanted him as desperately as a drug.

And no one would ever know. St. John wouldn't remember. Michael would never find out. Only she would even know what had happened between them. *Never again,* she thought. It was almost offered as a condition in this bargain she was making. A bargain for her soul, which she knew was already lost.

Only this once, her heart begged. *Only now. Only here.* Her lips opened in anticipation as his head continued to lower. And when his mouth finally covered hers, the feel of his kiss was as devastating as it had been in the dark cave.

His tongue demanded, pressing hers to answer. To answer him. To surrender to his surety and control. And she wanted to. There was nothing she wanted in this world now more than this.

As his lips continued to caress, his trembling fingers moved to the neck of her kersey dress. They loosened the small buttons, working slowly, opening them one by one. The resulting rush of cold air against her skin was another almost unbearable sensation. Her body seemed suddenly more sensitive. More responsive to everything around her. To him. Lost in his touch. Drugged with it.

When he slipped his hand inside her bodice, cupping his wet palm over the heat of her breast, she gasped, her mouth opening in shock under his. With that indisputable response, he deepened the plundering kiss. And suddenly she, too, was mindless with need, with desire. Nothing mattered but this. His mouth. His hands moving against her body.

His fingers captured the softness of her nipple between them, rolling it. The sensation of their hardness against the delicate nerves and tissue was so exquisite it was almost pain. Almost joy. As incredible as the feel of his lips, trailing now down the length of her throat, which was fully exposed for their caress. Welcoming, as his mouth moved intractably lower.

She knew what he intended. And her body reacted to that knowledge in anticipation. The liquid response was scalding in its intensity, rushing through her lower body in waves of heat.

What she was feeling was shattering in its newness. She would never have dared to dream of this, because she could not have envisioned it. She had no guides to the place where he had taken her. No experience in its wonders.

Suddenly, St. John's head lifted, his fever-bright eyes narrowed and directed upward. Even passion-drugged, she knew she should have been the one to realize what was happening. After all, this same shower of pebbles had been dislodged by her own descent down the slope that stretched above them. They had bounced noisily down the decline to land at the water's edge. Just as these did. Dislodged, of course, by someone above them.

Judith turned her head, tilting it back, trying desperately

to see who was there. From the angle at which she lay, there was little to see. Little that could be recognized.

Animals. Horses or donkeys. She could see hooves and legs, milling restlessly at the top of the decline. From the horses' position at the edge, she knew that their riders were looking down the slope, as she had looked down on St. John.

And he had been clearly visible here at the water's edge. Just as the two of them would be clearly visible now to whoever was up there watching.

Chapter Eight

Judith. Insuring her safety had been Kit's first thought, of course, when he realized the party of horsemen was above them. From what he could see, they didn't appear to be wearing uniforms, but he knew that might make them even more dangerous. Bandits? French deserters?

His fevered brain was slow in determining exactly who those riders might be. That primitive part of him, however, the part which had been shaped by generations of warrior ancestors, had already ordered his body to react and to do it quickly.

St. John began to struggle to get up, surprised at the unresponsiveness of his legs. It felt as if he were moving through water, his limbs slow and weighted.

Vaguely, he remembered *being* underwater. It had been so cold against his burning skin. He was still cold, he realized. And although he didn't think he was in the water anymore, it still seemed very hard to move. And harder even to think.

Whoever was up there had started down the slope toward them, he realized, as a stone bounced down the decline to land almost beside him. As he lay here, stupidly trying to remember something about being in water, they were coming to take Judith.

Kit rolled off her body, ineffectively kicking at the sodden wool of her skirt, trying to free himself. Somehow his legs had become tangled in her clothing. Maybe that's why it had been so hard for him to move. Maybe that's why it was hard to think, but even as he thought that, he knew it didn't make sense.

The men were saying something. Shouting at him as they came sliding down the slope. They were speaking Portuguese, he knew, but the words wouldn't quite fit together in his head.

But they were not the French, and that was good, because he had just discovered that someone had taken his uniform. He realized its loss only when he had finally stumbled to his feet.

The world swam sickeningly before him, and when he looked down to clear his head, he could see his right arm. There was no familiar crimson sleeve over it. He was wearing only his shirt, and it was very wet. He looked farther down and was reassured to find that he was still wearing his regimental pantaloons, their fine knit plastered against his legs and lower body. And for some reason he had taken off his boots.

Why had he begun to undress? he wondered in bewilderment. *Because he had been making love to Judith,* he suddenly remembered. *Judith. Where the hell was Judith?*

He saw that she was still on the ground at his feet, half reclining, her clothing disarrayed and her upper body propped on her elbow so she could see the top of the slope. Her eyes were moving back and forth between him and the approaching men.

Men, he remembered. He couldn't let them reach her. She would be raped. Repeatedly. Brutally. And then she would be killed, her slender white throat cut with one of their daggers. He could almost see that happening, too vivid in his mind's eye.

He had touched her throat with his fingers. He had watched them tremble over the pale smoothness of her skin, but he couldn't remember when he had done that. Why the hell couldn't he remember?

The men were still shouting, still clambering down the rocks toward them. *Not Judith,* he prayed silently. *Dear sweet God, not Judith. Angel,* flickered in his head. He couldn't recall who had called her that, but he knew it had been a long time ago.

God himself takes care of his angels. That's what they said. But God wasn't here. Not on this bloody, battle-ravaged peninsula. Despite the churches and shrines, St. John had not found the Almighty anywhere here. And he had not found that He was willing to intervene in the natural horrors of this war, despite the repeated prayers Kit had sent up in the last three years on behalf of wounded friends.

So it was up to him to save Judith, he decided. That seemed very logical, and he was relieved that he had finally been able to reason his way to the decision.

Kit fumbled for his pistol, but its familiar weight was not at his side where it should be. Nor was his saber. So he had no weapons. Nothing to fight them with. Nothing except his body.

He glanced down again at the woman at his feet. *My precious love,* he thought. There was something wrong with thinking that, and he knew it. Judith Haviland could never be his love, but he couldn't remember the exact reason for that either.

After all, she had been *making* love to him. He could remember the feel of her lips under his, the softness of her breast enclosed in his hand. He even remembered how her mouth tasted, her tongue hot and sweet, moving against his own. He remembered touching her. So why…

"St. John," she whispered, her eyes wide and her hand outstretched to him.

She must be so frightened, terrified because she knew as well as he did what these men would do to her. And he couldn't let that happen. Not to Judith.

Kit began to run toward the men who had now descended the slope. He hit the first one with his right fist. The blow seemed to have no force behind it, and that surprised him because he had always been considered a fair hand in Jackson's practice ring. But this, of course, was very different from that gentlemanly London pastime. This was life and death.

Despite Kit's doubts about the effectiveness of his fist's impact, however, the smaller man went staggering backwards into one of his companions. Kit struck out wildly at the next man, rushing him, but again the blow wasn't well-timed or well-aimed.

Kit knew that, but he didn't seem to be able to do anything about it. His arm moved too slowly, as if it were still fighting against the force of the water that had surrounded him. Some water. Some time. Why the bloody hell couldn't he remember?

And suddenly there were too many of them. All of them were gathered around him. Kit tried to raise his right arm again, but one of them must have gotten behind him, holding it. He could hear the man there. He tried to turn around to confront him, but, head spinning, he staggered with that too-sudden motion.

They were still shouting at him, more loudly now, but he couldn't make sense of what they were saying. The words beat at his brain like insects, droning and meaningless. So, jerking his right arm free, he hit another one.

Suddenly someone grabbed his left elbow, wrenching his injured arm backwards and twisting it high behind his back. An incredible agony shrieked through his head. He wondered if that sound were *his* inhuman shriek. Wondered if it had come through his throat or if, as he hoped, it had echoed only in his mind.

Judith, he thought, the blackness roaring into his screaming brain. The pain seemed to be trying to drown the remembrance of the woman he knew he must protect. It was rushing in like the water. So damnably cold and dark.

Judith, he had time to think again, and then Major Lord Christopher St. John fainted from the agony. And he wouldn't think about anything else for a very long time.

It's more than I deserve, Judith thought in voiceless gratitude. *Far more than I deserve after what I have done.*

Still thinking that, she pulled the coarse woolen blanket she had been given more tightly around her shoulders. Despite its warmth and the cheerful fire that blazed on the hearth she was huddled before, she didn't believe that she would ever truly be warm again.

She smiled at the old woman who walked across the hard-packed earthen floor to hand her a steaming mug. Judith took the cup, looking down into the dark, aromatic liquid. It was soup, she realized, thick with meat, its fragrance rich with fat and pungent with some unfamiliar spice.

Judith couldn't remember the last meal she had eaten. She remembered the poor draft animal Cochran had sacrificed. A question about the source of this meat appeared briefly in her mind and was then ignored. She raised the cup to her lips, having to hold it with both hands. But they were still shaking so much that she was forced to reach out to capture the cup's elusive rim with her lips.

The first taste whetted the appetite she had suppressed for days, and she gulped the thick, hot liquid, as unthinkingly greedy as a starving child. For a moment her responsibilities and anxieties were pushed aside in savoring the incredible pleasure of the soup sliding down her throat, warming a passage through the center of the endless cold all the way to her stomach.

"*Bom?*" the old woman asked, smiling. It was one of the few Portuguese words Judith knew, and she nodded her agreement vigorously, returning the smile. The black eyes filled with amusement at the Englishwoman's approval of her simple offering.

The old lady said something else, obviously pleased to find that Judith understood her question. However, her sentences had been too rapidly spoken, the gist of them beyond Judith's limited vocabulary. Helplessly, she shook her head.

The woman pointed to the cot where the villagers who had found them had placed St. John. They had had to subdue him first in order to bring him here because he had fought, trying to keep them from reaching her, she knew.

It was not a battle he could have won, of course, no matter whom he was fighting, but St. John had attacked the men as soon as they made it down the slope. Once Judith had been able to see them clearly, it had been obvious to her that the men who had stumbled upon them as they lay together by the stream were not the same as those who had attacked the camp.

For one thing, they had no weapons. For another, they didn't attempt to harm the English officer, not even when he charged them. In his weakened condition, however, they had had little trouble subduing him. All it had taken was for one of them to grasp and twist St. John's left arm.

PLAY

RUN FOR THE ROSES

...and you
can get

FREE BOOKS and a FREE GIFT!

Turn the page and let the race begin!

PLAY
RUN
FOR THE
ROSES

and get
THREE FREE GIFTS!

HOW TO PLAY:

1. With a coin, carefully scratch off the silver box at the right. Then check the claim chart to see what we have for you —**FREE BOOKS** and a **FREE GIFT**—**ALL YOURS FREE**

2. Send back the card and you'll receive two brand-new Harlequin Historical™ novels. These books have a cover price of $5.99 each, but they are yours to keep absolutely free

3. There's no catch. You're under no obligation to buy anything. We charge nothing — ZERO — for your first shipment. And you don't have to make any minimum number of purchases — not even one!

4. The fact is, thousands of readers enjoy receiving books by mail from the Harlequin Reader Service®. They like the convenience of home delivery...they like getting the best new novels months before they're available in stores...and they love our discount prices

5. We hope that after receiving your free books you'll want to remain a subscriber. But the choice is yours — to continue or cancel, any time at all! So why not take us up on our invitation, with no risk of any kind. You'll be glad you did!

This surprise mystery gift
Will be yours **FREE** –
When you play
RUN for the ROSES

PLAY
RUN FOR THE ROSES

Scratch
Here
See Claim Chart

YES! I have scratched off the silver box. Please send me all the gifts for which I qualify. I understand that I am under no obligation to purchase any books, as explained on the back and opposite page.

RUN for the ROSES	Claim Chart
♚ ♚ ♚	2 FREE BOOKS AND A MYSTERY GIFT!
♚ ♚	1 FREE BOOK!
♚	TRY AGAIN!

Name _____
(PLEASE PRINT CLEARLY)

Address _____ Apt.# _____

City _____ Prov. _____ Postal Code _____

(C-H-H-10/98)   **349 HDL CJCJ**

The Harlequin Reader Service® — Here's how it works:

Accepting free books places you under no obligation to buy anything. You may keep the books and gift and return the shipping statement marked "cancel." If you do not cancel, about a month later we'll send you 6 additional novels, and bill you just $4.19 each, plus 25¢ delivery per book and GST.* That's the complete price — and compared to cover prices of $5.99 each — quite a bargain! You may cancel at any time, but if you choose to continue, every month we'll send you 6 more books, which you may either purchase at the discount price...or return to us and cancel your subscription.

*Terms and prices subject to change without notice.
Canadian residents will be charged applicable provincial taxes and GST.

With her heart pounding wildly in her throat, Judith had watched him collapse, passing out from the pain or from the cumulative effects of the fever and his recent immersion in the icy stream. She had rushed to him, pushing aside the Portuguese peasants who gathered around him.

Judith didn't understand what they were trying to tell her, but the tone of it had been reassuring. And respectful. When she finally realized from their signs that they were offering to take the two of them with them, she nodded gratefully, tears of relief gathering in her eyes.

They had put the unconscious major up on a horse in front of the bulkiest of their number, handling him now with an almost exaggerated care. She was mounted on another of the animals, whose rider walked beside her until they reached this village, tucked into one of the valleys that separated these rocky ridges. The journey had taken them less than an hour.

Once here, their destination had been the house of the old woman. Acting on her instructions, the men had stripped off St. John's clothing, laying it carefully before the fire to dry.

Then the English officer, totally nude now, had been placed on the room's single narrow cot. Their wizened hostess had issued orders the entire time, watching over their shoulders as the men rushed to follow her instructions.

Those had apparently included directions for removing the bandage from St. John's arm. Her gnarled fingers had reached to gently touch the grotesque swelling around the inflamed wound. The tisking sound she had made with her tongue was universal.

But she had done nothing else about that injury, nothing for St. John beyond seeing to the placement of the blankets they piled over his shivering body. She had instead turned her attentions to her other guest, bringing first the blanket

that was draped warmly around Judith's shoulders and then
the soup.

Now Judith's gaze followed the old woman as she moved
back to where St. John lay, as pale and unmoving as an
alabaster statue. Despite the piled blankets, Judith could see
the small, steady rise and fall of his chest. His breathing
was shallow, but at least, she thought, offering up another
prayer of thanksgiving, at least he was still alive. Despite
everything, he was still breathing.

Again the old lady spoke, and Judith's eyes came back
to her face, trying to make sense of what she was saying.
With those twisted, arthritic fingers, the woman touched her
own left arm at a spot in the approximate location of St.
John's wound. She then made a slicing motion in the air
with the flat of her hand, mimicking, Judith believed, the
movement of a saber.

Judith nodded agreement. Again the tisking sound came
in response. The next question was indecipherable, and
mutely, Judith shook her head, raising both hands, palm
upward, to indicate her puzzlement.

The woman nodded, and then she moved nearer to the
low cot. Without hesitation, she pulled the blankets away,
exposing St. John's bare chest. She bent to take the swollen
left arm gently into her two hands, probing the area around
the wound with her distorted fingers. As she did, she
glanced over her shoulder to make an occasional comment
to Judith.

Although she was concentrating fiercely, Judith was able
to pick out only a few words and even most of those she
was not perfectly sure of, or of their context. Once she
thought she heard the word for *knife,* but she might have
been mistaken.

The commentary which accompanied the old woman's
examination ended in an inquiry. That was clear by its in-

flection and by the black, waiting eyes focused on her face. A question, Judith knew, but which one? And what about the reference to a knife?

It must be obvious to the woman that the arm needed to be taken off or St. John's condition would worsen. Gangrene would set in, if it hadn't already, and he would die.

Was it possible that there was someone locally who could be sent for, someone who might be able to accomplish that amputation? Was that what the old woman had said? Hope flared within Judith's breast. And was then as quickly extinguished.

What would a Portuguese surgeon, living in these primitive conditions, know about such an operation? Judith, who had watched the best surgeons England had to offer while at Wellington's headquarters, might even be more proficient.

Or, she wondered suddenly, was it possible that these kind and cooperative villagers who had found them might carry the two of them through the mountains to the English lines? Was it possible now to get St. John to those very same English surgeons?

Except how would she make any of those questions clear to the old woman? As she thought, trying to remember every Portuguese word she had ever learned, the old woman turned away from the cot and disappeared into the adjoining room, whose doorway was hidden by a colorful cloth hanging.

It was only minutes before she returned, carrying a leather pouch, which she put down on the table near the fire. She smiled at Judith before she removed the black cauldron from the hook which swung over the fireplace and carried it to the table.

As she passed by, the smell of the soup drifted out of the iron pot. Judith's mouth began to water, but the old

woman had already generously shared her limited resources. She certainly couldn't ask for more.

The woman dipped out a portion of the soup and added
cool water from an earthenware jar. She held out the cup
to Judith and then gestured with it toward the bed where
St. John slept.

Judith nodded and, still clutching her blanket around her
damp clothing, rose. She wasn't sure that she could get any
of the diluted soup down the major's throat, but she was
very willing to try. This was exactly the right thing for an
invalid, she thought, as she took the cup from the peasant's
hands and carried it carefully to the cot.

Judith's attempts to feed St. John, however, were not
particularly successful. More of the soup trickled out of the
slack corners of his mouth than went inside. And there had
been no response when she sat down on the bed beside him
and slipped her arm behind his neck. She tried to lift the
major's head, but it lolled lifelessly until she bent her arm
to hold it in place.

Not, of course, that it had done any good. His face was
almost waxen now, his lips still tinged with blue, despite
the covering of blankets and the warmth of the small hut.
Her eyes filled with helpless tears, and she blinked them
away, turning her gaze from his still, sunken features.

The old woman was rummaging around in the leather
bag she had brought from the back room. When she had
found what she was looking for, the crone dumped the contents of the paper twist into a wooden mortar and began to
grind whatever it was into a powder.

Medicine? Judith wondered. Some herbal remedy?
Maybe this old woman knew something about the plants
that grew in this region. Perhaps that's why the men had
brought them here.

When she had finished her grinding, the woman returned

to the fire and swung a smaller cauldron out to dump the contents of the mortar into the liquid that simmered there. And then she removed an object from above the fireplace.

It was not until the crone held the knife out over the bubbling pot that Judith realized what it was. The firelight caught the metal of the long blade, a flare skating along the keen edge like lightning.

An amputation knife? Although it was not curved as the English surgeon's tools were, it was certainly large enough. And more efficient looking than anything Judith might have been able to put her hands on.

When she glanced at the wall above the hearth, she could see other instruments, some hanging on pegs and some, as the knife had been, lying on a board above the fire. One appeared to be a saw such as the English surgeons used to cut through bone.

Judith swallowed her sickness, knowing that instead she should be feeling elation and relief. This woman seemed to be just what Judith had begun to suspect she was—the local healer or witch-woman or whatever the proper term was in Portugal.

Amputation of the diseased arm was what Judith knew in her heart would be necessary now to save St. John's life. She had known that almost from the onset of the inflammation, so she couldn't understand the thick knot of emotion that crowded her throat. She looked down into his face, too still and pale.

That mutilation would not in any way diminish St. John's virility. It couldn't change the man he was. The kind of man who, ill, burning with fever and handicapped with an agonizing injury, had tried to fight off a half-dozen unknown men in order to protect her. Judith would never forget his gallant and heroic defense.

And this operation was necessary to save his life. She

had prayed for the knowledge, the proper tools, and the courage to do it herself. Why then was she suddenly not ready for this to happen? She forced her eyes up from St. John's face, again fighting tears.

She watched as the old woman plunged the blade of the knife she held into the boiling water. At one time surgeons had applied heated irons to a wound to stop its bleeding. Maybe the healer didn't know about tying off arteries, and she intended to use the heated knife to try to seal them.

Judith had heard that hot tar was once used for that purpose, a horrifyingly damaging way to prevent the victim of the amputation from bleeding to death. Maybe the woman didn't know about tourniquets. There were so many things the surgeons had learned, knowledge that wouldn't have reached this isolated and primitive location. Knowledge that the old woman...

Judith took a deep breath, denying her growing fears. Together they could do this, she told herself. The Portuguese healer had the instruments and apparently the courage Judith lacked. Perhaps she had experience, too, but Judith had seen this done so very many times. She understood the most modern way of performing such an operation. Together, she thought again. Together they would succeed.

The men were back. They had come in answer to the old woman's summons. Following her direction, they had pulled the cot away from the wall and carried it to the middle of the small room, handling the bed and St. John easily, despite the weight of his still solid muscle. Now they were all gathered around, waiting for further instructions.

The old woman had looked at her strangely when Judith began to make sewing motions. She shook her head, brow wrinkled in puzzlement, but Judith had persisted. There were few things, however, that might be mistaken for the pantomime she was carrying out, and eventually the woman shrugged and produced exactly what Judith had asked for.

The needle was straight and small, rather than the large curved one the English surgeons used. The coarse thread was not the waxed shoemaker's kind she was accustomed to either, but it appeared to be strong enough to do the job. So Judith nodded her approval, smiling her thanks.

Then she curved her forefinger into a crook and pointed at the wall above the fire where the saw and the other implements hung. The woman's eyes followed the direction of Judith's finger, but then she looked back in bewilderment, shaking her head.

Judith then pulled her crooked finger toward herself, mimicking the motion necessary to pull the arteries out of the newly incised stump so that they could be tied off. The woman glanced toward the wall and back. Judith repeated her gesture.

The crone again shook her head, but finally she went into the other room and returned after a few moments carrying a small hook which appeared to be carved from bone.

It was certainly not the surgical hook Judith had requested. It looked like the sort of thing one might use in making lace. But, she decided, since it was small and sharp, there was no reason it wouldn't work just as well.

Carrying the hook and the threaded needle, Judith walked to the side of the cot. The old woman had begun issuing a stream of instructions to her helpers, who were scurrying obediently to carry them out. One brought the steaming cauldron from the fire and put it down on the left side of the cot. The handle of the long knife still protruded from the simmering liquid.

Others stationed themselves around St. John's unconscious body. Two of the men pulled the blankets off and grasped his legs. Another held his right arm. Two more stretched out the injured left, turning it so that the ugly, swollen wound was accessible.

The old woman's eyes met Judith's. The Englishwoman realized that she had been almost holding her breath, silently praying for success. They had come this far. She would not let St. John die now under the shock of the amputation or from blood loss. He *would* not die, she repeated like a litany.

Suddenly, the healer smiled at her, the movement disturbing the deep wrinkles around her mouth and revealing a set of teeth that looked surprisingly white and intact in her aged face. She reached out, patting Judith's arm reassuringly. The understandable gesture was accompanied by unintelligible words.

Comfort for her fear, Judith supposed. And it was welcome, of course, because the healer didn't seem to be the least bit afraid. Her calmness was infinitely reassuring. So Judith nodded, and the healer nodded again in return.

Then the old woman sat down on the floor beside the bed, crossing her legs under the skirt of her shapeless dress. Surprised, Judith knelt beside her, determined to make sure that whatever happened, St. John would not bleed to death. When the woman reached for the knife, Judith stopped her.

"No," she said sharply, pushing her hand away. There was no tourniquet above the wound. That was the simplest precaution, something that was done routinely in English field hospitals before any incision was made.

The eyes of the men standing around the cot were focused now on Judith's face, shock and puzzlement reflected in each pair. Apparently, judging by the way they had rushed around obeying her instructions, no one ever questioned the old woman's methods. This time, Judith thought with determination, someone would, and it didn't matter to her whether they liked it or not.

"No," Judith said again, shaking her head. If they didn't know the word, they would surely understand the gesture.

The old woman's hand had hesitated, but now she said something, her tone as sharp and demanding as Judith's had been. Her hand again moved toward the knife and was again pushed aside.

The crone turned to one of the men who was watching this exchange, wide-eyed in surprise. In response to the old woman's unspoken command, he moved to where Judith was kneeling and grasped her arm, trying to pull her up and away from the bed.

"No," she said again, jerking her arm away. As she did, she noticed that he was wearing a rope belt tied around the waist of his loose trousers. Excited by her discovery, she pointed to the belt, and startled, the man took an automatic step back.

Judith pointed at the rope again and then turned her palm upward in entreaty. He looked down at the belt, then at Judith, and finally his eyes moved to the old woman. The crone shrugged, apparently signifying permission.

When the man had handed her the rope, Judith slipped one end under St. John's outstretched arm. Then she twisted the two strands together, high on the upper arm, near the shoulder. Looking around, she indicated to one of the unoccupied men that she needed the pestle which was lying on the table where the old woman had ground whatever she had put into the cauldron.

His eyes sought permission from the healer and again received it, along with a verbal acknowledgment this time. The woman appeared to be fascinated by whatever Judith was doing. They all watched as she wound the handle of the pestle into the rope and used it to tighten her makeshift screw tourniquet.

When Judith was finally satisfied that it was tight enough

to stop the flow of blood, she reached up to take the hand of the man whose belt she had borrowed. She placed it over the stick, curving his fingers into position around it and then patting them to let him know that he should keep them in exactly this same place. She glanced up at his face to make sure that he understood. When his eyes indicated that he did, Judith turned back to the old woman and nodded.

The woman said something, pointing to Judith's left hand. The men laughed. Judith glanced at her hand and realized it was empty. She had laid the hook and the needle in her lap while she fixed the tourniquet. She picked them up again, smiling at the old woman.

This time when the crone's hand moved toward the knife, Judith made no protest. There was nothing else she could do. She had done her best, and the rest was in the hands of God. And in the bent, misshapen fingers of this old Portuguese peasant.

Chapter Nine

Something had gone wrong, Judith thought, *dangerously wrong.* Despite her efforts to see this operation done correctly, exactly as the surgeons would have performed it, nothing was happening as she had anticipated.

Before she could think how to voice her protest, the sharp edge of the knife the old woman held sliced into the swollen flesh. Not, however, where the incision should have been made, at least three or four inches above the climbing redness. Instead, the woman had made a cut on top of the original wound.

"No," Judith protested sharply and was ignored. "No," she breathed again, more softly this time because the healer was paying her absolutely no attention. She had not even looked up. She was intently watching instead what was happening under the pressure of the knife. And suddenly so was Judith.

They all were watching, Judith realized after a moment, all with that same horrified intensity. The evidence of the terrible inflammation gushed out of the cut the woman had made, the smell of its corruption strong in the small room.

One of the men hissed, but the old woman said "Ahhh" in the same tone with which one might express admiration for a beautiful woman, a well-prepared meal, or a fine painting. That drawn-out syllable had sounded exactly like an expression of delight.

As if in verification of Judith's thought, the healer looked up to smile and nod at her. Then she turned to grin broadly at the surrounding circle of faces, her strong white teeth again flashing in the dark, wrinkled folds of her skin. Her left hand made a flourish, as if celebrating some accomplishment, and the watching men nodded in admiration.

The old woman handed one of them the knife and voiced a demand. The man hurried across the room to put the knife on the table and returned with several pieces of cloth. These the healer laid on St. John's chest, except for the one she placed on the mattress under his arm, which the men were still holding up.

Then she began to press with both hands on the swelling above and below the cut she had made. The thick discharge increased, flowing out around the outstretched arm and down onto the cloth below.

Judith watched, the hope that had been so strong before fading quickly to despair. The old woman had never had any intention of cutting off the infected arm. That's why she hadn't taken the bone saw from the wall. That's why she hadn't applied a tourniquet.

All of Judith's expectations that this primitive healer might be able to save St. John's life had only been foolishly misplaced hopes, she realized. This old woman couldn't know, of course, the lessons the surgeons had drummed into Judith's head for the last three years. This *healer* didn't know anything.

But the crone was again issuing orders, rapidly and decisively, just as if she knew a great deal. The men had released their holds on St. John's limbs, except for the injured arm. The woman dipped a cloth into the liquid in the cauldron beside her and began to swab at the incision she had made.

She worked for several minutes, seemingly intent on making sure that the fluid penetrated, cleaning out the wound. Then again she pressed all around the area until she was satisfied that no more of the suppuration could be gotten out.

She threw the cloth she had been using on the floor and took a clean one from the pile. This she folded into a thick square and dipped it into the liquid in the cauldron until it was soaked. Then she placed it over the reddened area. Finally she replaced the stained cloth that had rested below St. John's arm with a fresh one from the stack.

When she was finished, she looked up at Judith again and pointed at the tourniquet, questioning its release. Shaking her head, Judith touched St. John's arm at a place an inch or two below the tight clamp of the rope. She made a sawing motion with the edge of her hand there.

The woman's eyes reflected her puzzlement. Judith pointed at the streaks creeping up St. John's arm and again made the sawing motion. Then she pointed to the saw above the fire.

The jet-black eyes followed. When she turned back to Judith, those knotted fingers made a similar sawing motion over her own left arm. Judith nodded. Had she finally made herself clear? Did the old woman now understand what must be done?

The woman laughed and made some comment to the watching men. Her jeering words were accompanied by the same sawing motion over her own arm. They looked shocked, their dark eyes turning in horror to study Judith's face.

Despite her mockery, the crone reached out to touch Judith's hand, the left one, gently patting the back of her fingers, just below the knuckles, and then smoothing her own hand over them. Another gesture of comfort, Judith supposed. Or reassurance.

Was it possible, she wondered suddenly, that the healer's incision and the fomentation, whatever it was, might really work against the poison? Even in England there was a long tradition of less radical treatments than those the surgeons now demanded.

She had brought to Spain numerous recipes for herbal remedies that her elderly friends had sworn were efficacious for a wide variety of maladies. And when she could find the ingredients they called for, she had used them with some success through the long months. Was it possible that this *could* work?

The woman was saying something to her, Judith realized. Then she reached up and grabbed the hand of the largest of the watching men, the one who had carried St. John's unconscious body here by supporting it before him in the saddle. The old woman pushed his hand up until he was holding his arm straight out in front of him. It was corded with muscle that stretched the material of his sleeve tightly.

The healer pointed to that strong arm and nodded. Then she pointed to the bandage she had placed over St. John's arm and nodded again, her head moving vigorously up and down.

Almost against her will, Judith found herself slowly nodding agreement with the woman's confidence in her treatment. *Please, dear God,* she prayed, *please let her know what she's doing.*

Her eyes fell to St. John's face. Deeply unconscious, he had not moved during the entire procedure. He had not flinched under the blade or when the woman applied pressure to the red, swollen arm or placed the steaming cloth over the raw flesh. There had been no response at all in the still, white features.

Unable to resist the impulse, she lifted her hand and placed her cool fingers against the fevered heat of his brow. She did not realize that the firelight, which had earlier illuminated the sharp blade of the knife, played now over the gold wedding band which she wore on her left hand. Or that its gleam had been reflected in the circle of dark eyes surrounding her.

With Judith's help, the old woman replaced the steaming cloths as soon as they cooled. As day faded into night, their vigil over St. John continued, although the men had been banished from the house hours before. The woman lit no lamps, but even after nightfall the light from the fire brightened the room enough for them to carry out this simple task.

Later Judith was given more soup, and too tired and hungry to think of refusing, she smiled her thanks and drank it down. The warmth of the room, the flickering, shadowed light cast by the fire, and the satisfying and unfamiliar fullness of her stomach inevitably took their toll, as the healer had known they would.

When the old woman finally lay down before the fire, pulling the blanket she had earlier given Judith around her own shoulders, she did not disturb the other woman who was already deeply asleep. The Englishwoman's dark head was pillowed on the bent arm she had propped on the edge of her husband's bed as she sat on the floor beside it.

The old woman smiled again in the fire-touched darkness when she thought of the Englishwoman's ignorance. Why should she want to cut off a perfectly good arm because of a little pus?

She shook her head, making again the tisking sound she had voiced before. So foolish. So primitive a method of healing. But then the girl was very young. Who could blame her if she knew no better? One must be taught the proper way to do things.

Tomorrow, the crone thought. *I will show her more tomorrow.* And with the pleasure of having someone to instruct in her arts, the old woman pulled the blanket closer and drifted off to sleep, her mind untroubled and supremely confident.

Far more than I deserve, Judith thought again, looking down at St. John's arm. The wound was still inflamed, still swollen, but she could see it was definitely improved. An incredible improvement over its appearance yesterday.

She studied St. John's face as the old woman pressed around the swelling. He was still asleep. Not asleep, Judith amended, seeing that there was not the slightest response to what the healer was doing. He was unconscious. Deeply unconscious, his breathing as shallow and thready as it had been yesterday.

But he was still alive, she thought, holding on to that. And apparently the old woman knew what she was doing. Judith glanced down again to watch the arthritic fingers moving over the wound. Satisfied by her examination, the woman reached into the pocket of her voluminous dress to remove a small, squat bottle whose stopper had been sealed in place with wax.

She pried out the stopper and dipped one finger into the bottle and began to rub the glutinous ointment it contained over the incision she had made last night. The ointment was faintly blue-green, and a strangely familiar odor drifted upward from it, teasing Judith's memory. So…evocative, she thought, but she couldn't seem to place it.

When the woman had finished applying the salve, she laid a clean, folded square of cloth over the area. As the healer closed the bottle and was about to return it to her pocket, Judith placed her hand on the reed-thin arm and pointed to the container. She raised her brows in question.

The peasant smiled, but not broadly as she had yesterday. This was almost secretive, almost amused. She rose from where she was seated on the side of St. John's bed and gestured for Judith to follow her. With only another quick look down at St. John's face, Judith obeyed.

The room to which she was led was like nothing Judith had ever seen before. It looked like an alchemist's workshop or a medieval apothecary. Her eyes circled it, fascinated by the objects hanging from pegs and strings all around the walls.

Almost everything that could be culled from the bounty of nature was here, both flora and fauna. Some of the plants she recognized, but many more she did not. Even her herbalist neighbors had had nothing like all this.

The woman seemed unaware of Judith's examination of her treasures. She placed the ointment bottle on one of the tables and then opened a small wooden box, from which that same tantalizingly familiar odor escaped.

It reminded Judith somehow of the forest. Dark and dank. Or perhaps more like the cave where they had hidden from the bandits. But still, she couldn't quite grasp the elusive memory.

Suddenly, the healer turned and motioned her closer. For some reason Judith hesitated. It was almost as if, now that she was here, she didn't want to know what the box contained. Hers was an almost superstitious response to the atmosphere of this room, to the secrets it held. Or to the miraculous improvement in St. John's arm, despite the fact that the woman had done nothing that the surgeons believed should be done in such a case.

Medieval, Judith thought again. Even smacking of witchcraft. The dark arts. She took a breath, the very air around her seemingly filled with the scent. Then, berating herself for her irrational fear, she gathered her courage and walked across the room to stand beside the old woman.

At first she didn't recognize what the healer had revealed. And when she did, she realized that it was no wonder she had been reminded of the damp loam of the forest floor or of the cave.

She could not tell what the old woman had originally put into the box. Whatever it had been, it was now covered over by a thick blanket of blue mold. This, then, was where the ointment had gotten its strange color.

The salve that the old woman had just rubbed all over St. John's arm had been made from this decaying mess of organic material. Sickened, Judith lifted her eyes from the contents of the box and back to the healer's face. The woman smiled, nodding her head.

The Portuguese word she said was unfamiliar, of course. But Judith didn't need a name for this. Whatever good had been done by the knife yesterday would surely be undone by the application of this rotting substance to the wound. Despairing, Judith shook her head.

The woman's smile faded, her eyes again puzzled. *"Bom,"* she said, nodding and pointing again at the mold.

At least she understood that, Judith thought, and it was apparently the limit of the verbal communication they would be able to share. But this was *not* good, of course. She looked back at the contents of the box. Nothing that looked like this could possibly be good, not for someone as sick as St. John.

* * *

The days and nights of their endless nursing drifted into a week. Despite Judith's protests, the old woman continued to spread the bluish-green ointment on St. John's arm. And the wound continued to improve. After the third day, Judith had not bothered to object, because the evidence of her own eyes outweighed the natural repugnance she felt at what the healer was growing in that dark, revolting box.

The troubling thing was that St. John's condition did not seem to improve, even as his arm healed. In addition to the salve she smeared on his wound every day, the old woman brewed a decoction which she insisted Judith get down the major's throat.

Although she was more than willing to try, of course, it was a time-consuming process. Judith spent hours every day attempting to get St. John to swallow some of the fluid. And she succeeded, she knew, despite her growing fear and the frustration over his continued unresponsiveness.

However, at the end of six days she could see no improvement. The fever continued to burn through his body unabated, perhaps no longer quite so high as it was when they had been brought here. With each passing day Judith's despair deepened. What did it matter if the old woman could heal the arm, if she could not save the man?

Judith slept beside the bed, curled in the blanket she had been given. She had worried at first about St. John's displacing the healer from her cot, but sleeping on the floor in front of the fire didn't seem to bother the peasant. The old woman awakened each dawn to rush around the cottage with a briskness and energy that made Judith almost envious.

Early one morning, while the woman was fixing their breakfast, Judith again sat down on the edge of the mattress, preparing for the first of the day's many attempts to get some of the witch's brew down St. John's throat. That thought was unkind, she knew, given all that the old woman had done for them, but still there was something almost unnatural about the potions and poultices she used.

Perhaps only unnatural in that, unlike most medicine Judith was familiar with, these seemed to work. Thinking that, her lips curved into a smile, reluctant admiration for the Portuguese woman's knowledge and skill.

For some reason, she seemed to be having more success than usual in getting this particular potion down, Judith realized. She glanced up, and found that the blue eyes which had once, in a faraway London ballroom, skimmed with boredom across her face were now focused intently on it. The shock was so great that her breath caught, and it was several seconds before she remembered to draw another.

"Hello," she whispered.

"Judith?" St. John said. His voice was as low as hers, and it seemed hoarse from disuse. His tone when he said her name had been questioning. Disbelieving, even.

She knew he would remember little of what had happened to bring them here. And probably less of what had happened between them. That was, of course, something she devoutly wished for—that St. John would never remember those embarrassing encounters.

But he had never before called her Judith. *Mrs. Haviland.* Or *Ma'am.* Never Judith. And so she found herself wondering exactly what he did remember. She could feel the hot blood climb into her throat and spread over her cheeks.

"Where are we?" St. John asked. He tried to look around, but then he closed his eyes quickly, and let his head fall back to the pillow. He would be fighting the vertigo she knew he would suffer after so many days spent lying flat on his back.

"It's all right," she reassured him.

Without her volition, her hand reached out to touch him, pushing the black silk of his hair away from his forehead and feeling beneath her palm its unaccustomed coolness. The long fever had finally broken.

In response to her touch, the dark lashes lifted again, and the sapphire eyes fastened on her face, moving over it as if he had never seen her before. As if he were trying to recognize her features. Or memorize them.

"It really is going to be all right," she said again, "now that you're awake. Will you drink something for me, Major St. John? It's very important that you try."

His gaze held on her face a long time, searching it, and then he nodded, the movement very small, but obviously signifying agreement. She smiled at him, feeling a resurgence of lost hope balloon within her chest, and it lightened all the black despair of the past few days.

She slipped her arm under his head. She fitted the rim of the cup against his lips and held it there as he drank. He finished most of the liquid before his eyelids drifted downward.

Still she held him, savoring the weight of his head against her breast. Then, once more, briefly, the heavy lids lifted, and his eyes found hers. Found and held. Some silent connection, a message that he was not able to fully communicate to her before they closed again.

Judith gently placed the dark head back against the pillow. He was asleep, that instant slumber into which invalids fall so easily, his now-frail strength suddenly exhausted. He was gone from her again, the bond once more broken, but she was elated.

St. John had just drunk more of the healer's decoction than she had managed to get down him all week. He had been awake. He had known who she was. All of those were wonderful signs.

She had not even realized that she was crying until one of the tears fell onto his sunken, whisker-roughened cheek. He did not react, but Judith smiled, the movement slightly tremulous, to see it there. With one finger, she wiped the teardrop away, and hurriedly blinked back the rest, before they, too, could fall and wake him.

After that first morning, St. John's recovery was rapid. More rapid than Judith believed to be wise, but the old woman encouraged him. And because she had been right about everything else, Judith acknowledged, perhaps she was also right about that.

The major had insisted on sitting up a little in bed the day after he woke. Propped on pillows, he had managed to swallow almost a cup of broth. St. John's command of Portuguese was far greater than hers, Judith decided, when he also talked the old woman into shaving him.

She used the keen-edged blade with which she had opened the abscessed wound, and he looked more like himself without the black whiskers. Much more like the man she remembered, Judith thought, but she acknowledged privately that perhaps that was not something to be desired.

Those small efforts seemed to exhaust him, and St. John had fallen almost immediately into a deep sleep and had thankfully, from her perspective at least, slept away most of the rest of the day. While he was awake, Judith found it very difficult to pretend that nothing had happened between them.

She was too aware that this was the man she had kissed, eagerly covering his warm, seeking lips with her own. In the cave she had lain over his body, her breasts pressed like a wanton's against the hard muscles of his chest.

And this was the man who had begun to make love to her beside the mountain stream. The man she had *wanted* to make love to her. To touch her. The notorious London aristocrat, whose conquests with the fairer sex were legendary.

Only here, Judith, could someone like you possibly be interesting to a man like St. John, Michael had told her. That was reality. What had happened between them there was only a fevered dream, and she prayed she could remember that and prayed conversely that he wouldn't remember anything at all of what had occurred.

But when he woke again, late that afternoon, almost at twilight, his eyes followed her as she moved around the small room, helping the old woman with their simple evening meal.

His gaze remained focused on her face as she fed him. Once she looked up to find the sapphire eyes tracing again over her features in what looked like speculation. She was forced to wonder exactly what he did recall because it was obvious, even from the few words they exchanged, that there had been a subtle change in their relationship.

That lingering question was somewhat answered as she began to prepare St. John for the night. When she unthinkingly tried to carry out the more intimate nursing duties that she and the old woman had shared while he was unconscious, the eyes she had been avoiding throughout the day suddenly flared in anger.

"What the hell do you think you're doing?" St. John demanded as she began to pull the blanket down to expose his body.

Her hand hesitated in the completion of that familiar action. "I was only going to…"

The words faded, stopped by the hardening of his features. As it had in the stream, his face suddenly turned to stone. But it happened now for a very different reason. St. John was clearly furious, and that fury was directed at her.

With his right hand, he jerked the blanket out of her fingers. "What the bloody hell *have* you been doing?" he demanded. A flush of color had crept under his pale skin.

She didn't understand why he was so angry. This was only a necessary part of caring for the sick. It was something she had certainly done a thousand times in the field hospitals.

And then suddenly, inexplicably, she was as furious as he. Perhaps her quick rage was a result of exhaustion. Or perhaps she was angry because of the unfairness of his reaction. After all, she had worried about him, cared for him, risked her life for him. *And* her immortal soul, she thought bitterly.

Even in her fury, she could not blame him for that sin, which was hers alone. But, she decided unreasonably, she could certainly blame him for what he had just said. And for the disgust that had been evident in his voice when he said it.

For days she had prayed for his well-being. She had worked like a slave dribbling endless drops of liquid into his mouth in an attempt to keep him alive. She had cleaned his helpless body. She had loved him...

...*had loved him*. The unbidden thought quenched her outrage as suddenly as one might pinch out a candle's flame. Because, of course, it was true.

And it was a truth she could no longer deny, at least not to herself. But the words were sacrilege to the vows she had made before man and God. Even thinking them, allowing them to form, was betrayal. *They* were betrayal, even if they were also true.

Judith Haviland was not a creature of impulse, nor was she given to gestures. Another woman might have poured the basin of water she had brought to the bed over St. John's ungrateful head. Or might have thrown the cloth she was holding at his set face. Judith did neither, of course.

She marched across the room and set both items carefully and deliberately down on the old woman's worktable. Then she opened the door and stepped outside into the coolness of the March night. She leaned against the wall of the small house, partially sheltered from the rain by the overhang of the eaves, and pressed shaking hands against her cheeks.

She had worked side by side with the surgeons for so long that she had apparently forgotten whatever natural modesty she had once possessed. She had tended to Major St. John throughout these long days as if he were an infant.

But he was not, of course. He was a man. A proud, virile man, and she had just treated him like a child. Perhaps it had been acceptable for her to care for him when he was unable to care for himself. Why had she not realized that he would resent and despise her attempt to do so now, especially without consulting him? Without asking his permission.

She could imagine his distaste. No other woman of his acquaintance would ever do what she had done during the last three years. They both knew that. No well-bred, delicate London lady would ever attempt to… Again her mind skittered away from those intimate services she had been accustomed to performing.

But she was *not*, after all, a delicate London lady. She had never been that. And really, what did it matter what St. John felt about her? she asked herself bitterly. Whatever had happened between them would never happen again.

That brief romantic interlude had only been a product of their circumstances. Of her fear. His illness. There were a hundred legitimate reasons for what had happened. Only she would ever know the real one.

So it didn't matter, of course, what he thought about her. It didn't matter if he found her behavior disgusting or crude. Even if he thought her as common as the old peasant woman who grew mold in boxes.

Together they had saved his life. She and that old Portuguese healer. Judith removed her hands from her cheeks and unconsciously lifted her chin. That was really all that mattered. And as for the rest…no one would ever know about the rest, of course. No one.

She took a breath and allowed her mind to linger again on the very few times he had touched her. In the cave, when his fingers had trailed gently and yet so seductively against her throat. In that stream where he had held out his hand as if inviting her to waltz, and where his darkly beautiful face had begun to lower, his mouth open and again seeking hers. And when they had lain together beside the water…

Unnoticed, her anger had dissipated. Her lips had curved into a smile. *And this, too, is sin,* she thought, when she realized what she was doing. The small, remembering smile faded.

Soon they would be back in the English camp, and Michael, who was her husband, would be there. That was her reality. And her future.

A brief, unholy alliance. A fantasy. That's all it had ever been. And now it was over. St. John would again be her friend, and he would never be anything more to her, she knew. Still she fought against the regret, the deep sense of loss.

He was alive, she told herself, and she was at least partially responsible for that. That could not be cause for regret. Never could she regret *anything* she had done to keep St. John alive.

Again her lips tilted upward. This time her smile was resigned. Reflective. Perhaps even slightly satisfied.

Only here, Judith, could someone like you...

Deliberately, Judith Haviland banished the memory of those mocking words. Not even Michael could take this victory away. Major Lord St. John was alive.

Only here, Judith could someone like you...

Desperately, Judith Hawkend beheld the memory of those moments before. No, even Michael could not ride his victory away. Major Lord St. John was alive.

Chapter Ten

Judith had no warning and was therefore unprepared when St. John finally asked her the question she had dreaded so long. The question that had been in his eyes after he'd awakened had gradually faded with the passage of time. With its disappearance, she had begun to breathe again, believing that he must have assigned whatever remaining fragments of memory he had about their encounters to the fever. His gaze didn't follow her around the room anymore, and so she had begun to believe that her secret was safe and would remain so.

She smiled at him that afternoon as she brought the bowl of stew to his bed, but she was careful that it was exactly the same smile she had given a hundred other wounded men she had tended. She felt a slight trepidation, however, because they were alone for the first time since they had arrived in this house.

The old woman had gone into the nearby village to deliver a baby. At least that's what Judith believed, judging from the joyful excitement of the man who had come to fetch her and the few words she had been able to pick out of his message.

"Thank you," St. John said as she held out the bowl to

him, but he made no effort to take it. Instead, he looked up into her eyes, holding them with the sheer physical intensity of his.

"I believe I must owe you an apology, Mrs. Haviland," he said.

Her pulse quickened, trying to think how to answer him. Judith knew that whatever she said, she would be treading on very dangerous ground.

"I'm afraid I don't understand, Major St. John. An apology? For what?" She controlled her breathing, thankful to note that the bowl she held did not tremble. Not even now.

"I seem to remember..." His deep voice hesitated over the words, and she held her breath. "If I did anything that was improper, Mrs. Haviland..." Again the sentence faltered. "I hope you know that I would never willingly offer you insult. If, in my illness, I said or did anything that caused you distress—"

"Major," she interrupted. "There was nothing for which you need apologize. Or explain. Nothing...improper," she added.

He held her eyes, trying to read them, she supposed. But she had already dealt with her own guilt, standing one rainswept night outside this house. She hoped that her eyes reflected only her certainty that nothing of what had happened was his fault.

There is nothing for which you need apologize. That was truth, and she let him see it in her eyes and in what she prayed was the calm serenity of her face. He truly *had* done nothing she hadn't wanted him to do.

In time they would both forget. He because he would believe those fading memories were only dreams. And she... She would forget because she must.

"You need to eat," she admonished almost brusquely. She put the bowl of stew into his hand and turned away, hopefully before he could see those emotions she didn't intend for him ever to find in her eyes.

"English. English."

The Portuguese word had been repeated perhaps three or four times before Kit understood the distant shout. Apparently there was some lingering effect from the fever, which still clouded his thinking.

The feeling that he was operating in a daze would soon be over, he had reassured himself through the long days of his recovery. Soon everything would become clearer, and he would be able to remember all the events of the last few weeks, which seemed to him only a jumble of impressions, their images bleared and distant.

And not all of them made sense. Such as what he seemed to remember about Judith Haviland. Were those images created by his hopeless fantasies, by the strength of his unspoken love? Or was it possible that the encounters between them had really occurred?

The images lingered tantalizingly in his mind, seeming far too vivid to be dreams. Was it possible, despite Judith's denial, that he had touched her? Possible he had kissed her? That they had even lain together—

"English."

The man who had been shouting the phrase outside burst into the hut where they had been living with the old woman for almost a month. St. John had no clear remembrance of their arrival here or of the woman's treatment, but under her care and Judith's he had slowly been regaining his strength.

Mrs. Haviland had told him only that the woman was the local healer. And despite everything that had happened—his wound, the inflammation and high fever that had resulted from it—he seemed finally to be on his way to recovery. Therefore the title Judith had given the old woman apparently had validity.

When the man entered, Judith's eyes had found St. John's face. Kit was aware that the emotion reflected in their dark depths was not one he should now expect to find.

Judith Haviland should be relieved and excited, but somehow he knew that she was not. He could not have explained how he'd arrived at that conclusion or why he was so certain of it, any more than he could explain the uncanny perceptions about her feelings that he had had since he'd awakened.

"English on the road," the man said, still speaking in Portuguese. He was almost gasping in his excitement over having this important news to deliver.

Apparently Haviland had gotten through, Kit thought, and Wellington had finally sent out a party to look for them. And to look also for the wounded that Smythe had placed in his care. St. John felt again a deep sense of regret and even of guilt. None of those men were alive, of course. Only he and Judith were left, the two lone survivors from the entire regiment.

That had been the first question Kit had asked after he'd regained consciousness. He had been grateful when Mrs. Haviland had answered him truthfully. As she answered his other questions which had followed her painful recitation of the events at the cave. Sanctuary, he had thought when Cochran guided them there. But, of course, it had not been. Not for any of the others.

Now Kit listened to the peasant's excited explanation about the English presence in the district with only half his attention. Judith's eyes never left his, holding on his face as he questioned the man. She was waiting, Kit supposed, for some news of her husband.

But there was none. The villager had come away as soon

as he spotted the English column moving along the main road. He thought it would be better if he had something to give them, he explained to St. John. Some sign, proof of their existence. The soldiers would accept some physical evidence of their identity better than they would accept his word.

Given the treachery of the local bandits, the man's suggestion made sense. No British commander would send a detachment into these mountains based solely on the word of a Portuguese peasant.

"My coat," Kit suggested to Judith.

She hesitated only a moment before she obeyed. She brought the mutilated uniform to him and placed it in his hands. Kit tried to think what would be the best thing to send. Not the entire garment, but something that would identify him to whichever English commander Wellington had sent to find them.

Finally he stripped off the regimental insignia and his rank. Those would probably have been enough, after Haviland's message, but there were more than a few stolen British uniforms in Portugal, of course. And more than a few deserters. Reluctantly, Kit also took the gold signet from his finger.

It was the ring his father had given him when he attained his present title. It was the only thing here that he had from the earl, almost the only thing left of what he had brought with him from home. But the signet would identify him more clearly than anything else he could think of.

"Yours, too, I should think," he suggested, looking up from his ring into Judith Haviland's eyes.

"My wedding band?" she questioned.

"I think it's best they have no doubt of who we are."

Judith glanced at the man who had brought the message. Kit knew what she was thinking. There was nothing they could do to prevent the peasant from stealing their possessions, which had more sentimental value, of course, than they had monetary worth. And she was right. There wasn't anything they could do to insure that the man would take these items to the English commander.

"They have shown us nothing but kindness," Kit reminded her softly. Her gaze came back to his face. "We have to trust him, Mrs. Haviland. And we have no reason not to."

Finally she nodded, slipping the slender gold band off her finger and placing it on his outstretched palm along with the things he had chosen. Kit only hoped that his Portuguese would suffice to explain to the peasant what he should do with them.

The English patrol arrived in the village in the late afternoon of the following day, but not before St. John had begun to despair that his message had been conveyed to the column. The lieutenant in command of the detachment was no one he knew, not even by reputation, but it was obvious the opposite was not true.

"I've heard a lot about you, Major St. John," the young officer said in greeting, after Judith and one of the villagers had helped Kit outside.

"Indeed? Lieutenant...?" Kit wondered, as he waited for the man's name, which of his very different reputations had preceded him.

"Standish, sir. Carter Standish, at your service."

"Wellington sent you?" Kit suggested.

There was a flare of surprise in the officer's eyes. He glanced at Judith, and then back at Kit. "No, sir. Advance patrol for the main army. No orders about you, sir."

"Then the army's on the move."

"We left winter quarters two days ago with the intent of

driving the French across the border. Old Hooky's chomping at the bit, pardon the expression. He can't wait to push north.''

"But no one..." Kit hesitated to ask the vital question, his eyes tracing over Judith Haviland's pale, composed face.

"No one...?" Puzzled, the lieutenant repeated the broken phrase.

"No one has reported us to Wellington as being in need of help?" Kit asked, deliberately forcing his gaze away from Judith and back to the young officer.

"Not that I'm aware of, sir. Not that I was told of. Where are the rest of your men, Major? How did you and your wife—"

"My *wife?*" The tone of Kit's question was too sharp, and he watched Standish's eyes widen. They, too, moved to Judith's face and then came quickly back to his.

"This is Mrs. Michael Haviland, Lieutenant," Kit corrected.

"But the villagers told us that the two of you were—"

This time the abrupt interruption was internally triggered. Standish clamped his lips closed over the words he had been about to utter, but he glanced again at Judith, his manner now full of unease. When Mrs. Haviland's dark eyes met his with the same open and steadfast regard which was so much a part of her character, a small flush of embarrassment spread beneath the fine-grained skin of his cheeks.

"Did you say Haviland?" he asked suddenly, pulling his gaze back to Kit. "Mrs. Michael Haviland?"

"That's correct."

Standish's eyes found Judith's again, and his lips tightened briefly before he opened them to speak, his tone softened now with sympathy. "Then I'm afraid, ma'am, that I am the bearer of very bad news."

"Michael's father?" Judith whispered. "My husband's father is General Sir Roland Haviland. Have you had news of him?"

Standish's regretful eyes returned quickly to St. John's, reading in them the realization that Judith had not yet made.

"No, ma'am. No news concerning General Haviland," the officer denied. Then he hesitated, obviously trying to think how to soften the blow he was about to deliver. "It's your husband, Mrs. Haviland. I'm afraid his body was found more than two weeks ago. May I offer you my sincerest condolences on your loss."

Without his volition, Kit's eyes searched Judith's face, which had drained of color. He fought against the urge to hold her, simply to enfold her in his arms and offer what comfort he could. He might have despised Michael Haviland, but as Judith had once reminded him, Haviland was her husband.

There were no tears, however, in the wide dark eyes. She had made no outcry, had expressed no outward sign of grief. And with what he knew about Judith Haviland's abusive marriage, Kit could not in all honesty blame her for that. In fact, it even gave him some small hope that her loyalty to her husband had been only that and not some deeper attachment.

Despite the intensity of his gaze, Judith never looked at him. Her eyes, the pupils starkly distended with shock, remained on the young lieutenant's face. Finally at the continued, painful silence, St. John turned back to Standish.

"Are you sure?" Kit asked softly. "Are you absolutely certain of Captain Haviland's death?"

"There's no doubt, I'm afraid," Standish said. "I understand he was identified by his own batman."

"His batman?" Kit asked in surprise. "A Private Reynolds?"

"I'm afraid I'm not certain, Major. If I heard the man's name, I've forgotten it. Is it important?"

"I suppose not. It's simply... I had thought Reynolds died with the rest of the regiment."

"The *rest* of the regiment, Major?" Standish asked, his voice disbelieving. "How could the two of you... Begging your pardon, ma'am, but how did the two of you...?" Again the question faded, and the color deepened in the boyish cheeks.

"The regiment was massacred by the French advance. By the reinforcements Napoleon sent Massena," St. John explained.

"Reinforcements, sir?" Standish repeated. There was a thread of doubt in the question. "We had no word that Massena had *been* reinforced."

This was the first time St. John would hear the tone. The first time he would notice eyes deliberately shift to avoid meeting his. The first time he would see a gleam of speculation in a man's gaze as it moved across Judith Haviland's beautiful features. All of those would become very familiar to him during the next few months, but Kit would remember this man's reaction to their story as the beginning of the horror that was to follow.

"Because Smythe's messenger and mine were both killed before they could deliver the news. I was ordered to see the wounded and the women safely to the coast road," Kit said, controlling his quick anger at the lieutenant's doubt. "We were sent to make contact with Trant and the militia, but the bridge was blown."

"Then there are other wounded here?"

"No," Kit said softly, reluctantly remembering the

friends he had lost. "There are no other wounded. Just as there is no longer any regiment."

"I see," Standish said. His tone, however, indicated that he certainly did *not* see how something like that could happen.

"Probably not," Kit retorted, the old aristocratic arrogance answering the unspoken but implied suspicion. "But I assure you I'll explain every circumstance," he added coldly. "That explanation shall be made, however, to his lordship. And at the proper time and place, of course."

Surely, St. John thought angrily, his standing with headquarters was such that whatever action he had taken to safeguard the wounded and to carry out his orders should not now be questioned. Not by this green boy, who had probably never seen an action, much less been involved in one.

"Certainly, Major St. John," Standish said, his tone more respectful, a response, no doubt, to Kit's obvious fury. "How long will it take you to pack, sir, and be ready to move out? I'm sure Colonel Prescott will be happy to send an escort to accompany you and Mrs. Haviland to headquarters."

"I should be grateful," Kit said, his words coldly formal. He turned to Judith. "You have my deepest sympathies, Mrs. Haviland, on the death of your husband."

"Thank you, Major St. John," she whispered. She looked at him then, dark eyes luminous now with unshed tears.

She really loved the bastard, Kit thought in despair. *She truly loved him, despite it all.*

Kit turned and walked back into the hut, not bothering to wait for help, from Judith Haviland or from anyone else.

"There is no question, Major St. John, of any misconduct on your part," his lordship said. "I do not wish you to feel that I am in any way censuring the decisions which you and Mrs. Haviland were forced to make during those desperate days. However…''

Wellington's deep voice hesitated. The piercing eyes above the famous hawk-like nose, which had earned him his nickname among his troops, rested on Kit's thin face.

It was the first day St. John had dressed in full regimentals since his return, and the effort of this appearance before the allied commander had taken a toll on his still uncertain strength. He was determined, however, that Wellington would not be aware of that.

Several of the garments Kit wore had been borrowed. None of his fellow officers had begrudged those loans, he knew. Their manner had been as accepting as his rank, position, and military reputation demanded. And thankfully there had been no condemnation in their faces.

They felt, so he had been led to believe by their supportive comments, that if he said Boney had sent reinforcements, then the emperor bloody well had. And if St. John said Smythe had directed him to take the wounded, himself included, out of harm's way, then of course that was exactly what had happened. Not one of them seemed to doubt those statements.

It was only the other that was still whispered about in the officers' mess. And it was the other which had occasioned the kind of titillating gossip that swept like wildfire through the ranks of a bored army, especially one which has gone without anything so interesting to talk about during six long months in winter encampment.

An enlisted man heard to utter such remarks about an officer or an officer's wife might be flogged. But among the members of the officer corps itself, physical punishment could not be used to quash the rampant gossip about the relationship that had existed between Mrs. Haviland and the handsome, aristocratic Major St. John, whose reputation with women was not only well-known, but apparently well-deserved.

Standish and his superior, Colonel Prescott, had clearly heard the peasant's explanation. The translator had repeated his words loudly enough that none of those who had been nearby that day could possibly have any doubt about the situation the peasant described. And of course, the inclusion of the wedding ring seemed to reinforce the story the man had told.

Major St. John and Michael Haviland's widow had been living openly as man and wife for several weeks in the small Portuguese village where they had been found. There was no doubt at all about that part of the oft-repeated tale.

Exactly how that scandalous arrangement had come about was, however, at the core of the gossip. And about that everyone seemed to have an opinion. However, Kit reminded himself, the only opinion that really mattered was the one he had been ordered here today to hear.

"You must know, St. John, there has been a great deal of talk," Wellington went on.

"Talk, sir?" Kit repeated, although he was as well aware of what was being said as was his commanding officer.

"Gossip concerning you and Mrs. Haviland, I am afraid. Somewhat natural under the circumstances, I suppose."

"I was unaware, sir, that you…entertained gossip," Kit suggested softly.

In his voice was an echo of the long generations who had borne the noble name he carried. It was a tone of unconscious arrogance which Kit had acquired from his father. Its coldness might have stopped a lesser man than Wellington from pursuing this line of inquiry.

"Colonel Prescott was told that you and Mrs. Haviland were living together as man and wife. Standish confirmed that was the impression which the villagers had of your relationship,'' the general continued, seemingly untroubled by Kit's disdain.

That was a question, of course. It was not stated as such, but both men understood what information the commander sought.

"I'm afraid, sir, that neither I nor Mrs. Haviland can be held responsible for...impressions,'' St. John said. His tone had not changed. It was still frigid and immensely formal.

But neither had Wellington's eyes changed. The general's lips pursed slightly and were then controlled. "You know that Haviland is dead, of course. His body was found during our advance. It has been positively identified by his batman.''

"Reynolds,'' Kit said, his tone slightly altered.

In response to that, one of the general's dark brows quirked, questioning perhaps. "Private Reynolds reached our lines a month ago. He left camp after the battle and made his way south. You are acquainted with the man?'' Wellington asked.

"I had believed Private Reynolds was killed with the rest of the regiment. I was...somewhat surprised to find that was not the case. Were there other survivors then, sir?''

"None that I am aware of,'' Wellington said, not unkindly. "The two of you seem to be the only ones who escaped the destruction of Colonel Smythe's forces. You two and Mrs. Haviland, of course.''

Kit said nothing, remembering again the men he had led. Men who had fought bravely beside him. Who had protected him, followed him, honored him with their trust. Now they were all gone. Perhaps the emotion of that renewed realization left him unprepared for what came next.

"And the question is, of course,'' Wellington went on, "what should be done about Mrs. Haviland.''

"Done, sir?" Kit asked, pulling his mind from the past into this equally painful present.

"You must realize that even her status as a widow leaves her unprotected from the unkindness of this scandal, particularly since she was at the time...not yet a widow," Wellington said, obviously choosing his words with care. "That makes the situation even more difficult, I think."

"I'm afraid I don't understand," Kit said, but he was beginning to. The direction of Wellington's comments went a great way toward explaining why the general had sent for him.

"Whatever the truth of what happened in that village, Major St. John, it is the stain of speculation about it which will mark Mrs. Haviland's life. And your own, of course."

Kit said nothing, working to control the growing tumult in his chest, working to remain outwardly calm as the parameters of his world shifted and then realigned themselves.

He had dreamed of Judith Haviland while the idea of loving her had been morally and legally forbidden. And now... Now it seemed that Wellington himself was about to propose that he—

"I had thought to suggest," his lordship continued softly, "that you might wish to do the most honorable thing in this very difficult situation." Wellington's dark eyes had dropped to consider his long-fingered hands, resting together on top of the cluttered desk.

"The honorable thing?" Kit repeated, fighting his sheer physical response to the idea. There was no honor involved in this. There was desire, hot and powerful, coursing through his body. And there was love. He had realized that a long time ago, even when he had thought Judith forever out of his reach.

"No one can force you to do so, of course," Wellington said. "And I do appreciate the differences in your stations.

There is not, I believe, anything in Mrs. Haviland's background that might prevent such an alliance. Her father is General Aubrey McDowell, as you know, a respected retired member of His Majesty's army."

The commander's eyes lifted again, fastening on Kit's face as if awaiting a response to that commonplace. That was not, of course, what he was seeking.

"You are suggesting that I should offer Mrs. Haviland the protection of my name," Kit said. Despite the pounding blood at his temples and the incredible sense of anticipation, his voice was calm. He also knew from long experience at the gaming tables of the more elegant London hells that his features would reveal nothing of his true feelings. Nothing of his growing excitement.

"I believe that might be the honorable thing. Under the circumstances, of course."

"I see," Kit said softly. He wondered if Wellington could hear his heart, which seemed as loud to him as the frantic French drums that beat a prelude to every battle.

"If, however, despite my recommendation, you feel that you should consult your father—" Wellington began, only to be sharply cut off.

"My father—" Kit said, his voice like a whiplash. He stopped, sought a breath and control. "My father has *nothing* to say about this."

Again the dark eyes of Wellington probed and then lowered from that handsome face. "Then may I expect you to carry out this…obligation?" he asked.

"You may," Kit agreed.

"May I also suggest you move with all deliberate speed, Major," the general said. "Before this talk becomes more disruptive than it already is. And before the lady herself—"

"I understand," St. John said. "You have made yourself very clear, sir." He saluted his commander, forced to do so improperly with his right hand. Then he turned on his heel and quit the room.

Behind him, Wellington pushed himself out of the chair behind the desk and walked across the office in the small municipal building they had commandeered to serve as his headquarters. He looked out the window and watched St. John stride purposefully across the uneven paving stones of the plaza.

Apparently St. John didn't appreciate having his actions questioned, the general decided. Or perhaps he resented suggestions as to the direction his life should take.

Wellington didn't blame the major for his resentment. Being told what he must do was something he himself had never enjoyed. In that, they were very much alike, he thought.

The earl of Ryde's son had, of course, enough natural arrogance, money and position to protect both himself and his wife from the cruelly wagging tongues. Perhaps this marriage would stop the rumors before they could reach London. That would protect McDowell, whom his lordship knew and respected.

The best thing for them all, Wellington thought, believing he had truly achieved that goal. And as far as the British commander was concerned, the minor social affair of Major St. John and Mrs. Haviland had been satisfactorily resolved.

He would not be aware for several days that it was not. And by the time he *was* aware of that fact, it would be far too late to do anything else about the tragedy that was unfolding.

Judith Haviland had spent the last few days simply waiting for whatever came next, her mind numbed by the enormity of what had happened. She had sent her husband to his death, and she could not even be sure within her own heart that that had not been her intent. And if *she* were not sure…

She closed her eyes, trying to think about Michael. She had been attempting to visualize him as he had been the first time she'd met him. Handsome. Charming even. But he had been sober, and that was an occurrence which had happened less and less frequently until, at the last…

Judith took a breath, wondering why she was dwelling on Michael's failings. They had been many, but now he was dead. *And may he rest in peace,* she thought. She really wished that for him. Just to let Michael rest in peace.

Apparently, her husband had been true to his sworn word. He had been killed on his way to Wellington's headquarters. He, then, had kept his part of the bargain. As she would keep hers.

"Mrs. Haviland?"

She knew before she looked up who had spoken her name. Major St. John and the officer's wife with whom she was living were standing in the doorway. She hadn't seen him since the escort Prescott had arranged brought them to Wellington's temporary headquarters.

It had been a much longer time since she had seen him like this. If she had not known of St. John's illness, it would be very difficult to find evidence of it in his appearance today.

His handsome features were still too finely drawn, but it was very hard to criticize them. He was dressed in full regimental regalia, and few men wore the uniform as well as St. John. None, she would venture, had ever worn it better.

She should be delighted to see him so fully recovered, she thought, and yet there was within her heart an emptiness. Never again would their relationship be what it had been through those weeks they had spent together, during those days when she cared for him and had, through sheer determination, kept him alive.

St. John looked more like the man she had so briefly met in London than the man who had once touched her. The man whose fingers had loosened her hair and brushed tantalizingly against her breast. The man whose mouth had ravaged her own.

"Major St. John," she said, fighting those memories.

She nodded dismissal to her hostess. "Thank you, Mrs. Stuart." The woman's brows climbed, but she left them alone, only after she had made her reluctance to do so obvious.

Judith waited until the door of the parlor closed behind her hostess before she turned to St. John. She smiled at him, but he didn't return it. His face was composed, almost set, the blue eyes distant.

"Mrs. Haviland," he said finally.

She was aware that his gaze had scanned quickly over the black gown she wore, a mourning dress she had borrowed from Mrs. Stuart. It was not only too large, but both the color and style were vastly unbecoming, she knew.

At that thought, the guilt she had felt since they had been rescued assaulted her again. She was thinking about how unbecoming her clothing was, about how she appeared in St. John's eyes, when she should instead be lost in grief over her husband.

"I hope you are well," she said.

"Very well, thank you," St. John responded politely.

She had had more comfortable conversations with strangers, Judith thought. And more meaningful. An impossible distance now stretched between them. They seemed to have lost even the friendship and respect they had once shared. She wondered again what St. John remembered and if those

memories colored his present treatment of her. The word
wanton brushed through her mind.

"Mrs. Haviland, you may be aware that..." St. John
began before his voice faltered, but his eyes still held hers.

"Aware of what?" she asked finally when he didn't go
on.

"I would like to offer you the protection of my name,"
St. John said simply, abandoning whatever explanation
he'd begun.

It took a moment for the words to penetrate. It was the
last thing she had expected him to say. The last she might
have dared wish for. Hope for. Dream of. And so she
waited, repeating the phrase again and again in her head,
trying to think of any other possible connotation for those
words.

"Protection?" she whispered finally.

Despite her attempts to rationalize what he had said, the
physical reaction had already begun. Desire roiled through
her body as it had before. Within the dangerous darkness
of the cave. And later beside the water, the paralyzing cold
of the mountain stream burned away by the heat of his lips.

"There has been some gossip, I'm afraid," he said
softly. His eyes were shuttered, hidden. They had always
been open, honest in their regard and their appraisal.

Of course, she thought in despair. Why had she not expected this? They had spent several weeks alone. St. John's
very honorable offer was the natural result of that time.
Offer, she repeated. It was a word whose meaning she had
not thought about since those far-off days of her brief London Season.

"This isn't necessary," Judith said softly. "Thank you,
Major St. John, for your consideration, but I assure you..."

She found that she couldn't continue, couldn't force her
mind to compose the formal words of denial. The images

were suddenly too clear in her head. All of them crowded into her brain and into her heart, blocking any rational thought.

The memory of the day he had removed his shirt, revealing that darkly bronzed expanse of muscle and bone. The feel of her breasts crushed against his chest. The trembling hand he had held out in invitation. The incredible pleasure of his body on top of hers. The solid weight of it. The breathless anticipation with which she had watched his mouth descend to hers...

To Judith Haviland, marriage had been a prison. A soulless excursion into the empty void of abuse and alcoholism. Now, finally, she had found the man with whom it might be all that it should be. What her father's and mother's union had once been. Joy and companionship. A glory of mind and body joined. One.

But not like this. And not for these reasons.

"I can't marry you, Major St. John," she said softly, denying what she did not deserve. *More than I deserve* echoed again in her head as it had in the old woman's hut.

St. John was alive. And Michael, her husband, was not. Because she had sent him to his death. Perhaps she had even sent him to die because she desired another man. This man.

If this were punishment for her sin, it was apt, and it was even just, she acknowledged. Because she had just been forced to say no to the one thing she would willingly have given up her immortal soul to possess.

Chapter Eleven

"**I** can't marry you," Judith had whispered.

Whatever Kit anticipated when he had come to her today, it was not this, not an unequivocal denial. He had never before proposed marriage, but Lord St. John had seldom been refused any other request he'd made to a woman. And this was the only one that had ever truly mattered.

"I'm not sure you have a choice," he warned softly.

Her dark eyes widened. He wondered if it were possible she didn't know what was being said about their relationship. But Judith Haviland's innocence was something he had never doubted.

Despite the brutality of these last three years, despite the duties she had undertaken, there was a quality about Mrs. Haviland that proclaimed her lack of cynicism and her belief in the inherent goodness of people. That characteristic had been evident in her dealings with the men of the regiment, and even the roughest had responded with unfaltering respect.

It had also shown, of course, in her dealings with Kit himself. In spite of her denial, he knew that something had happened between them. She had lied to him about that to assuage his guilt for what he had done under the influence of his delirium. Kit was sure that the images which lived in his memory were far too clear to be mere fantasies.

Once he had kissed Judith Haviland. And he had touched her. He knew that, no matter what she said. He was ashamed that he had pressed his unwanted attentions on a defenseless woman, even if his actions had been a result of his illness.

His unwanted attentions, he thought grimly. And apparently they still were. But Mrs. Haviland had been married then, and all of what he felt for her had been forbidden. As had been, of course, whatever happened between them. And now it was not.

"I don't understand," she said.

"Lord Wellington believes it will be better that we marry and put a quick end to this gossip."

It was his strongest argument, and Kit was not opposed to using any card which fate placed in his hand. He had no doubt that once Judith belonged to him, he could win her love. And he was determined to have with Judith the true marriage that Michael Haviland had foolishly thrown away. Even if she had loved her husband, Kit still believed, arrogantly perhaps, that given enough time and the depth of what he felt for her, he could defeat the hold of Haviland's ghost.

"Lord Wellington sent you here," Judith said, interrupting his pleasant fantasy. "Of course," she added, speaking so softly that the comment seemed only to herself.

Her voice was flat, and the words held a trace of bitterness. He wondered if she expected him to deny it. Wellington's suggestion was not the reason he had come, of course, but rather the impetus for acting so soon. The general had given him permission to seek Judith's hand. That was a privilege he had not expected, had not believed appropriate, given her recent bereavement.

"I think he was concerned about the damage to your reputation, Mrs. Haviland. And concerned about your father's reaction to the story when he hears it," Kit added.

He realized that her father's reaction was not something she had considered. Her eyes dilated with shock at his words, the rim of brown almost disappearing in the expansion of her pupils. She had apparently never thought how her father or society would view what had happened. Or what people *thought* had happened, Kit amended. However, his name and position could offer her protection, he knew, if she would only agree to accept them.

"My father?" she repeated disbelievingly.

Despite her question, that argument had obviously had an effect. Kit saw the pain of it reflected in her eyes, and of course, given his own father's undeniable influence in his life, he understood her anxiety.

"We were together for some weeks. The villagers had the impression we were man and wife. That's what they told Prescott. I'm afraid the story has now been too widely circulated to hope to contain the damage it might do to your reputation."

"Damage to *me?*" she asked.

Her eyes seemed to ask another question, but before he could guess what it was, the long lashes fell, hiding whatever had been in their dark depths.

"Not to me, in any case," he said. "I'm afraid my own reputation is such, Mrs. Haviland, that it makes your present situation more difficult."

Her eyes came up at that, and what had been in them before was gone. They were again clear and open to his scrutiny.

"Believe me, I am truly sorry for that," Kit said softly.

He *was* sorry. He had wondered before what she had heard about him, and then that concern had been lost in the friendship she had offered and in her acceptance of the man he had become here on the Peninsula. Now his previously reckless life had stained her. Judith Haviland didn't deserve that blotch on the sterling reputation she had acquired through her service here.

"You have *nothing* for which to apologize, Major St. John," she said emphatically. "And you have certainly done nothing for which you need offer to make this sacrifice."

Her lips had moved into the small, heartbreakingly familiar smile with which she had greeted so many disasters throughout the last three years, and his heart responded. There was no sacrifice in his proposal, of course. Only need. And a desire such as he had never felt before. A desire to cherish and protect this woman. And to love her.

"Mrs. Haviland—" he began, only to be interrupted.

"You have most gallantly defended me, Major St. John, when there were real threats. I promise you that it is not necessary now that you continue to do so. My father knows my character. I assure you he will disregard whatever unpleasant gossip he hears. And perhaps, if we are fortunate, he will hear none."

It was not the answer he had hoped for, of course, but Kit had learned from his years as a soldier. One of those lessons concerned the wisdom of outflanking his opponent. He had come here determined to secure Judith Haviland's agreement to marry him, and he would worry about other considerations only after that particular goal had been accomplished.

"But *your* father is not the only person involved in this situation, I'm afraid," he said. "Or the only one touched by its possible ramifications."

The emphasis was deliberate. The generosity of Judith Haviland's spirit was well-known. If she believed his own reputation was at stake, or his father's regard for him, then she might give in. The silence stretched through several heartbeats, and her eyes again examined his face, seeking answers.

"You believe that—" she said finally.

"I believe," he interrupted, "that this is truly the best solution for everyone involved. I beg you to reconsider. I promise you that this marriage will in no way encroach on your natural grief and regard for your late husband."

Again some emotion touched her eyes and was quickly controlled. Kit had given her his word, and he intended to abide by it. He was not by nature a patient man, but he had once believed Judith Haviland to be forever out of his reach. And now, suddenly, everything he had once only dreamed of was within his grasp. He could wait.

Michael Haviland had mistreated his wife. He had marked her life with violence and dishonor. Kit sought only the privilege of making her forget. And if he did, then the rest of what he wanted would follow eventually.

Again the silence grew, the rush of blood in his ears almost overpowering as he waited. Finally Judith moved. She put out her hand, and surprised by the simple, almost masculine camaraderie of the gesture, Kit took it into his.

It was small and fragile, so vulnerable that again he had to fight the inclination to take her in his arms. To close out the world that whispered scandals about her name and linked it to the notoriety of his. An almost undeniable urge to protect her.

She didn't smile at him as her fingers rested in his. But he saw the breath she drew, almost shuddering in its intensity. And he read her answer in her eyes long before she gave it.

"Then, yes, Major St. John," she said, her voice soft

and very calm. "Given those considerations, I *will* marry you."

Wellington proved as adept at arranging a wedding as he was at supplying his vast army. Kit had no real friends among his lordship's colorful staff, but several of the officers whom he had known socially in London attended the ceremony. As did the woman with whom Mrs. Haviland had been living since their return.

Judith was dressed in another borrowed gown, but Kit was relieved to find that it was not the stark black she had worn on the day he proposed. This was a soft violet-gray, an acceptable color for the latter months of mourning, and its pleasant hue produced an answering blush of color in Judith's cheeks. She looked far less fragile than she had in the too-large, scarecrow black she had worn before.

Jewel tones to bring out the dark perfection of her skin and hair, Kit found himself thinking as he watched Judith walk down the aisle of the chapel on Lord Wellington's arm. At one time Lord St. John had been considered to have a great deal of expertise in feminine fashions.

Kit's mistresses had been reputed to be the best-dressed women in the capital. He would delight in clothing Judith in the finest the London modistes could produce. To be allowed to dress her as she should be would give him infinite pleasure.

Her hand was shaking when she placed it in his. Her fingers were cold, the vibration in them strong. Suddenly Kit remembered touching her like this. Cold and trembling, her lips had once opened under his. Not in fear or disgust, but in an undeniable response to his own passion. Judith Haviland's body had lain acquiescent under his, her lips parted in anticipation of his kiss. His hand cupping the warmth and softness of her breast.

The image was so vivid he knew he hadn't imagined it. He could not have imagined her willing participation in their lovemaking. But it was there, complete and perfect, in his head.

Finally, in spite of the power of that memory over his senses, he remembered to breathe, to think, and even to repeat the vows the clergyman spoke. This was one more thing to be gotten through before Judith Haviland belonged, finally, to him.

The ceremony seemed dream-like. And when it was over, Kit turned to face Judith, aware that others were watching. Aware again that this was little more than a performance. He lowered his head to find her mouth and it, too, trembled under the warm caress of his lips. A contact too brief. Too quickly ended.

He did not release her hand when it was over. She left her fingers trustingly in his, and his was the voice that answered the few well-wishers in attendance. His were the practiced and graceful phrases that carried them out the door and across the plaza to the small suite of rooms that had been provided them.

And finally, after the seemingly endless ordeal involved in satisfying the conventions and expectations of this small, close-knit society, they were once again alone.

"Will you tell me the truth?" he asked.

Judith's eyes came up from the well-cooked slice of the roast he had cut for her. She had prodded it with her fork throughout the meal, between sips of the wine his lordship had thoughtfully sent them, but she had eaten very little.

The woman who owned the house had tried to produce a proper wedding supper, and Kit supposed he should be grateful. Judith, however, had toyed with the rich food. And in the end he had found himself simply watching her pretense at eating. It was another performance, of course, this one for his benefit.

"The truth?" she asked cautiously.

"The truth about what happened between us during those days. The days I was ill. The days you cared for me."

She smiled at him before her eyes fell to her nearly untouched plate. Deliberately, she laid the fork she'd been playing with down and put both hands in her lap. When she looked up at him again, her eyes were amused.

"The days I cared for you?" she repeated, a thread of self-derision coloring her voice. "Do you mean perhaps the day I let you wander into the middle of a mountain stream? I left you alone for a moment, and when I returned, you had taken off most of your clothing to go swimming. Except the water was more suitable for an ice fair than a bathing excursion."

She hesitated, her eyes no longer smiling, before she finished. "I thought you were going to die, in your stocking feet and without your uniform, and it would have been my fault."

Kit laughed. He was pleased to see a spark of answering amusement lighten the seriousness of her eyes at his unexpected shout of laughter.

"I don't see how my stupidity could in any way be considered to be *your* fault," he said.

"You were desperately ill, and I should have taken better care of you. I knew you weren't…entirely rational, and still I left you alone in a vain attempt to see where the trail we were following led."

"That's when the villagers came," he suggested. He allowed his eyes to release hers as he waited for her reply, taking the opportunity to pour wine into the glass she had almost emptied.

This was the crux of the matter. Whatever had happened

by the stream. That was the image he had remembered so clearly during the ceremony today. Kit found that he wanted her to tell him about it, to confess to what he believed he had read in her response.

"Very soon thereafter," she agreed. Her hand closed around the delicate stem of her glass, and her fingers trembled slightly as she raised it to her lips. He met her eyes over the top of the glass and held them.

"And before that?" he probed. "What happened before they arrived?"

Slowly she set the glass down without drinking from it. Her chin lifted, but her eyes didn't evade his. "I'm afraid I don't understand what you're asking, Major St. John."

"I should think," Kit suggested, "that you might try for something a little less formal. Considering the fact…"

"That we are married," she said when he paused.

"There are some who will think it a very strange marriage indeed if you are determined to address me as *Major* St. John," he said. He smiled at her and was relieved at the slight relaxation of the tension that had held her.

"I didn't even know your given name," she said softly. "I don't believe I had ever heard it before today."

"And now you know it."

"Christopher." Her voice was low, the tone ordinary, so he was surprised by the physical response the whispered word evoked.

"Or more frequently Kit," he suggested, fighting that response. It had been a long time since anyone besides his immediate family had employed that childhood nickname. He was most often addressed by his title, of course. Only his mother and his old nurse and occasionally Roger still used the other.

"Kit," she repeated. "It…fits you somehow."

"I'm glad you approve."

"And would it matter if I hadn't?" she asked, smiling.

"It would have mattered a great deal to me," he said softly.

The smile faded, even from her eyes. There was a sudden tinge of color in her cheeks, but her gaze met his unflinchingly.

"Why?" she asked.

Caught by surprise, Kit laughed again. "Do you know, you are the only woman of my acquaintance who would have thought to ask me why," he said. "Most would simply have accepted a compliment they considered their due."

"Is that what it was? A compliment?"

"In your case, Mrs. Haviland, it was simply the truth."

The unthinking use of Haviland's name destroyed the ease that had been growing between them. That was clear from the pain in her eyes. And Kit cursed himself for forgetting and employing the habitual formality he had always used in addressing her. For so long he had forced himself to think of her as Mrs. Haviland. A married woman. Forbidden to him. And now...

"Mrs. St. John," she said.

He looked up to find that her eyes were forgiving, trying to tell him that she understood why he had made that cruel slip.

"Actually," Kit corrected, smiling at her, "it should be Lady St. John."

She returned his relieved smile before she said, "I don't believe I shall ever be able to bring that off, Major."

"Kit."

"And Judith. Safer, I think. At least until we become more accustomed to this...marriage."

"Is it so difficult for you to accept?" he asked.

"I never thought..." she began, and then she hesitated,

obviously considering her words carefully. "I never imagined I should ever be anything but Michael's wife," she
said softly.

Michael's wife. In spite of all Haviland had done to her,
she was still, in her own mind at least, Michael's wife. Kit
fought the thick rush of disappointment. Judith was now
married to him, but not by choice, not as she had chosen
Haviland. She had been forced to wed Kit by circumstances. In order to protect those she loved. And because
he had tricked her.

"Of course," he said. He rose, placing the linen napkin
carefully beside his plate.

Her eyes had followed his movement, and they were
questioning. He had promised patience, had vowed to give
her time, and already he was finding the constraints imposed by that vow to be impossible.

"Where are you going?" she asked.

He turned back and saw that she had also risen. She took
a step away from the table and nearer to him, but he knew
that if he stayed, he would eventually say or do something
he'd regret. Perhaps he was the one who needed time. And
distance.

He needed *something* to fight against the images that had
crowded his brain since the ceremony. The too-vivid memory of Judith willingly lying in his arms beside that mountain stream.

"There's only one bedroom," he said bluntly. "And it
contains one bed." Again her eyes widened, and color
stained her cheeks. "Did you intend for us to share it?"

She said nothing for a long moment. "But where will
you go?" she asked finally, destroying the small, fragile
hope that had begun to grow in Kit's heart.

"There are always places for a soldier to sleep. During

the last three years you and I both have endured conditions far worse than this town offers."

"There's no need—" she began, but he didn't listen. Suddenly he knew that he couldn't stay in this house tonight. He couldn't stay here with her. Not with the ghost of Michael Haviland between them.

"Good night, Judith," Kit said simply. He opened the door and stepped out into the waiting darkness.

"So you finally got what you wanted."

The voice was familiar, but Judith hadn't managed to place it before she looked up, straight into the vindictive eyes of Toby Reynolds. Michael's batman was standing beside her at one of the stalls of the open-air market.

Judith had borrowed a wicker basket from her landlady this morning, deciding that a dose of fresh air and sunshine might lighten her mood. The day had cooperatively provided both, and her small basket was now filled with fresh produce from which she planned to offer her husband a more appetizing meal than the heavy one they had pretended to share last night.

Her normally resilient spirits had responded to being out of doors and to the friendliness, despite her limited command of their language, of the peasants who had come here to sell their goods. She had been feeling better about the situation, despite the fact that Kit had still been absent from their rooms when she had awakened, alone and almost lost in the wide bed.

Now, however, Judith's heart plummeted at what she heard in Reynolds's tone. Perhaps that was because his accusation echoed the guilt her own conscience used to torment her. What he had just said was something she had already acknowledged as the simple truth. She *had* finally gotten what she wanted.

"Private Reynolds," she said, nodding at him. "It's very good to see you again. I'm so glad you escaped."

She was pleased at the normality of her voice. None of her sudden trepidation was revealed in its tone, but Reynolds grinned, apparently seeing through her in an instant.

"You always wanted our pretty major," he said. "Me and the captain knew that. I heard the two of you talking in the tent."

For a moment Judith froze, trying to remember anything improper that Reynolds might have overheard between them. And then she realized that, given his phrasing, he might have meant that he heard her and Michael talking. However, her hesitation caused the batman's leering grin to widen.

"You might'a fooled the others with your act, your *ladyship,* but I knew what you was. And I was right, I see."

"I don't know what you're talking about," Judith said. She could feel the guilty burn of blood in her cheeks.

"It didn't take the two of you long to figure a way to work it. I'll give you that. Clever you are. Sly and clever. A dangerous combination in a woman, I always say. What I don't see is how you got the captain to agree to make that run through the French lines. He weren't no fool. You and I both know that."

She took a breath, trying to think what she could tell him, trying to remember what he might already know. "Captain Haviland volunteered to carry word to Lord Wellington of our predicament and of the arrival of the French reinforcements," Judith said.

"Volunteered?" Reynolds repeated, still mocking. "Is that how it goes, now? I think I'm beginning to get the drift of this. Our noble major wants you, and all the while you're lusting for him. Obvious as a bitch in heat to those of us who really know you. Like your husband did."

"How dare you," Judith whispered. The nausea engendered by his words stirred in her throat.

"One order from the major, and the way is clear," he went on, still smiling at her. "And it worked, of course. He got his Bathsheba. Neat as a charm. St. John took a chance on the captain getting killed, and his bloody luck held, even in that. But then he always was reputed to be a fair lucky bastard."

David and Bathsheba. She remembered the story, of course, with all its Old Testament sin and guilt. King David had sent his captain, Uriah, to be killed in battle because he lusted after the man's beautiful wife. "That's not what happened," Judith denied. "You were there. You *know* what really happened."

Still she hesitated to even speak the truth aloud. But this man knew what had occurred. He knew of Michael's guilt and disgrace, and that her husband had been made a prisoner after that disastrous battle. He also had been in camp when Smythe refused to let Michael undertake the mission that she and her husband had finally forced St. John to allow. Reynolds knew the truth.

"I know that noble bastard tried to have me flayed," Reynolds said. His voice had lost the amused mockery and was filled instead with hate. Its venom chilled Judith to the bone.

"I promise you that Michael volunteered to take that message. He wanted to do something—"

She hesitated again, remembering the purpose behind her husband's gesture. *Something so valiantly right and honorable that it might make up for all the wrongs...*

That had eventually been Michael's wish as well as her own. The aim of that daring journey he had offered to undertake had been to protect his father.

Kit had had nothing to do with that. He had been opposed from the first to letting Haviland go. She and Michael together, however, had given him little option, so he had finally given Michael what he wanted—permission to go— and his own oath never to speak of what had occurred. And if she now revealed what had been done, then the sacrifice of Michael's life would have been made in vain. All of it would be thrown away. Wasted.

"Major St. John had nothing to do with Michael's decision to volunteer," she said.

"It just *conveniently* happened and got him something he'd wanted for a long time? Do you really think anyone will believe that? Especially after they hear that the two of you were already up to no good, and that the captain knew about it. St. John sent a man to his death in order to get you. I wonder if he's found you worth doing murder for."

"No," she said, horrified by the implication. "Nothing you've said is as it happened. Please don't ever suggest—"

Reynolds laughed, revealing stained and uneven teeth. "It's what *I* believe happened, your ladyship. And what others will believe, too. You might'a got what you wanted, you and St. John. But you ain't got off for free, neither of you. Don't you go believing that. Not so long as Toby Reynolds is around."

He insolently took an apple from the basket hanging over Judith's arm and bit into its white flesh with those broken, discolored teeth. His eyes mocked, but he said nothing else to her before he turned away and sauntered across the cobblestones.

Behind him, Judith eventually remembered to breathe, as long and as shuddering an intake of breath as when she had agreed to become St. John's wife. She had married Kit to make the scandal over the weeks the two of them had spent together go away. To protect those they loved. And now, with Toby Reynolds's vicious accusations, she knew without a shadow of a doubt she had failed.

Chapter Twelve

"Considering everything," Wellington said softly, "it might be wise to consider resigning your commission."

"There's no truth in what Reynolds is suggesting. You must know that." Kit's voice was controlled, but the rage that had been building inside him for days threatened to explode.

He had followed his lordship's urgings and the prompting of his own heart when he had proposed to Judith Haviland. Now Reynolds's poison had made their marriage the center of a scandal that was far worse than the previous whispers had been. Something much more dangerous, as Wellington had just acknowledged.

The batman had virtually accused Kit of murdering Haviland by sending him on a suicide mission, one which had already cost Lieutenant Scarborough his life. St. John had supposedly ordered Haviland to make that same impossible journey in hope that he, too, would meet that fate. Then the major could marry Judith, with whom, Reynolds hinted, he was having an adulterous affair.

The batman had woven a sticky web of lies, deceits, and half-truths, which, it seemed, nothing Kit or his superiors said could completely destroy. The story was too grotesquely fascinating, especially after the gossip that had gone before. And especially since it concerned someone like St. John.

Wellington had tried to stop the slander by sending for Reynolds. He intended to warn the man of disciplinary action if he continued his calumny, but apparently Reynolds had carefully walked the line between accusation and implication, walked it too adroitly for the general to take any official action against him.

A lot of what Haviland's orderly said was true, of course. The facts about Scarborough's death, the composition and vulnerability of the small caravan Kit led, the fact that Mrs. Haviland and her husband had both been part of it. But the central claim, that Kit had ordered Haviland to cross enemy lines, could not now be proven one way or the other. And nothing could stop people from making the inference it suggested.

Of course, the batman's story contained no reference to the charges Smythe had brought against Haviland, to his disgrace and subsequent arrest. Kit himself was honorbound not to reveal any of that information, which might have turned the tide in his favor, although, like the other, there was now no proof that any of that had happened.

His commander's questions had been pointed enough that Kit believed Wellington himself, on occasion at least, wondered exactly what had occurred. Only Judith and St. John knew the entire truth, and Kit had taken an oath not to reveal an important portion of it. And the reasons Judith wanted her husband's dishonor unexposed were, he knew, still as valid as when she'd explained them to him. So they were left with Reynolds's whispers, and no way to disprove what they implied.

Wellington's mouth pursed in thought, but his eyes met St. John's, their gaze considering. "Those of us who knew

Haviland," he said, "did not find him to be self-sacrificing. *Or* heroic. Perhaps that assessment of his character is one reason people are now listening to his batman's story."

"Those who are listening," Kit said, "do so because they *enjoy* hearing filthy gossip. Whatever Haviland was..." Kit paused, thinking about what Judith's husband had been.

Remembering his oath, however, St. John's lips closed over the true explanation for Captain Haviland's self-sacrifice. He stood silently before his commander, lost in bitterness, again reliving the decisions he had been forced to make.

It was Wellington who finally broke the strained silence. "Reynolds claims that Scarborough had already been lost in the attempt to get word through. Is that information accurate?"

"It is," Kit agreed reluctantly. "Scarborough had made it only a few miles before he was ambushed."

"Private Reynolds avows that you then requested Haviland be attached to your command. Is that also accurate?"

"It is *not*. Colonel Smythe had placed Captain Haviland with my detachment long before Scarborough's body was discovered."

"A detachment which included Mrs. Haviland?"

"And the other women," Kit reminded softly. A muscle tensed involuntarily beside his mouth, and was then controlled.

"Haviland was assigned to your detachment despite the fact that Smythe, shorthanded as he was, knew he would soon be facing a vastly superior French force? Despite the fact that due to your own injury he had already lost one of his best officers?"

Wellington's questions themselves seemed accusations, at least to Kit, although the commander's tone was measured. "I didn't question the reasons for Colonel Smythe's orders," he said. "I obeyed them. As I had always done."

"I see," Wellington said. His eyes remained on St. John's face. "And when you were forced to turn back from the bridge and found that the regiment had been wiped out? There was no one else within your command whom you might have sent to me with word of the French reinforcements and of your predicament?"

"There were only three of us who knew the country well enough to have any chance of reaching the English lines."

"You, Sergeant Cochran, and Haviland?"

"Yes, sir," Kit agreed.

Another silence stretched as Wellington referred to a document before him. St. John could only assume the paper contained Reynolds's sworn statements.

"We've been over this before," Kit said. "I have explained the entire situation as it existed at that time."

His commander's eyes lifted, but he ignored the protest, just exactly, Kit thought, as his father had always ignored him when he tried to defend his actions. "Cochran was too valuable to send, you said, because he was foraging?" Wellington asked.

Kit's mouth tightened, but determinedly he held his temper. "That is correct."

"And could not Captain Haviland have been assigned to see to that? Given that his wife was with your party, it seems that it might have been more appropriate to allow Haviland to remain with the command and send Cochran to me." The sentence had somehow become a question.

Kit took a breath, strong enough that it lifted the muscles under the white facings of his uniform. "I felt Cochran was the better shot," he offered.

"Not better than you, I should think. According to your reputation, at least," Wellington suggested. "But I had forgotten. You were wounded. In high fever by this time and being cared for by Mrs. Haviland."

"Are you suggesting—"

"I am suggesting," Wellington said, loudly enough that his voice overrode the obvious fury in Kit's. "I am suggesting," he repeated, his tone modified now that St. John's angry words had stopped, "that these are the very questions which will be put to you if you allow this situation to proceed to an inquiry. Don't be a fool, man," he advised softly. "Sell out and go home. You can do no more good here, considering these rumors. And your injury provides the perfect excuse."

"I'm not looking for excuses," Kit said. "I'm a soldier. I came here to fight the French. I think that perhaps even now we may agree that I have been effective in that endeavor."

His father would have recognized the glacial glint in the blue eyes. Apparently so did his commander. "You have proven to be an exemplary officer, St. John. With a record here you may be justifiably proud of. No one can ever take that from you."

Kit's tight-set features relaxed minutely, until the Beau added softly, "*Unless* you let them do so with this slander."

Kit's laugh was bitter. "I am already stained with 'this slander.' My name *and* my record. Resigning will only appear an admission of guilt. I don't intend to *run* from Reynolds's lies. There isn't one word of truth in what he's suggesting. I swear to you on my honor as an officer that nothing happened as he says it did. Not regarding Captain Haviland. *Or* his wife."

"*Your* wife," Wellington reminded him. "You married Judith Haviland to protect her. Why the bloody hell don't you do it? Take her home, St. John. Get her away before this becomes something I can't contain. Do it before some-one decides to write her father or yours or Haviland's with all the scandalous details. Then there will be nowhere for the two of you to go."

"I don't believe that will—"

"With you gone, the talk here will die," Wellington broke in. "I guarantee you that. They'll all be too busy chasing the French to have time to gossip like the old women they seem to have become. I'll see to it, damn it. I still have *some* authority over this army."

"Use it to force Reynolds to tell the truth," Kit argued.

"Do you suggest I have the truth *beaten* out of him?" the general asked, his own temper flaring for the first time.

Suddenly St. John remembered the flogging he'd over-seen that snowy morning. It had been Haviland's crime, of course, but it had been the back of his servant and confidant Toby Reynolds which received the stripes. In carrying out Smythe's command Kit had apparently acquired a bitter and vindictive enemy.

"Do it for her sake if not for your own," Wellington urged.

This time the silence grew until it filled the small room. Proud, stubborn aristocrats both, they also possessed equally brilliant, tactical minds.

"Retreat and cut your losses," the general suggested, as he would have advised any subordinate in a losing position.

"I swear to you, sir, on my honor, that Haviland vol-unteered for that mission. I never ordered him to go," Kit said stubbornly, but the anger had been wiped from his voice. It was tired instead, almost emotionless.

"I never believed you did. But your wife is a beautiful woman. And you're correct about the undeniable lure of a scandal such as this. This gossip will never disappear as long as you are here, living together, your marriage a constant reminder.''

Living together, Kit thought. The bitterest irony of all.

''I can arrange transportation home, if you like,'' Wellington offered. ''The ships carrying reinforcements have already begun to arrive. They'll be returning as soon as possible with the wounded and those whose terms of enlistment are up. I can get you and your wife a cabin on one of them.'' The general's voice was compassionate, but this battle was done, and he was certainly strategist enough to recognize when he had achieved his ends.

''I should be very grateful,'' Kit said.

He saluted, and, as he had before, he turned and crossed the room with the same purposeful stride as the day he had been given permission to propose to Michael Haviland's widow. Nothing in his movements betrayed the enormous difference between what had been his feeling of elation then and the cold desolation in his heart today.

''England?'' Judith repeated softly.

''Wouldn't you like to go home, Judith?'' Kit asked. ''To see your father again?''

Nothing of the agitation he had felt when he left Wellington was in his voice. St. John had walked for hours after that painful interview. He had even ventured outside the walls of the town and into the still dangerous countryside.

None of the English sentries had questioned his destination, either because they had identified him or because they were veterans who had long ago learned the signs of despair and battle fatigue which sometimes drive men to commit acts which are not entirely rational. Kit had walked off his rage and his disappointment. And he had eventually become reconciled to the wisdom of Wellington's suggestion.

He had joined the army because his father had ordered him to, and he had come to Iberia because he had been given little choice. Once here, however, he had found purpose and honor for his life, a sense of pride and accomplishment that had long been missing. Now he must give them up because of one man's lies and innuendoes. About himself and Judith. About their relationship.

But Wellington was right, of course, and Kit had been forced finally to acknowledge that at some point during his aimless wandering. One of the many reasons he had married Judith Haviland was to offer her protection against scandal, and considering the situation, he could no longer do that here.

Kit had discovered that trying to destroy the whispers that haunted their lives was like fighting shadows. They became fleeting and insubstantial when he attempted to confront them. No one said anything openly, or he would have called that man out, of course. What was happening was too subtle for that.

He had clearly witnessed the effects of the batman's libel in the uncomfortable reaction of his fellow officers to his presence. Read it in their eyes when they looked at him. Or at Judith. That had been the most difficult to bear.

"But to resign your commission—" Judith began.

"The surgeons say there are physicians in London I should consult about a course of treatment for my arm. To regain full mobility. To have any chance of success, that must be done before the muscles become completely atrophied."

Her eyes fell to his arm, which in truth was far less impaired than she had warned him it would be. She would probably know that was a lie, he thought. But at least a reasonable one.

"This is what you want?" Judith asked finally, her eyes again on his face, trying to read the truth there.

He smiled at her, his own gaze clear and serene. In those hours after he left Wellington's office, he had made his decision. And he had faced the only guilt he knew he bore for this situation. He had been in love with Judith Haviland—long before her husband had volunteered for that mission.

It was possible that his feelings for her had in some way colored his ultimate decision to let Haviland go. There had been nothing like what Reynolds implied, of course, but still he *had* loved her. Dishonorably, he had desired another man's wife.

Who was now his wife, he thought, and protecting her was what honor now demanded. That was more important than his small role in this war, which Wellington was already winning and would continue to do. Judith was the most important thing now, far more important than his career or even his father's regard.

"I want to take you home," Kit answered her truthfully.

Judith was still watching his eyes, and at what she saw within them, finally she nodded agreement.

The ship did not afford Kit the same opportunities for escape that the town they had left behind them had. There was nowhere for him to go other than the small cabin that had been allotted to the two of them. Space was at a premium, he'd been told, and they were man and wife, of course.

Kit stood in the open doorway of the cabin, still wearing his cloak. The thick red wool was darkened across the shoulders with the cold rain that had pelted them as they hurried from Wellington's private carriage and on board the transport.

He watched Judith press her palm against the mattress of the bed. She had removed her gloves and thrown back the hood of her cloak. A few droplets of rain glinted like diamonds in the dark tendrils that surrounded her features.

"The sheets are damp, I'm afraid," she said, looking over her shoulder at him. The pale oval of her face was alternately illuminated and then shadowed, as the oil lamp someone had thoughtfully lit for them swayed with the motion of the ship.

She was so beautiful Kit's heart lurched painfully in his chest. He could hear the nervousness in her voice, despite her seeming composure and her conversation about something as commonplace as damp bedding. That was an attempt, he knew, to talk about anything except what lay between them.

"But then so are we," St. John reminded her softly.

She smiled at him, but the corners of her lips were slightly tremulous. She would be as apprehensive about this as he. Kit had made her a promise, and he had kept to it scrupulously throughout the brief days of this unconsummated marriage. But occasionally there had been something in her eyes that made him question the conclusions he had drawn about Haviland's death and her grief. Something that reminded him of the image which had leapt into his mind as she put her cold, trembling hand into his the day they wed.

"Come inside," she invited.

She moved away from the bed and over to the low table where the sailor who had guided them to the cabin had placed their borrowed portmanteau.

Kit obeyed, closing the wooden door behind him, shutting out the rain and the low howl of the coastal wind. The resulting silence was almost shocking, as if they had finally managed to shut out the howls of the outside world as well. To be transported back to the few, quiet hours they had once spent alone together.

Judith looked up at the sudden silence, and the same memories he fought were suddenly in her eyes. *Will you tell me the truth?* he had asked, and he knew now that she never had.

"There's a peg for your cloak," she said.

Obediently, Kit loosened the fastenings and swung the military cape off his shoulders. He shook it once so that the moisture fell, leaving a pattern like rain over the scarred wooden floor. He was aware that Judith watched him as he moved across the cabin to hang the garment where she'd indicated.

He walked back to face her. He reached out to untie her cloak, and her eyes widened as his fingers came near. He deliberately ignored her surprise and continued to untie the black silk cording. Almost grateful for the opportunity to escape, it seemed, she turned her back when he had finished that task, allowing him to lift the cloak away from her body.

When they'd first entered, the room had been filled with the odor of brine, of tar and hemp; now these were joined by the unmistakable smell of wet wool.

And underlying them all was something that moved in Kit's memory, evoking feelings long denied. That undernote was the pleasant aroma that was uniquely Judith. He was standing so close to her that when he inhaled, the warm scent of her body filled his senses. A delicate combination of rose water and soap. Of clean skin. The fragrance of her hair, spread like a dark, perfumed cloud across his chest and shoulders.

That was fantasy, but the image was no less powerful because it was not real and had not been experienced. Imagination was, of course, the most potent of aphrodisiacs. As was anticipation.

They stirred in his groin, demanding. Needing. He needed Judith. Her comfort and kindness and her concern. Beyond those, he needed to lose himself in the hot, sweet oblivion of desire. To bury the frustrations and bitterness that had tormented him these last days in the welcoming softness of her body.

"The room seems very small," she said, turning back to him.

He was still holding her cloak, so he folded it carefully over his arm, working very hard to regain the control he had imposed on himself for so long. "There's nowhere else for me to go, Judith. I'm sorry for that."

"I'm not," she said, smiling. "I think it would be lonely here without you. And a little frightening."

"You don't like the sea?" he asked, turning to hang her cloak on the peg beside his. Then, as she had done, he put his palm down against the clammy coldness of the sheets. Both actions hid his face for a few moments so, he hoped, she would not be able to read in his eyes what he had been thinking.

"I am *not* a good sailor," she said. "I should have warned you." That appealing touch of self-mockery was in her voice.

"Then I'll play at nursemaid," he said.

"Perhaps if the sea is calm, you won't have to. If," she said, "you are very lucky."

The luckiest bastard alive, Kit thought. And when she smiled at him, there was not even an echo of irony or bitterness in the remembrance of that once-familiar epithet.

The crossing, however, was difficult from the first. The spring storms had apparently arrived early, and waves tossed the heavy transport as if it were a rowboat. Judith spent the first night alternating between bouts of extreme seasickness and exhausted snatches of sleep. Whatever nervousness she had felt at their enforced proximity evaporated.

Finally, she ceased to be ill only because there was nothing else within her stomach to be gotten out. That was when Kit had teasingly plied her with rum, its potency cut with a little water. He poured out a measure of it from an ornately engraved silver flask. A gift from Lord Wellington, he explained, a wedding present and a farewell memento.

Judith certainly didn't want the drink, but Kit had so charmingly cajoled her, she finally gave in. She found that her husband's teasing was very difficult to resist. And besides, she remembered his very practical and competent kindness in tending to her while she was so embarrassingly ill.

She had drunk down the first draught, which, surprisingly, given the state of her stomach, stayed down. She hadn't even protested the second, which produced a most pleasant lethargy.

And at dawn she had awakened to find herself in Kit's arms. Tucked very comfortably beside him, she realized, his body protecting hers from the endlessly rolling motion of the ship.

Her head was cradled on his chest, and her hand had found a very natural resting place on the opposite broad shoulder. He held her, as he had held her in one way or another, through most of the long, intensely uncomfortable hours of this night. And in those hours, she found that their relationship seemed to have moved beyond embarrassment or pretense.

"Are you asleep?" she whispered. She turned her head

slightly, but she couldn't see his face. Given what had gone before, and their positions, that was perhaps just as well.

He must be very sorry of his bargain *this* morning, she thought. One of His Majesty's bad bargains, the soldiers called someone who didn't meet muster. That's what she had been for Kit—a very bad bargain indeed. In so many ways.

"You're supposed to be asleep," he said. The sound of the soft words rumbled beneath her ear, his voice deep and pleasant.

"I have been," she whispered.

"Better now?"

"All better," she agreed. "I'm sorry," she added.

"For being sick?" His question was touched with humor. The tone of his voice was distorted by the position of her ear over his chest, but still, his amusement had been obvious.

"For everything," she confessed softly.

She *was* truly sorry for it all. For the scandal. For the disgrace she had unwittingly brought into his life. He had been forced to marry her, by the constraints imposed on him by his honor and probably by Wellington's command as well.

She knew very well the real reason Kit had sold his commission. A soldier's daughter, Judith knew, probably better than he, how the small world of the British army really worked.

"For everything?" he questioned.

She said nothing for a moment, wondering how she could adequately express her regret for the fact that she had ruined his life. She had never intended that. She had loved him, and because she did, she had allowed herself to reach out and grasp something she knew had never really been intended for someone like her. And now…

"If you mean last night," he said, interrupting that self-castigation, "then I think the scales are still tilted very heavily in your favor."

"The scales?"

"You cared for me far longer than I have cared for you."

"But not like this," she protested, thinking of the events of last night, thankfully clouded by the alcohol-induced haze that affected her this morning.

"No," he suggested softly, "your nursing was in fact far more..." He hesitated, but his deep voice was still relaxed. Still unembarrassed. "Far more intimate," he finished finally.

If she had been able to see his face, she might have been more inhibited. But here, held warmly against the strength of his body, the fingers of his right hand moving slowly, caressing small circles on her back, she felt safe from his possible disgust, and even from her own discomfiture.

"I didn't mind," she whispered, remembering those days in the old woman's hut, removed from the world and from all other considerations except tending to the needs of the man she loved.

"But I must confess that I *did* mind," Kit said. His voice, however, was still laced with amusement.

"Is that why you sent me away that night?"

"I sent you away..." he began, and then the words faded.

She waited a long time, feeling the slow, steady rise and fall of his chest beneath her cheek and listening to his heartbeat. It had quickened when she asked her question, but now it returned to the measured tempo it had held to before.

"I sent you away," he said finally, "because that wasn't the kind of intimacy I wanted."

"Not the *kind* of intimacy?" she questioned. But after

all, she had been Michael Haviland's wife for almost three years. There were so many kinds of intimacy.

"*Not* the kind that involved nursing," he said.

She thought about what he had said, trying not to read more into that simple statement than she should, although her own heart rate had accelerated.

"You cared for me," she reminded him softly.

She pushed up on her elbow so she could see his face. Sometime during the long night, Kit had turned the lamp down very low. The deep shadows it cast drifted again, back and forth, across those handsome, aristocratic features.

"Because you needed me to care for you," he said simply.

It was what he would have done for any comrade, she realized. For any of the men under his command. Whatever St. John had been when he had come to Iberia, he was now the kind of man who would always care for those who needed him. If they belonged to him. If they were his responsibility.

There aren't many choices where duty is involved, he had once told her. And he had been the kind of officer who made the difficult ones. That was all he meant, she had decided, when he added something else, the words very soft.

"And because I wanted to care for you," he said.

Her eyes stung, but she blinked away the moisture, hoping that in the shadows he had not seen it. And that he would never be aware of how much that simple phrase had meant to her.

Only here, Judith, could someone like you... Michael's taunt echoed suddenly in her heart. *Only here...*

Kit had married her because he had been forced to, she reminded herself. Now perhaps he had decided that, since they were wed, he must make the best of his bad bargain.

She could not allow herself to read too much into those idle words. Kit was her husband. Caring for her was his duty. And he would fulfill that duty, as he had all the others.

"Thank you for what you did last night," she whispered.

She watched his mobile lips tilt at her politeness. His lean face was relaxed and without tension, as she had not seen it in so many days.

"You're very welcome," he said softly.

His head began to lift. His eyes seemed to be focused on her mouth. As if he intended— Suddenly she was aware again, unromantically, of the more unpleasant aspects of last night. Instinctively, she recoiled, pressing her lips together and putting the tips of her fingers over them. It was a defensive gesture, not prompted by the interpretation he put on it.

"Are you ill?" he asked. He sat up, raising her carefully.

"No," she protested. "No, I'm..." She stopped, and took a breath, reading concern in his eyes now, and certainly not what she had believed might have been in them before. Wishful thinking, she supposed. "A little sick, maybe," she lied.

"Then fresh air," Kit said decisively. "And there's nothing more beautiful than the sea at dawn. Especially after a storm. Would like me to show you?" he invited.

She nodded. At least that would remove them from the confines of this small room. And perhaps she did need fresh air to clear her head, to blow away the remains of the sickness and even the effects of the rum he'd given her, because sometime during their conversation, she had begun to hope...

Kit suddenly swung his long legs off the bed and then stood beside it, stretching with the grace of a big cat. He ran his right hand through the black curls, which were still too short to have become very disarrayed in sleep.

He had removed his uniform coat before he lay down, and she could see the muscles in his back and shoulders, their movement delineated under the thin lawn of his shirt. Her eyes traced down his slim hips and over the muscles of his buttocks and thighs, clearly revealed by the tight-knit pantaloons he wore.

He reached to pull his cloak off the peg and swirled it with the ease of long practice over his wide shoulders. Then he took hers, holding it out with both hands despite his damaged arm, inviting her to step within the welcoming warmth of its folds.

Obediently Judith crawled out of the bed they had shared last night, brushing distractedly at the skirt of her borrowed dress. At least that gave her something to do with her trembling hands. And something to look at besides her husband's body.

The gown was too badly wrinkled, however, for her efforts to do much good, so she wisely gave up the attempt and moved to stand in front of Kit, her back to him. He laid the cloak over her shoulders and reached around her body to fasten the cords.

She looked down, watching the long brown fingers working competently just beneath her chin. They had been just as skillful in their ministrations last night. Holding her, pressing a cold cloth against her face, touching her with compassion. His hands had been as soothing as his calm, low voice had been through the long hours.

They stood a moment when Kit had finished with the cords. She fought the urge to lean into his body, against which she had sheltered last night. Somehow, she had lost the license to touch him, which her illness and the darkness had given her then.

Once more St. John seemed almost a stranger. Someone she didn't know very well at all, despite their enforced intimacy. *Intimacy*. Her mind repeated the word, remembering how it had sounded when he whispered it and what it had seemed to imply. *Intimacy*.

His hands lifted the hood of her cloak and placed the cloth protectively over her head. As she began to tuck in the tangled strands of her hair, she felt his hands fasten gently on her shoulders. He leaned forward and put his chin against the top of her head. He held it there for only a second before he moved, pressing his lips now at the spot where his chin had rested.

Then he stepped back and removed his hands from her shoulders, releasing her. She listened without moving as his footsteps crossed the wooden floor behind her.

Finally she began the prosaic task of pulling on the damp gloves she had stuffed into the pocket of her cloak last night. She could barely see her fingers, her vision blurred by the same unexpected rush of tears she had experienced before.

She had gone through so many things in the last few months, horrors that were truly worthy of tears, but she had not given in to them. Now it seemed she was destined to succumb to that very feminine weakness at the slightest excuse—a kind word or the impersonal touch of her new husband's lips.

The sudden rush of cold air from the door Kit opened was welcome. It broke the pull of emotion, clearing her head and sweeping away the stuffiness of the small cabin. Blinking at the light and trying to banish the moisture from her eyes, Judith turned and found that Kit was watching her from the open doorway.

In his eyes was an expression she had never seen there before. But then, there were so many things she didn't know about him. Still, they had survived the night, and they were leaving behind them in Portugal the painful scandal that threatened disgrace. Together they would build a new life in England.

Home, she thought, finally allowing herself the luxury of acknowledging how glad she would be to leave this country and the memories of the last three years behind. The thought of a new beginning was as welcome as the rush of fresh air into the cabin had been. It banished the shadows and destroyed the pervasive, damp miasma of the long night they had passed through.

From the doorway, Kit held out his hand, an invitation to join him, as clear and compelling as that same gesture had been beside the mountain stream. This time, however, the long brown fingers did not tremble.

This was not a man who needed her care, and not a man who would ever disappoint or abuse her. This was a man who was both strong enough to protect and gentle enough to shelter, as he had done last night.

She smiled at him, and perhaps even at the pink-tinged dawn that gilded the dark panorama of sea and unclouded sky that stretched beyond him. The long storm, it seemed, was finally over.

Chapter Thirteen

It was Roger who met their ship. Kit had written his brother, and Wellington had kindly offered to include the brief message in the diplomatic pouch. He could give no guarantee, of course, that the letter would arrive in England before the transports, but apparently it had.

The missive contained only the barest bones of what had occurred in Portugal. Kit included the news of his marriage, and Judith's parentage by way of an introduction. He also mentioned that his wife was a widow, but deliberately avoided any details about her previous marriage or her husband's death. It was not that Kit distrusted his brother, but the fewer who knew about the controversy they had left behind them, the better.

Despite the contrast between his stolid practicality and Kit's restless wildness, despite the nearly five-year difference in their ages, he and Roger had always been close. And he knew that his brother had protected him from their father's wrath on more occasions than they either would wish to recall.

"This is Judith," Kit said after he and his older brother had exchanged their somewhat restrained greetings.

Roger took Judith's hand, bringing her fingers to his lips. "I'm very glad to have finally acquired a sister," he said.

His blue eyes, very much like Kit's own, seemed to study Judith's face a moment before he said, "My mother asked me to make her apologies. I'm afraid she's been a bit unwell this winter. Nothing serious," he added, seeing Kit's quick concern. "She hopes you'll forgive her. She's waiting for you at home."

"There's nothing to forgive, of course," Judith said. "I'm very sorry she's been ill."

Roger smiled at her. Then his gaze left her face to examine his brother's. "The rest of your luggage?" he asked, rather than voicing the questions which were in his eyes.

Kit glanced down at the battered case which contained both his and Judith's meager possessions. And they were lucky, of course, to have those. "That's all of it, I'm afraid," he admitted. He could see the quick shock in Roger's face, but his brother made no comment before gesturing to the waiting coachman.

The man handled the portmanteau so gingerly that his reluctance to touch it was obvious. His manner bordered on impertinence, something that would surely have set off Kit's uncertain temper three years ago. Now he found the coachman's snobbery merely ridiculous.

Judith's eyes met his, and in them was an amusement that matched his own. *Even the servants are offended by our baggage,* hers seemed to say. *Baggages,* Kit thought, remembering the rag and tag collection of women and children who invariably followed in the tail of the army. That derogatory term might now be used to describe the two of them, he thought. And as he watched, his wife's small smile widened, almost as if she read his mind.

Reluctantly, he pulled his gaze from her face, breaking the connection that had sparked between them. On board the crowded transport, with its enforced proximity, he and Judith had at least reclaimed the friendship they had once shared.

There had still been moments of tension, of course, especially since they had to keep up the pretense that theirs was a normal marriage. They dined with the captain each evening and had discovered to their mutual delight that his love of books was as deep as their own. They matched wits over literary arguments, their discussions far-ranging and very pleasantly ordinary after the horrors they had endured.

Kit and the captain took a long walk around the deck each evening after they had escorted Judith to the cabin. By the time Kit returned, his wife had changed into her nightgown, another outsized garment loaned her by Mrs. Stuart, and was tucked safely between the damp sheets of the bed, pretending to be asleep.

Each night they shared the cabin, but never again the wide bed and so never with the intimacy he had confessed to her he wanted. Given the revelation he had made, Kit felt that the next move must be up to Judith. As yet, she had given him no indication she was ready to make it. Perhaps, he thought, that would change now that they were home.

Kit handed his wife into the carriage and was about to climb up into the seat when Roger stopped him by placing his hand on his arm. "He wants to see you," his brother said softly. "This afternoon. As soon as we arrive at the town house."

His father, Kit realized. "Let me guess," Kit said sarcastically. "Because he's missed me?"

"Because..." Roger began, and then he paused. "Because of what he's heard about Portugal. About what happened there."

For a moment sickness stirred in his throat, and then Kit

realized that this summons didn't necessarily have to be about the scandal. "And exactly what has Ryde heard about Portugal?"

"About her," Roger said, his voice still too low to carry into the interior of the carriage. "About your marriage."

Kit laughed, and shock touched his brother's eyes. He knew Roger could never understand the bitterness of that laughter. Nothing of what he had accomplished in Iberia had reached his father's notice. Or if it had, Ryde had chosen to ignore it.

St. John had led his men well enough to have earned their respect. And even, in some cases, their love as he had been very honored to realize. His actions had been mentioned in the dispatches on at least a half dozen occasions, and Wellington was not known for citing his officers except for extreme bravery.

None of that mattered, of course. Not beside the other. The scandal was all his father had taken notice of, it seemed. All he wished to speak to him about.

"Tell him," Kit said, his voice as low as his brother's, but each word enunciated distinctly, leaving no doubt about the import or the tone of the message Roger was intended to convey. "Tell him I'll see him when I can find time. But not today, Roger. Will you tell him that for me?"

"Don't be a fool," his brother warned. "You really can't afford to alienate him any further."

"I doubt that I could," Kit said truthfully. "Tell him I'll come when I can find time," he said again. Then he shook off his brother's arm and climbed into the waiting coach. It was several long seconds before Roger followed.

They didn't speak of it again. Judith and his brother made polite, idle conversation during the journey home, but Kit took no part in that. He looked instead out the window of the carriage at the countryside they passed, thinking how little anything had changed during the last three years. And how unlikely it was now that it ever would.

"Tell me the truth, damn you," his father said. "About her. The Haviland woman. About her husband's death."

"The truth, sir, is that Judith is my wife. And that Michael Haviland died while on an important and dangerous mission he had volunteered to undertake. He died trying to save the lives of wounded men and the women."

"That isn't what I've been told."

"But you asked *me* to tell you the truth," Kit said softly.

He had known how this would go. It was the same pattern as all their encounters. This one would be no different from any of the others, and he had acknowledged that before it even began. Except, he supposed, this might well be the last of them.

"Do you know that he's been here? In this house," his father said. Ryde was furious. His voice was controlled, as always, but there was a streak of color over his high cheekbones.

"Michael Haviland?" Kit asked with pseudo-politeness, while trying to imagine who his father could be talking about. But then, it didn't really matter who had been here, he decided. Obviously *someone* had rushed to tattle to the earl about the scandal. "If you've been a victim of ghostly visitations, sir," Kit said, "then might I suggest that—"

"Not Haviland, you fool," the earl interrupted, cutting through the mocking suggestion. "His damned batman."

"His batman?" Kit exclaimed, his voice wiped clean of mockery. They had left Reynolds behind them in Portugal, along with his lies. Or so he had believed. But if the batman was here in England, then that explained, of course, how the gossip had arrived before them.

"Only he's not a batman any longer. Or even, apparently, a soldier," his father said.

Wellington hadn't known that Reynolds fell into that group he had so casually mentioned—troopers whose terms of service were up. And with the destruction of his regiment, no one would even try very hard to convince Private Reynolds to reenlist. So, frightened by Wellington's warning perhaps, the batman had beaten them home, securing passage on one of the returning ships. And his first destination, it seemed, had been this house.

"What did he want?" Kit asked. Nothing about this nightmare could surprise him anymore. The gossip Reynolds spread seemed like the mythical Hydra. If one of its heads were cut off, it simply grew another.

"Money, of course," his father said. "A great deal of money, as a matter of fact."

"And did you give it to him?" Kit asked, knowing the answer before his father gave it.

"You know me better than *that,* I should think. I sent him packing."

"But you listened to all his lies before you did."

At the accusation in Kit's tone, the patchy color deepened in the earl's pale face. "Lies?" he asked sarcastically.

"Lies about how you sent *another* man to his death to secure something you wanted. Nothing has changed, St. John," Ryde said. "You *still* know nothing of honor."

Kit wondered if there was anything that would ever make a difference in his father's opinion of him. It was his own fault, he supposed. Or the fault of the man he had once been.

That all seemed so long ago. He had stood before this same desk and been told that Spain and Wellington might make a man of him. And in fairness, he thought they had. His father had at least been right about that.

"I know enough about it to realize that honor isn't what the world says about you," Kit said. "And I finally understand that if you have it, there is nothing anyone can do that can take it from you. They may destroy your reputation or even destroy you, but honor is inviolate. And indestructible. I have nothing I need to explain, not to you nor to anyone else, sir, about what happened in Portugal. You are quite free, of course, to believe whatever you wish."

His father's eyes had widened, and his face suffused with blood, but for once it seemed he was speechless. For the first time in Kit's memory, the earl of Ryde had nothing to say to his profligate son.

Kit turned, the movement unconsciously precise, almost military. He walked across the vast salon of the town house, his footsteps echoing, and closed its door behind him. His father had asked him for the truth, and what he had told him, Kit knew, was as near to that as he was ever likely to come.

"We don't have to stay here," Judith said. "We can go to my father's."

"I'm through running," Kit said. "We left Portugal because I let Wellington convince me it would be best. I find now that it wasn't. It has only been construed as an acknowledgment of guilt. I'm not leaving London."

He had been surprised that his father hadn't required that of him. Kit had not seen the earl since their confrontation almost two weeks ago, but he and Judith were still living in his father's London town house.

The first night, his mother had hesitantly suggested that they might wish to dine in their rooms, due to their exhaustion from the journey and their status as newlyweds. Kit had made no comment, and the practice had simply continued. Every day for the last two weeks their meals

had been laid in this suite, effectively isolating them from
the rest of the household.

Kit saw Roger and his mother on occasion, but never
Ryde. And he found that was no longer even a matter for
regret. He and Haviland really *had* been more alike than
he realized, Kit thought, remembering the captain's bitter
questions.

*"Do you love your father, St. John? Have you sought
his approval your whole bloody life and known that you
never quite lived up to his expectations? Do you have any
idea what it's like never to measure up? No matter how
hard you try?"*

Never to measure up, Kit repeated mentally. And he
never had.

"Why are you doing this?" Judith asked. "There's no
point. We both know now that we can't put an end to
what's being said. Not even by staying in town."

He nodded, his eyes tracing over her face. The strain was
beginning to take its toll, even on Judith's courage and
determined composure. The direct cuts and even the more
discreet whispers they had endured in London were far
worse than any of the hardships of war they had once faced
together.

Then there had been some purpose in the suffering. This
was...senseless, meaningless. And it was fueled by one
man's lies and innuendoes. When the earl refused to give
in to his blackmail, Toby Reynolds had apparently taken
the revenge he promised. As he probably would have in
any case, Kit acknowledged. He didn't blame his father,
because he himself would have given Reynolds the same
answer, of course.

"I never meant for this to happen," he said. "I thought
I was doing what was best for you."

"If we go to my father's..." she said again.

The suggestion faded when he caught her hand. "I can make arrangements for you to leave tomorrow," he offered.

"For *me* to leave?" she repeated.

"I'm not leaving London, Judith. I'm not running away from their whispers again. I've done nothing wrong."

Nothing except to love you, Kit acknowledged, *long before I had the right.* Although he had searched his conscience, he truly believed that there was no other decision he could have made in Portugal than the fateful one he had come to. The one that had allowed Michael Haviland to undertake the mission that had ended in his death. The mission which had, ironically, saved Haviland's honor and destroyed his own.

"I know," she said. "If you're staying, Kit, then so am I."

"It might be better—" he began.

"No," she said. "If you're staying in London, then so am I."

He still held her hand. He realized that her slender fingers had finally taken on the smoothness they deserved, that he had wanted for them. He released them reluctantly and watched as they fell against the rich fabric of her skirt. Judith Haviland had at last become his lady, and she looked the part.

The gown she was wearing had been cut to Kit's exacting demands. The garnet silk was as becoming to her coloring as he had known it would be. Her darkly shining hair, highlighted with gold by the myriad candles, had been piled high on her head in loose curls. The style emphasized the slender length of her neck and the oval perfection of her face. Under his supervision, Judith had come into her own, as beautiful now in the eyes of others as she had always been in his.

Not always, he acknowledged, mocking his own arrogant

stupidity when he had first seen her, more than five years ago. It was a meeting he had never been able to remember, and it had taken place here in London. So they had come full circle, he supposed. Except now he was the outcast, the one who didn't fit in, and she...

She was the most intriguing woman in the capital. Even Roger had commented on the flattering masculine attention that followed Judith the few times they had gone out to the opera or the theater. Of course, the whispers had followed them as well.

Part of the fascination the *ton* felt was no doubt because Judith was the woman who had lured the infamous St. John astray. A woman worth committing murder for, they whispered. Although he hoped Judith was not, Kit was certainly sophisticated enough to understand that the men who watched her speculated about what she had done to win London's most notorious rake.

They would probably never understand her true attraction, Kit thought. Her honesty and courage had won his heart. They, of course, were looking for quite different attributes from the woman who, they supposed, had ensnared St. John so strongly that he had arranged her husband's death so he could have her.

That belief was in their eyes. Kit saw it clearly, although he believed Judith was unaware of it, at least, he hoped, as yet unaware. But realizing that he couldn't protect her from what was being said, he had finally stopped taking her into society.

Kit himself still visited his clubs and the other haunts he was accustomed to frequent when he was in town. He would be damned if that bastard and his lies would drive him into hiding. But he would no longer allow Judith to be subjected to the snubs and the covertly vicious tongues of the London *ton*.

Nothing was said openly, of course, or within his hearing. Given his reputation with a pistol, few men were brave enough to give him a direct cut. He almost admired those who did.

They were his fellow officers. He had called none of them out, of course, but their actions, and the realization that his own kind had rejected him, hurt far more than the other. He did not even recognize the irony that he now considered himself one with that group of veterans rather than with the far more select circle of aristocrats to which he had belonged since birth.

"St. John?"

Kit raised his eyes from the paper he had been pretending to read straight into those of the speaker. The man who had questioned his identity was no one he recognized.

He was elderly and obviously frail, but the posture was unmistakable. His thin shoulders were erect, and his spine held as straight as a ramrod, despite the ebony walking stick he carried. His black eyes were as piercing, as accustomed to staring down subalterns apparently, as were Lord Wellington's.

It was afternoon, and a pleasant drowsiness had settled over the few inhabitants of White's, the foremost gentleman's club in London. There were none of Kit's onetime cronies here at this hour, of course, which was why he had chosen it.

He made frequent appearances at his club, determined not to let the gossip drive him away, but he seldom came when he might expect his former friends to be in attendance. Kit had found he could no longer bear to be coldly shut out of the circle of which he had once been the acknowledged leader.

"I'm St. John," Kit said. *A friend of his father's?* he wondered. The age was right, but somehow...

The rest of the thought faded as the old man began to pull off his gloves. His hands were as pale as his face, blue veins prominent under the thin skin. Kit's eyes came back to the man's face, and for the first time, apprehension stirred in his gut. There was something in those eyes he should recognize. Something so familiar that it pulled at his mind, urging him to remember.

"Would you stand up, sir," the old man demanded. He held his gloves loosely now in one hand, but his dark eyes had not wavered from Kit's. The words were a command, uttered in a voice that expected nothing less than obedience.

Conditioned during his years on the Peninsula to respond automatically to that exact tone, Kit closed the *Times,* holding its flimsy pages in his right hand, unconsciously using his forefinger to mark his place before he rose. Standing at his full height, Kit almost towered over the visitor.

The old man's eyes were still intent on his. He moved slowly enough that Kit could have avoided the blow, but by that time he understood what was happening, of course. And he knew whose eyes these reminded him of.

The leather gloves were supple from age, but the sound of the blow Roland Haviland struck with them was as shocking in the quiet confines as if it had been a gunshot. Heads turned at the noise, and a few that had been nodding over an afternoon brandy jerked upright. Kit himself, however, didn't react in any way, except for the uncontrollable draining of blood from his face.

The gloves struck again, moving in the direction opposite to that which they had taken before. The shock had faded enough that Kit felt the second blow. And he was humiliatingly aware of the horrified fascination with which the

members of this elite establishment were watching this encounter.

"A coward as well as a murderer, I see," Sir Roland
Haviland said. His voice had not been raised, and St. John
was probably the only one who had clearly heard the accusation.

"I didn't kill your son," Kit said.

"You ordered him on a mission that you hoped would
result in his death," the old man accused.

"Not even that, I swear to you. Your son volunteered
for a task which he knew was dangerous and necessary. He
died a hero's death, Sir Roland. But not, I swear to you, at
my instigation."

The dark eyes held to his, wanting to believe him, Kit
thought. And he was aware when the decision was made
not to.

"Will you not meet me, you bloody coward?" Haviland
asked.

"There's no point in this. There's no basis for the story
you've been told. It's only one man's vindictive lies."

"You killed my son so you could marry his strumpet
wife," the old man said, his voice raised to carry throughout the quiet room. At what he saw in Kit's eyes, Haviland
smiled, triumphant, believing that he had succeeded in what
he had come here to accomplish. "Send your second to
me," he suggested.

Honor isn't what the world says about you, St. John had
told his father. It was not, of course, what the world said
about Judith either. She would be the last to wish this meeting, or to forgive him for it, no matter what the old man
said.

"I won't fight you, Sir Roland," Kit denied. "Our meeting will serve no purpose."

"It will serve *my* purpose."

With those words, Haviland raised the stick he carried in a whistling arc high above his head and brought it down on Kit's shoulder. Again the shock of the old man's action was great enough that Kit didn't try to ward off the blow. St. John didn't move until the stick lifted again.

This time Kit caught it before it struck, and wrenched it out of the frail, trembling fingers. He threw the cane from him, hearing the wood clatter and bounce across the marble floor, the noise it made far too loud in the stunned silence of the room.

"Meet me, damn you," Haviland demanded, "or I'll have my coachman thrash you like the sniveling coward you are. And then I'll have her dragged through the streets like the whore *she* is."

Haviland's voice had risen so that it echoed now against the marble and the fine oak paneling, the words as jarring to the room's normal tranquillity as the obscene clatter the stick had made. Almost against his will, his body flooded with fury and adrenaline, Kit nodded.

Satisfied, the general nodded in return. Then Michael Haviland's aging father turned on his heel, his back still militarily straight, and marched across the marble floor toward the street. He didn't bother to retrieve the walking stick.

Behind him the silence in the club welled like a chorus of condemnation. St. John was not aware of it, of course. He was thinking instead about Judith. And about all that he had lost.

He knew now what he must do. Everything was clear in his mind, the plan of action formed in its entirety as had sometimes happened to him on the battlefield. It was all laid out before him, as plain as if someone had drawn him a map.

There was no doubt and no decision to be made about

what would happen next, because it was exactly as he had already told his father.

They may destroy your reputation or even destroy you, he had said to Ryde, *but honor is inviolate.*

Chapter Fourteen

"You can't fight Haviland," Kit's brother said.

"He didn't give me a choice, Roger. Believe me, I did everything in my power to avoid meeting him."

"This is beyond the pale, Kit. Even you must see that. If you kill that old man, you'll be an outcast."

"I'm already an outcast," Kit said truthfully. "But I won't kill Haviland. I promise you that."

"You didn't *intend* to kill Edmonton either. Things happen in a duel that are beyond anyone's control. But even your intent to meet Haviland—"

"He threatened to have his coachman thrash me in White's. Would you and Father have preferred the notoriety engendered by that display?" St. John asked softly.

The reasonable question gave his brother pause, but as the earl would have done, Roger rose to the occasion. "Father and I would have preferred that none of this ever came to pass," he said stiffly. "It's simply another blot on the family name."

"I never meant for it to happen, Roger, I assure you."

"You never do. It's your damned recklessness. If only you would—"

"Please, don't treat me to a lecture," Kit broke in.

"Once you're Ryde, you may control your sons as you wish, but I ask you to remember that you are *not* my father."

His brother's mouth tightened, but he didn't make the rejoinder that almost echoed between them. *Thank God for that,* Kit was sure his brother wanted to say.

"The only thing you must answer for," St. John went on, ignoring Roger's anger, "is whether or not you're willing to serve as my second. And before you refuse," Kit added, modifying the edge that had crept into his own voice, "I should warn you that there is no one else I can ask. At least no one who would agree. I'm depending on you, I'm afraid, and hoping that you may have still have some family feeling for me."

"Kit, surely you must see—"

"No more," Kit said, holding out his hand to stop the flow of unneeded advice. He had known there was no way to avoid the duel when he had looked into Roland Haviland's eyes.

They had been filled with an inflexible determination Kit had seen only once in the eyes of Haviland's son during the entire three years he had known him. And that was on the day Michael Haviland had talked Kit into allowing him to undertake the mission to Wellington.

"Will you second me or not?" Kit asked again.

The brothers' eyes met and held. In Roger's were unanswerable questions and regret. In the other pair was simply resignation. And the carefully concealed knowledge that what had begun in Portugal was, at last, almost over.

Finally Roger nodded. Kit clasped his brother's shoulder quickly and squeezed, exactly as he had once done, he remembered suddenly, with Sergeant Cochran. "Good man," Kit said softly.

This time, however, there was no respect in the eyes that

met his. But, Kit realized gratefully, nor was there within them the slightest awareness of what he intended.

News of the upcoming duel spread throughout the *ton,* as all rumors in London eventually did. The Season was winding down, and aristocratic boredom had set in.

Matches had been made and relentlessly examined to determine which party had gotten the advantage. Fortunes had been won, or more frequently lost, on a horse race or the turn of a card. And there had been at least one affair of honor, but whatever it had been about had apparently been settled to everyone's satisfaction with the first prick of a rapier.

This meeting, it was understood, would be something very different. Haviland was out for blood, of course, seeking revenge for his son's murder. St. John had already killed one man, it was whispered to those who might have forgotten, and his unquestioned skill with the pistol was well documented.

And, it was ventured by those knowledgeable about such things, this duel would be little more than a slaughter. It was true that Haviland had once been a notable shot, but given his age and recent stroke, it was almost certain St. John would be the victor.

The general consensus was that, considering those factors, St. John should never have accepted the old man's challenge. None of those who so vehemently voiced that opinion bothered to explain how he could have avoided it, given Haviland's actions in White's that day. The word murderer was again being bandied in the clubs and gaming hells and even in shocked whispers in spacious, flower-scented ballrooms. And eventually, of course, it reached the ears of the ladies.

The thought that Judith might hear of the challenge never

crossed Kit's mind. With the help of his man of business, St. John had made the necessary provisions for the settlement of his estate. He would instruct Roger to see that they were carried out. Judith would be taken care of. He had seen to that.

What he had not seen to, because he could not have anticipated it, was his wife's reaction to the duel. And ironically, Judith's reaction was the one thing which might have prevented St. John from reaching the fateful decision he had come to that day in White's.

The musicale was no duller than those she had endured during her Season, Judith supposed, but somehow, given her far more exciting, although sometimes terrifying experiences on the Peninsula, the afternoon seemed endless.

She had agreed to attend the entertainment today only because the countess insisted. She wondered if Kit's mother had any idea of what was being said about Judith and her son. She also wondered if this afternoon's public appearance might possibly be some misguided attempt on the part of the Countess of Ryde to try to redeem them both in the eyes of society.

If so, it was destined to fail, of course. No one had been openly rude as the countess had taken her around the room to make her introductions. Most of the women in attendance were old friends of her mother-in-law's. The countess had, therefore, every confidence that this outing could be accomplished without incident. And it almost was.

The newest twist to the scandal was far too exciting *not* to have been a topic of conversation, however, even in these genteel environs. Since the countess and Lady St. John were fellow guests, it had, of course, been a very discreet one. It was not until the harpist had finished her performance and the polite farewells had begun that Judith learned about the proposed duel.

She and her mother-in-law had already reached the entryway, their coachman called and their wraps brought, when the countess discovered she had left her fan in the salon. Judith dutifully volunteered to fetch it.

The comment she overheard when she reentered the room had never been intended for her ears. And she would never have heard it had Lady Marbury been a little less hard-of-hearing or a little less given to making decisive pronouncements on every topic.

"Then there will be the blood of *two* Haviland men on St. John's hands, my dear. You mark my words," the old woman said.

The ringing tones in which she ventured that opinion might well have been heard in the back row of the Haymarket Theatre. They certainly were loud enough to carry to the ears of the slender woman who had hesitated in the doorway of the elegant gold-and-white salon.

"I beg your pardon?" Judith said. At her question, the shocked gaze of every one of the gossiping women focused on her white face. Lady Marbury's mouth opened and then closed, rather like a dying fish, but apparently she thought better of whatever explanation she had been about to make. Her spinster daughter, who was standing beside her, blushed such an unbecoming shade that her complexion almost blended with the puce of her gown. But neither of them attempted to deny the import of the comment.

"Were you speaking of my husband?" Judith asked calmly, her eyes far more demanding than her voice had been.

"Which one, my dear?" Lady Marbury parried adroitly. "I find it so difficult to keep them straight."

"Lord St. John," Judith said evenly. "Who, I assure you, has *no one's* blood on his hands."

"Indeed?" the old woman questioned with feigned politeness. "I admire your loyalty, my dear, but that isn't what we've been told."

"Whatever gossip you've heard about my husband, I assure you that you may discredit both it *and* the talebearer. There's not a word of truth in those malicious rumors now circulating. I was in Portugal. Surely I'm in a better position to know exactly what occurred there than anyone here in London."

"Then why has he agreed to Sir Roland's challenge?"

"Sir Roland's challenge?" Judith repeated. Her breathing was suddenly constricted and the rush of blood through her head so strong she was almost faint with it.

"The duel is to take place at dawn day after tomorrow, I believe. I'm surprised you didn't know, Lady St. John," Lady Marbury suggested archly. "Given your very *close* relationship with both parties involved."

Judith didn't respond to the gibe. She walked across the room, deliberately holding her head high, and retrieved her mother-in-law's fan from the chair in which she'd been sitting. No one said another word as she walked past them and back to the entry. Lady Marbury's smile was triumphant, she noticed, probably because she was sure she had had the best of this encounter and because it would make such an entertaining story.

Judith, however, wasn't concerned with that. She was dealing instead with what she had just been told. Given what she knew of Michael's father, she knew she shouldn't be surprised that he had sought out St. John. The only question was: Why hadn't Kit told her?

When Lady St. John reentered her father-in-law's town house that afternoon, she thanked the countess for the af-

ternoon's outing and then hurried up the stairs. She did not
linger in her bedchamber longer than was necessary to remove her gloves and her pelisse before she opened the con-
necting door to the part of their suite which had hitherto
been her husband's private domain.

She found him writing at his desk. If Kit was surprised
at her unannounced and unprecedented visit, he hid it well.
The blue eyes which lifted to meet hers were filled only
with polite inquiry.

"Why?" she asked softly and watched as they changed.

St. John could not know, of course, what she had been
told or how much she knew of the situation, but at least he
didn't pretend not to understand.

"Because he left me no choice," Kit said simply.

"Could you not—" she began.

"If there had been any other option, Judith," Kit said,
"I assure you I should have taken it."

"You won't..." Although her husband had made no interruption this time, her voice faded over the impossibility
of voicing what was, to her at least, unthinkable. And she
knew Kit wouldn't kill Sir Roland. She knew the kind of
man St. John was far too well to believe he would shoot
Michael's elderly father.

"No," he agreed finally when the silence between them
had lasted a very long time. "Of course, I won't," he said.
"We both understand that."

"Kit," she whispered.

At what was in her tone, finally he smiled at her. His
blue eyes were very calm, but then he had had several days
to come to terms with this. As she had not.

"You have to explain to him what really happened," she
said.

"I gave my word, Judith, on my honor, that I would never divulge what occurred. And Michael gave me his."

"And kept it," she said softly, remembering the circumstances surrounding her first husband's death.

Kit nodded. "I have to do the same. Surely you understand that. I can't tell General Haviland or anyone else the truth."

"But you had *nothing* to do with Michael's death."

"No one believes that. Only you and I know what happened. And nothing I've said so far has made any difference in what they've chosen to believe."

"Then I will say it," she said. "*I'll* tell them the truth. And I'll *make* them believe me."

He smiled at her again. Almost for the first time since they had arrived in London, she realized, Kit's smile was as it had been before this had begun, without any trace of bitterness.

They had believed that in leaving Iberia, they could escape. They both knew now that they had been wrong. He had accepted that, but she could not, because if she did...

"They won't believe you," Kit advised. "Even if you tell them the truth, it will make no difference. Except it will defame Haviland's memory."

He was right, of course. She would not be believed. She had already been judged guilty, as had Kit. The truth would only give the gossips more grist for the slow-grinding mill of rumor. Perhaps Toby Reynolds had begun this, but they had all had a hand. All the scandalmongers.

Telling them the truth would not stop the talk because they would simply choose not to believe. The truth was not nearly so interesting as the lies they had devised to explain it away.

"Then I'll go to him. To Michael's father. I'll tell *him* the truth," Judith said. "And I'll make him listen to it."

"You're the one who wanted Michael to have a chance to redeem himself. Remember your reasons? To protect his father and yours—two fine old soldiers—from that very truth. And what we agreed to accomplished that. Would you destroy it all now?"

"If I have to," she said truthfully. "If that's the only way in which I can protect you." Something moved in his eyes at her words, an emotion that appeared briefly, burning within the blue as strongly as a rocket's flare.

"Thank you for that," he said softly. "But I think you, as much as I, are bound by the agreement we made. Haviland gave up his life to protect his father, to prevent him from finding out how far from his image of his son Michael really came. We agreed to those terms. *Neither* of us can now go back on our bargain, no matter how inconvenient it may now seem to be."

"*Inconvenient,*" she repeated, her tone full of disbelief. "This isn't inconvenience. It's foolish, Kit. And it's incredibly dangerous. There is always the possibility…" The thought was too painful to put into words.

"There is nothing you can do to prevent this meeting, Judith. And nothing I can do. Haviland is determined. And you can't in honor reveal Michael's actions which led to his death on that mission, any more than I can."

He was right, she realized. Although she had sworn no oath, she, too, was bound by the sacrifice Michael had made to prevent his father from ever being hurt by his cowardice. And she was, after all, the one who had suggested her husband volunteer. In that, she bore far more guilt for Haviland's death than Kit. She had always understood and sympathized with Michael's reasons for wishing to protect his father. How could she now be the one to destroy the old man's hallowed view of his dead son?

"But I can talk to Sir Roland," she said. "At least I can

try to convince him that you had nothing to do with Michael's decision. I was Michael's wife. Surely he'll listen to me. He'll want to believe that Michael was everything he had hoped he would be. A hero who died a hero's death. I'll *make* him listen," she vowed desperately.

"Judith, he's already made up his mind. He's lost his only son, and he wants someone to blame. Or perhaps he believes that this scandal stains Michael's sacrifice. For whatever reason, he has chosen to hold me responsible for his death."

"But you weren't. Not in any way. Surely I can—"

"He thinks you were part of this," Kit warned softly. "Believe me, nothing you can say to him will change anything."

"But I have to try, Kit. This is my fault. All of it. Surely you see that I have to try."

But Kit had been right, of course. When she left General Haviland's house that evening, she had finally been forced to acknowledge that probably nothing *anyone* could say would change the old man's mind. Michael had been his son, and despite what her first husband had believed, his father had truly loved and admired him. And had convinced himself that Michael was all he wanted him to be.

Sir Roland had chosen to believe instead that she and Kit together had planned his valiant son's murder in order to satisfy their own lusts. Toby Reynolds's poison seeds had found fertile ground to grow in within the old man's stroke-damaged mind.

The realization that she had failed hurt far worse than the ranting denunciations her former father-in-law had made about what he imagined to be her role in Michael's death. Adulteress was the kindest of the appellations he had bestowed. And she knew now how he had managed to force

Kit to agree to meet him. Sir Roland himself had taken great delight in telling her.

She could never explain the impulse that caused her to stop at the door of her father-in-law's study before she climbed the stairs to her rooms. She had lived in his house for weeks, but she had not yet been introduced to Ryde, obviously because he had no wish to meet her. And, considering what she knew about his relationship with his younger son, she hadn't particularly wanted to meet the earl.

However, she acknowledged, the earl of Ryde was a very powerful man and no one, including herself, had more influence on Kit than his father. Her husband would certainly have denied the reality of her assessment, but almost every action he had taken since she had known him had been with some consideration of his father's opinion of him. Before she could change her mind, Judith opened the massive oak doors of Ryde's study.

The man who was seated behind the desk in the center of that vast room was not at all what she had expected. He was smaller and a far less intimidating presence than she had envisioned. His build was slight, narrower than Kit's tall, strongly muscled frame, and his thin face was deeply lined. And his hair, she realized, was almost as white as General Haviland's.

As the doors opened, the earl of Ryde glanced up from the papers scattered over the surface of his desk. His eyes examined her briefly through the lenses of the lorgnette he'd been using. A enormous cabochon ruby, set in the ducal ring he wore on the elegantly pale forefinger of his right hand, had gleamed in the lamplight when he raised his glasses.

She could see nothing of her husband in his features, but she didn't have long to make that evaluation. Apparently uninterested in what he saw, the earl's gaze returned to the material he had been perusing on her arrival. Rudely, he said nothing, treating her almost like one of the servants, who were supposed to be invisible, of course.

Undaunted, and having faced far more terrifying prospects than the earl of Ryde's studied disinterest during the last three years, Judith crossed the expanse of rich Oriental carpet. She stood before his desk in silence for several seconds, but her father-in-law didn't look up again.

Despite the gravity of the situation that had sent her here, Judith fought a smile, amused by his determined attempt to ignore her. She was not, he would find, so easily gotten rid of.

"I have come to ask for your help," she said finally.

Ryde's head lifted, his eyes meeting hers. "Indeed?" he inquired softly, one brow arching in question.

"I am Kit's wife."

"St. John," he corrected her, but at least he was listening.

"St. John," she amended dutifully. "Who plans to meet General Sir Roland Haviland at dawn on the day after tomorrow. I was not sure you had heard."

There was a brief silence, and then Ryde said, boredom injected almost theatrically into his voice, "What St. John does is of little moment to me. My son and I are *not* on terms. I think you, of all people, may imagine the reasons why," he added, before his gaze returned to the papers on his desk.

"Because of me?" Judith said. "Because of what is being said about what happened in Portugal?"

His eyes lifted again, and this time they focused on her face. She supposed Ryde was not often asked to explain himself, especially by a woman.

"I do not approve of my son's actions. I have told him

so. I am taking steps to see that St. John's scandals no longer reflect on this family."

"You're going to disown him," she guessed.

"It's something I should have done long ago. Family feeling, as you may imagine, prevented me. And, I suppose, the misguided hope that my son might change. I have been disappointed in that."

"Disappointed in your son?" Judith questioned softly. "Do you even know him, I wonder?"

The brow quirked again, but the cold eyes did not change. "I have known St. John all his life. Far better than you, I should think."

"Yet you believe what Haviland believes about him. Did you ask Kit to tell you what happened?"

"I did," Ryde said. His eyes said nothing beyond that.

"And what did he say?" Judith demanded softly.

"That your first husband volunteered to give up his life. A very convenient response on Haviland's part. And it certainly accomplished what you and Kit wanted. The story might even have worked, had not someone else survived to recount a very different version than the one you and St. John were putting about."

"Kit told you the truth," Judith said, ignoring the sarcasm, "but not the entire truth. Perhaps when you know it all—"

"I have no wish to 'know it all,' I assure you. The particulars of your sordid affair do not interest me in the slightest. Nor did the story St. John told."

"But it should," Judith said. "Because it *is* the truth."

The earl's features sharpened in distaste, and in his eyes was simply resignation. Judith took a breath, knowing that she would have only one chance. One opportunity to change his father's lifelong perception of St. John.

"Michael *did* volunteer, just as Kit told you, but there

was a very good reason for why he was willing to do so. And a very good reason for why Kit agreed to let him undertake the mission.''

"I really am not interested—'' Ryde began, but Judith interrupted him.

"This concerns your son. Your own flesh and blood. You *should* be interested.''

"I see that you are determined to tell me this sad tale,'' the earl said sarcastically. "Can I not convince you—''

"No,'' Judith denied, shaking her head.

There was another silence, and then the earl put the lorgnette he was holding down on the papers and folded his hands. The long, aristocratic fingers appeared to be perfectly relaxed.

"Then I will beg you simply to be brief,'' he said.

"If you knew your son at all...'' she began and realized her mistake. "But obviously you don't. I know, however, the kind of man St. John really is. I know his unquestioned and well-documented bravery in battle. You may verify that with the Horse Guards if you wish. But what won't be in those records is how St. John's men felt about him. They trusted him with their lives, and he never betrayed that trust. He cared for them. And in the end they not only respected him, they loved him.''

The dark eyes considered her, but she could see no emotional response in them. To those who had never been in battle, perhaps it was difficult to understand how important those attributes were in an officer.

Judith took another breath, trying for calmness, trying to think what she might possibly say that could make a difference in a relationship that had become set and static long before she met Kit. And when she spoke again, it was not really about St. John at all.

"I have just come from Michael Haviland's father,'' she

said. There was a brief reaction to that in the dark eyes watching her, and she knew she had surprised him. "Whose son was a coward and a drunkard whose men despised him," she added softly.

Judith had not told General Haviland about his son because of what Kit had said to her, but she did not feel that telling Ryde broke the unspoken agreement she had made with Michael. And as she had told Kit, she would do anything to protect him. Perhaps now only his father could do that.

"Despised him? As did his wife, of course?" the earl suggested. One corner of his mouth moved, twitching in amusement.

"I won't make excuses for the failure of our marriage. I will tell you, however, that Michael's drunkenness caused him to make an error in judgment that cost the lives of men under his command. It was not the first time that had happened. This time, however, Michael also disobeyed a direct order not to engage the enemy, and then, when he had, he ran away from the battle, leaving his men. He was disgraced, and we both believed news of it would kill his father."

Her voice was very soft, but there was no other sound in the vast room. In the earl's eyes for the first time was something other than boredom.

"And your son," Judith went on, "who had been wounded when he led his men into that same battle to rescue Michael's troop, was given the job of guarding my husband. Along with the task of seeing that the women and the wounded were taken to safety."

"A task at which he failed," Ryde said.

"Perhaps," Judith acknowledged. "Ultimately. But not because he was a coward or because he didn't do his duty. And not even because he made bad decisions. Kit failed because of circumstances beyond his control, by acts of war. He was forced by those same circumstances to let Michael go for help. And because..." She hesitated, remembering her role in this. "Because we both begged him to give Michael a chance to redeem himself. In exchange, Kit gave his sworn oath that no word of Michael's disgrace would reach his father.

"And the ironic thing is," she said, her voice almost a whisper now, "Haviland would probably not have believed it, even if it had. We tried, all of us, to protect him from the knowledge of Michael's guilt, but I think he would have found it impossible to believe his son could do such a despicable thing."

"Misguided faith," Ryde suggested sarcastically.

"But faith, in any case," Judith reminded him softly. "Faith in a son who didn't deserve it. And you, on the other hand..."

"I know my son," Ryde said stubbornly.

"No," she said. "Not if you can believe what Toby Reynolds says about him. If you can believe St. John would send a man to his death in order to win a woman, any woman, then you don't know your son at all." Again a silence fell between them, but there was a subtle difference to the quietness this time.

"Why would Reynolds lie?" the earl asked.

"I don't know. The simplest explanation is that Kit had a hand in punishing him for something he didn't do—or rather for something Michael had ordered him to do—and he wanted revenge. I think it's far more complicated. I think that, as Michael did, Reynolds saw in Kit what he himself lacked. Courage and honor."

"Honor," the earl repeated quietly, but there was no mockery in his voice. "Is that what you believe this duel represents? Honor? Neither of St. John's choices will be honorable," Ryde said, "I assure you of that."

"Neither of his choices?"

"There are only two, of course. He may kill Sir Roland—"

"He won't shoot General Haviland," Judith interrupted. "Kit isn't the kind of man who would ever do that."

The earl's mouth moved again and then was still. "A fascinating observation. Especially given St. John's past. May I ask your basis for that…insight on my son's behavior."

"He won't shoot General Haviland because it would be wrong," she said simply.

The earl laughed. "Because it would be wrong," he repeated.

"Wrong to kill a sick old man. A man who believes he himself is doing the right thing. The honorable thing. Kit won't do that."

"Then he must delope and admit that what Haviland accuses him of is true."

"No," Judith said again, thinking about that possibility. "For *your* sake, he won't do that. And because it isn't true."

"For my sake?" the earl said sharply.

"Because he loves you," she said softly.

The earl said nothing for a long time. His fingers had found the lorgnette and turned it idly, over and over, but he didn't look again at the work on his desk.

"There's nothing I can do, you know," Ryde said, and she believed she heard regret in his voice. And, for the first time in the course of this painful interview, emotion there as well.

"If you are right in what you say," Ryde continued, "and mind you, I do not concede that point…but if you are right, then there is only one thing St. John can, in all honor, do.''

"In all honor," Judith repeated, thinking about all the implications of that simple phrase.

"If he refuses to delope and admit he is in the wrong, and if, as you assert, he will not shoot Sir Roland, then..." The earl's voice faded.

Judith knew very little about dueling, but the earl, who knew far more than she about how such things were done, understood, of course, the decision St. John had already made.

"Then the best shot in London will deliberately miss his target," Ryde finished softly. "And after he has, he will simply stand and wait for his opponent's bullet to kill him."

the fact that there should be only one thing sure here, for this time only.

In all honour," Judith repeated, drawing strength from the acceptance of this simple power.

Chapter Fifteen

It was a long time after she left Ryde's study before Judith again opened the door which connected her rooms to her husband's. She almost expected to find Kit still seated at the desk where he had been working this afternoon.

He was not, of course. The room was empty, the low, banked fire in the grate its only light. She walked across to his desk. It seemed that she could still smell the candles which had burned there. The scent of their expensive wax filled the room, along with the completely masculine odors of fine leather and starch and sandalwood.

There was a gilt-edged volume on the desk, its thin pages opened to a passage in the Psalms. It was too dim in the firelight to read the text, but the words were familiar, of course. They had both listened to them read aloud beside isolated graves on the Peninsula too often to ever forget their import. And their undeniable comfort. *Yea, though I walk through the valley of the shadow…*

Lying beside the Bible were several envelopes, all of them addressed in her husband's bold scrawl. Each had been sealed in wax and stamped with the signet he wore, the same one he had sent as a means of identification in Portugal. She touched the top letter, tracing with one finger the imprinted design the ring had left, and she realized in surprise that the wax was still soft.

Her eyes lifted, circling the room again, but she had not been mistaken. Apparently Kit had finished his correspondence and gone out. Judging by the scent of the candles and the softness of the wax, she had missed him by only a few moments.

If only she had gathered her courage more quickly, she thought. But that phrase encompassed almost the whole of their relationship. *If only...*

She looked at the letter she had touched and, without thinking about the propriety of her action, turned it over. It was addressed to his brother Roger. She pushed that one aside to read the next, which said simply "Ryde." There was another for Kit's mother. And the last...

The last was addressed to her. *To my beloved wife Judith.* The words blurred suddenly as she looked down on them. She drew the tips of her fingers slowly across the inscription, as if she could feel with them the phrase she could no longer see. *To my beloved wife...*

She had been Michael Haviland's wife, but she had never been Kit's. She had been wed to him, but nothing of what the other implied had ever occurred between them. A fevered kiss. An unspoken, delirium-induced invitation, accepted and then interrupted by the cruel circumstances of war. That was all they had ever had.

And now the word he had written would never have meaning. There were too many barriers, and far too little time left to attempt to overcome them. If only they had had enough time, she thought. *If only...*

Unconsciously, she picked up the letter. She was not sure what she intended to do with it. Perhaps carry it with her back into her chamber. Or maybe the urge to hold it, to touch the phrase he had written, had grown so strong that it was irresistible. She could not have read it. Not here in the shadowed, fire-tinged darkness. Not through the blur of tears.

"That's not for now," Kit said.

She looked up to find him standing in the doorway that led to the balcony. With the breath of the night breeze behind them, the sheer draperies swirled and billowed into the bedroom as if they were alive.

Obediently, she laid the thick letter back with the others. She knew what they were. Farewells, dutifully written to his family. And, of course, that word *did* include her. Not his wife, perhaps, but now at least part of St. John's family.

He had given her that. He had freely offered her his name in Portugal. To protect her, and instead...

"Part of the dueling ritual, of course." His voice was dispassionate, perhaps even a little amused.

"Did you write these before? Before the other duel you fought?"

"Every duelist pens his farewells," he said, his voice still mocking. "And when the duel is over, he throws them with a great deal of relief into the fire. Exactly like the rubbish most of them are."

She looked down on the letters. Her eyes had adjusted to the dimness enough that she could now distinguish the individual elements of the seal. The rampant lion, the crest, and the Montgomery motto. Automatically, she translated the archaic Latin phrase. *Without honor, there is nothing.*

"And your opponent's letters?" she asked. "What do you suppose happened to those?"

But instead of answering her, he asked, "What are you doing here, Judith?" He stepped into the room and turned to close the doors behind him. The silk that had seemed so alive suddenly went limp, falling still and dead against the black glass.

"I know what you intend to do," she said.

When he turned, his voice was still calm, his eyes unreadable in the darkness. "What do you think you know?" he asked. He didn't move any nearer to her. He stood before the shrouded windows, little more than a silhouette.

"Your father told me."

His laughter was a breath of sound. "My *father* told you?" he repeated unbelievingly.

"He said there are only two options in a duel. And you, of course, won't take either of those. Because in this situation, both of them would be wrong."

"Then...it follows there must be a third option," he said softly.

She knew suddenly that he was smiling. She could hear it in his voice, and her heart ached with the need to see him smile at her again.

"Ryde says you'll deliberately miss your shot and let Haviland shoot you."

Still he had not moved, but she knew that the smile was gone. He really had not intended her to know, of course.

"When did you speak to Ryde?" he asked calmly. But she was aware that he hadn't denied what his father suggested.

"Tonight. After I returned from General Haviland's. And you were right, of course. Sir Roland didn't believe me."

"I know," he said, his voice now almost comforting. "It doesn't matter, Judith. None of it matters anymore."

"Will you do what your father said?"

"I always do what my father says," Kit said. Again his voice held amusement. Whatever decision he had come to, he was at peace.

He was a man who had faced death a hundred times. In battle and sport. His peace with dying had been made long ago, she supposed. Long before she had known him. Certainly before she had become his wife. *My beloved wife Judith.*

"But there's nothing for you to be afraid of," he said. "Whatever happens, you'll be taken care of. And after a while, even the talk about this will die. Some new scandal will distract them. All this will simply be...a memory."

She nodded, her eyes on the letter because she could not see his face and because his voice was too much now as his father's had been. Without emotion.

Whatever she had hoped for when she came here, there was nothing, apparently, that he needed to say to her. He had given her his name. For honor's sake. That was all he owed her. More than he *owed* her, she amended. Telling him what she felt for him now would only be another burden, she knew, added to this heavy one he already bore.

Please don't die, because I love you. And because I need you. I need to know you. I need long days to learn about the man you are. And I need time to make you love me.

Those were not words she had any right to say to him. And even if she had that right, would saying them make anything about this better? He had been ordered to marry her, and he had obeyed, out of his sense of honor.

Now her own honor forbade that she voice the demand she had no right to make. *Please don't die, because I love you...*

"Go to bed," he suggested, his deep voice touched with the same kindness it had held when he cared for her on board the ship the night of the storm. "There's nothing to be afraid of," he said again.

"I know," she whispered.

But before she turned away, her fingers closed over something, and furtively she took what they had grasped from the desk. Like a common thief, without honor, she crushed the letter he had not intended her to see between the folds of her rail. And she carried it with her when she left his room.

In the quiet darkness she left behind, Kit finally remembered to breathe. He thought of what she had said about meeting his father. Ryde and Judith, he thought, savoring the image. His mouth curved again, almost a smile.

In Judith, his father had probably met his match. In many ways, they were alike. People who never took the easy way out, who never bent or faltered, no matter what was demanded of them.

Not like him, he thought, remembering what he had written. It had taken him a long time to compose those two letters. They both contained things that would perhaps have been better left unsaid, but he had been unable to control the impulse that made him put it all down. That made him write the words he had never had the courage to say to either of them.

To his father. For whom his life had been a constant disappointment.

And to Judith. For whom he had been... *For whom he had been nothing,* he acknowledged with painful honesty. Whatever he had imagined happened between them beside the stream that day must have been only that—the product of his fevered imagination.

He was her friend, and she had never indicated by word or deed that she desired any other relationship with him. And now that was just as well, he supposed. She had lost the husband she loved. And in all probability...

He drew another breath, inhaling deeply enough that the sound was audible in the stillness of the room. There was no point in revealing to her what he felt. There was nothing to be gained, of course, by telling Judith that he loved her. That he *had* loved her, long before he had the right.

The confession he had written would do nothing but make her unhappy. He knew her well enough to know that she would regret that she hadn't understood what he felt. And regret, perhaps, that there had been nothing of what he wanted between them. Without that letter, at least her memories of him would contain no loss beyond the loss of his friendship. And they both had endured the loss of friends. She would endure again.

He was a fool, Kit decided suddenly. There was no point in hurting Judith. If writing down his feelings had been cathartic, so would be the destruction of what he had written.... *Thrown into the fire like the rubbish most of them are.*

He walked across the room and looked down at the letters he had left on the desk. He pushed them apart, trying to find the one with her name. And then, not finding it, he went through them again. But for some reason there were only three of them. And the one with Judith's name...

When he flung open the door to her room, she didn't even look up from what she was reading. She had not taken time to light the lamp. She had knelt instead by the fire, holding the letter out to the soft, golden light of the flames.

He could smell the wax from the seal she had broken in her haste. It had fallen in scattered pieces on the hearth, and they smoked and sizzled there in bloodred droplets.

It was too late. If there had been any doubt before, that hope was destroyed when she finally raised her face to his. Her eyes reflected the firelight, golden and luminous with her tears.

"Why didn't you tell me? Oh, Kit, why didn't I know?"

Her low words were anguished. Tortured. He knew that he had been right before. This was a burden that he had no right to ask her to bear. Because tomorrow...

That thought was like a blow, stunning in its intensity,

sickening. He believed he had been prepared to face with honor whatever vengeance Haviland wanted to take. His father was right, of course, as he usually was. Because there had always been only one other option. One outcome.

"How could you not know?" she asked softly. "How could you not know how I feel? How I've felt about you for so long."

He felt the pain of that. The initial, protective numbness of shock had worn off, to be replaced now by a sense of loss that was deeper and more agonizing than any he had ever known.

She laid the letter down on her lap, its whiteness disappearing against the pale cotton of her gown. He could still see her hands, slender fingers holding his letter, their skin a darker cream than the gown, touched with the gold of the fire.

"I never intended for you to know," he whispered. "It's too late. It's all come too late."

"No," she said simply.

She put the letter aside and rose. There was no awkwardness in the motion. He watched as she crossed the room toward him. She moved silently, on bare feet, coming to him out of the darkness, as if she moved in a dream. And it was his dream, of course. Long held. Long denied.

When she was very close, she hesitated, her eyes tracing over his face, and then she smiled at him. "First," she said, "I admired you for what I knew you were. I watched you silently, from a distance. Then you became my friend, and I was so honored by your friendship. I thought it was far more than I deserved. And then somehow..."

She paused, her dark eyes glowing. What was in them was unexpected. Unasked for. But, as the gift of his name had been, he knew it was freely given.

"I loved you long before I should have," she whispered.

"Long before I admitted it, even to myself. Long, long before I ever dreamed of this."

She held out her hands to him, both of them, and unthinking, he caught them tightly in his. "But I could not know…" she whispered. "That you, too… And I would never have known."

"Judith," he said softly. His throat closed with the force of how much he loved her. Courage and honor and strength. She was all that he had learned to value in the last three years.

And she was his. Finally, in every way that God intended, she was his. That, too, was in her eyes. It would have taken a far stronger man than St. John knew himself to be to have refused.

He had once imagined the scent and softness of her hair tangled over his chest and shoulders. Now the fragrance of it surrounded him. They lay together like spent swimmers, at peace, safe at last on this new and alien shore. The ocean might pound behind them, but here the threat of its waves was nothing. Less than nothing.

He watched as his fingers found one dark, curling tendril of her hair and held it up to the light. It blazed suddenly, a thread of gold running along the long darkness of the strand.

The memories ran through his mind as quickly. Droplets of rain caught in her hair, flashing like diamonds, as the ship's lantern swung slowly back and forth. Her lips parted in anticipation as he lay on top of her, their legs entwined, caught in the cold, wet fabric of her skirt. Her eyes when she had placed her trembling hand into his on their wedding day. *Why didn't I know?* she had asked, and his heart repeated it.

It had been revealed tonight in every movement of her

body. Every response. Every sighing breath he had evoked as he made love to her. Every vow and promise. Like lovers' promises, whispered into the darkness, those would melt away in the sun.

St. John's eyes moved to the windows, but there was as yet no hint of dawn behind their blankness. Time. Even hours, perhaps, to know her. To claim her. To brand her with the heat and power and force of his love so that no matter, in the long years ahead, whoever else touched her...

For them, of course, there was no future. As there was no past. No echoes of guilt or regret. Here there were only the two of them. These hours. These minutes which were moving out of his grasp as the tide slips inexorably away from the shore.

She turned her head, and her eyes opened. What was in them had changed. The wonder of discovery had been joined by the knowledge of desire and need. Fulfilled and yet still wanting. Exactly as it should be.

"I thought I was to blame for what I couldn't feel," she said softly. "For what I couldn't be to him."

He didn't answer her with words. He turned, pushing his mouth into the now familiar softness beneath her jaw. Her head moved, tilting upward, welcoming his caress.

His lips trailed down the ringed column of her throat, tasting the salt-slick dampness of her skin. The scent of her body, heat released, drifted around him, perfumed subtly like her hair. Clean and faintly rose-sweet.

His tongue laved the shadowed hollow at the base of her neck and then traced over the delicate collarbone. Examined its fragility. Caressed. It touched finally against the small, hard nub of her nipple. Circled slowly before his mouth closed over it and suckled. Pulling strongly. Demanding.

She gasped, the sound an indrawn breath, almost lost

against the silk of his hair. At that, his head lifted, and his eyes examined her breast, its rose areola surrounded by the dark cream of her skin and the hard masculinity of his fingers.

Fire-touched, heat-scented, her body at last lay open to him. He had explored its mysteries and had shown them to her. And he would again. He lowered his head, nuzzling against the dampness his mouth had left on the nipple. He turned his face so that the beard-roughened skin of his cheek moved over and then around her breast. She moaned, and his knee pushed between hers. Demanding still.

Her legs opened and then drifted apart. Boneless. Welcoming. Her slender body arched upward, searching for his. He lifted over her, aligning their bodies into a position as old and unchanging as time. His palms cupped the outside of her breasts, and he lowered his head between them. Breathing in. Inhaling the fragrance of her skin. The essence of her body.

He pushed into it. Despite the times he had made love to her, he was so hard, so tight, engorged with a need that was as sharp and painful as starvation. Never to be fully sated. Never satisfied.

Her hips responded as they had before, moving upward to meet his thrust. He raised his head, and his palms found now her face, shaping themselves to its contours, feeling the fragility of bone. He held her, watching her eyes as his body lowered again and again to hers. An invasion that was slow and measured and controlled.

The first time had been little more than an explosion of need. His and hers. He had not left her behind, despite the pain of what he felt. The boiling force of his desire had seemed to take over his body, overpowering, but he had, even then, protected her from it. This was Judith, and he would always protect her. Without thought. An instinct only, perhaps, but one that could never be overridden, not even by his want.

This was something different. Deliberately different. A subtlety measured in millimeters of motion perhaps, but precise as a fencing lesson.

As he had written what his heart contained, never intending that she should read it while he lived, he wrote now what was in his soul, inscribing it on her body. Indelibly. One chance to make it last forever. The unchanging expression of his love. One unfading memory to shine in the darkness of loss.

"I love you," he said. *My beloved wife Judith.* There had been nothing of what he had written on those pages that was not true. As was this. Truth and honor. And courage, finally, to confess it all. No matter what happened tomorrow.

Her fingers lifted to touch his mouth. To trace its shape. To press against the words he had finally uttered. Then she brought them to her own lips and held them there. Her eyes were still locked on his.

His body swelled with love. Need. Want. Desire. Heat. The force of it drove him against her. Out of the coldness and into her warmth. After a long time, her eyes closed and the tears seeped slowly from beneath the dark sweep of her lashes and, touched by the firelight, shimmered over her temple to be lost in the cloud of hair that spread across the pillow.

He lowered his head, even as his body arched and thrust above hers. Slender hips answered, responded, as he had never dreamed they could. Her eyes opened only as need exploded and then dissolved, the hot moisture of his seed spilling into the receptacle of her body as her tears had slipped over her skin.

And, as the response he felt moved in shivering force

throughout her frame, he watched it also happen in her face. The wonder of it was reflected clearly in the darkness of her eyes, as had been the golden firelight when she knelt before the hearth and read what he had written.

My beloved wife Judith... Finally, and always, she was.

He dressed without waking her. He moved through the dark room, pulling on familiar garments that now seemed terribly strange. And when he was dressed, except for the cloak he had thrown over the chair near the door, he came back to stand beside the high bed. Her body lay fully exposed, the forgotten sheets at the foot, twisted and disordered by their lovemaking.

Judith was lying on her side, her hair spread across the pillow behind her head as if blown by an unseen wind. One hand was before her face, and he imagined the feel of her breath feathering against it, just as it had whispered over the skin of his body while he lay, unsleeping, beside her. Holding her.

He wanted her again. Even now. Even given what had passed between them during the long hours. He had taken her again and again, beyond satisfaction into exhaustion. She had refused him nothing. Her generosity of spirit extended even to this.

And he had made love to her in every way he could devise, imprinting the memories of each on his brain and his heart, just as he had pressed the signet into the warm, soft wax of the seals. Indelibly fixed there. These memories would be the last he would think of as he waited today for Haviland's shot.

His spirit would not be there, not under the shadow of the tall trees that sheltered the secluded site from the growing light of day. It would be here. Still. Sheltered by something very different.

St. John did not believe in ghosts. Not in the coldly rational part of his mind. But he had seen things on battlefields that he could not explain away. And now no longer tried.

If it's possible, my Judith, he thought. *Here. Always.*

He wanted to touch her. To run his fingers one last time over the warm, alabaster velvet of her skin. To feel her shuddering response to his touch. To see in her eyes...

But he could not bear what would be in her eyes. It was better then that this goodbye never be made. Last night had been enough. *Far more than he deserved.*

Involuntarily, without his conscious direction, his strong brown fingers, tanned and hard from years of war, reached out and found a solitary tendril in the dark curling mass of her hair. He wrapped it slowly around one finger, being very careful to put no pressure on the strand. He held it there a moment, its warmth and softness almost alive. Almost enough.

And then he slowly unwound the curl and let it fall. It did not lose the shape of his finger. It lay instead beside her cheek, moving slightly, up and down, with the deep, even breaths she took as she slept.

When he turned away in the near-darkness of pre-dawn and walked to the door across the silent room, still she did not awaken. Not even when it closed, very softly, behind him.

Chapter Sixteen

The morning that broke over the tall trees represented England at her finest, the pale light of dawn as golden as the firelight had been the night before. A light fog hovered, floating over their boots, softening, with its white peacefulness, what would happen in this place.

Ritual, he had told Judith. And now, most of that had been completed. The recitation of the rules they all knew. The examination of the grounds. The loading of the two beautiful and very deadly pistols. All of that was done. Finished.

His brother asked finally if he had any messages. Kit was forced by the question to pull his mind from where it had found refuge, a fire-touched distance, infinitely far away.

"Nothing, thank you, Roger."

His brother nodded, regretfully, St. John thought, but still he resisted the urge to touch Roger's shoulder comfortingly as he had done before. His brothers were all dead, their bones and ashes scattered across battlefields almost as far away in time and distance as the bed he and Judith had shared last night.

Kit did not bother to examine the pistol he had been

given. The pair had belonged to his grandfather, and he knew them well enough to know that there was no need. They always fired straight and true. There would be no mistake.

The clatter of the arriving carriage was loud enough to drag him again from his self-absorption, especially when he recognized the crest on the door. Large, black, and well-sprung, the coach, pulled by four magnificent grays, flew across the grassy expanse toward them. The small assembly watched in silence as the earl of Ryde's carriage was pulled to a halt, just before it seemed that the racing horses would careen into the participants.

Kit couldn't imagine what his father was doing here, and for a moment he wondered if the occupant of the coach might be Judith. It was the kind of courage she possessed, of course.

Could she have come in another attempt to change Haviland's mind? he wondered. It was obvious to him that would be fruitless. And Judith could not know that her presence here was the one thing that would make this unbearable.

The slight figure who descended from the carriage was not his wife, however. Ryde's eyes briefly met his before they found his brother's and held a moment. Kit wondered if his father were surprised to see Roger here, his attendance such a departure from his conventional lifestyle. It was not to either of his sons, however, that the earl spoke.

That he spoke at all, interrupting the formality of these proceedings, was as stunning as his unexpected arrival. The rules about that were very clear as well. Those not parties in these contests had no role. Ryde knew the ritual, of course, although to Kit's certain knowledge his father had never engaged in anything so scandalous as a duel.

"I'm afraid I have very bad news for you," Ryde said

to Roland Haviland. He had not looked again at either of his sons.

"I am not interested in your 'news,' Ryde," the old man replied. His eyes shifted purposefully to his opponent, evidently intending to ignore the earl's interruption.

"I have proof that what has been said about my son's action in Portugal is false. You should be interested in that."

The general's eyes came back to him. "What kind of proof?"

"A sworn statement to that effect from the same man who told you those lies. Who has told us all that same lie."

"A statement you coerced from him? Or more likely bribed him to make?" Haviland suggested contemptuously. "It makes no difference what Reynolds says now. We have all heard the truth."

"What he says *now* is the truth," Ryde asserted, his voice still calm. "And truth should always make a difference."

"My son is dead. Murdered under the cover of battle so his wife could become your son's whore. That is the only truth of this. I need hear no other."

"Perhaps this might change your mind," the earl said, his voice still controlled and yet somehow ringing through the clearing. He held out a small, flat packet.

Kit knew immediately what it was. So would Haviland, because they had both seen such packets a hundred times. Military dispatches, still folded as tightly as they always were.

"These were found among Toby Reynolds's belongings when I had them searched. He had given me the address of his lodgings, of course, in hopes that I might change my mind about paying him to keep quiet. And he had been foolish enough to hold on to these. I suppose it's possible he did that because he intended to use them later to black-mail you.''

"Me?" Haviland questioned, his eyes widened a little in surprise. "How could he possibly have thought to black-mail me?"

"These dispatches were written by Colonel William Smythe shortly before he was killed in battle. They are addressed to his commander, Lord Wellington, and they concern *your* son, Sir Roland. They detail *his* actions in Portugal. His very disgraceful and cowardly actions. You will find, I'm afraid, that they have great bearing on this matter."

Of them all, only Kit could know the full significance of what his father had found. Smythe's dispatches had never reached Wellington, of course, because his chosen courier had not gotten through. He had been found by Sergeant Cochran, his throat cut and the dispatch case he had carried missing.

For an instant the image of that smiling, boyishly freck-led face invaded Kit's mind. Scarborough, who had tended his wound on the battlefield and had probably saved his life. Scarborough, who had died alone, and apparently at the hands of a comrade. Someone he would have trusted.

"Have you come here in an attempt to blacken my son's name? In a fruitless effort to save St. John's worthless life? It won't work, Ryde, no matter what lies you've paid Reyn-olds to tell. Or to write."

"The writing is Smythe's. That can easily be verified at the Horse Guards if you wish."

"I *don't* wish," Haviland said bitterly. "I don't need to have anything verified. I knew my son. Nothing you can say makes any difference to this. I have issued a challenge to St. John, and he has already accepted it."

The old man's eyes shifted from the earl to St. Jo'

"Do you wish to admit your guilt in my son's death and withdraw from this meeting like the coward you have proven yourself to be?"

Only one option, he had told Judith. There should still be only one, but before he could frame an answer, Kit found himself caught within the golden, seductive net of memory, reliving the short night they had shared. Remembering those brief dark hours.

What did it matter what anyone said about him? He knew he had done nothing wrong, as Judith did. Did it really matter then what anyone else believed? Did anything matter beside what he had found, finally, with her?

His eyes met his father's. The earl was still holding out the papers that would damn Michael Haviland as the drunken coward he had been. That would brand and disgrace his family forever.

It was even possible, Kit realized suddenly, that Haviland was the one who had sent Reynolds to stop Scarborough. With orders to see to it that these papers never reached headquarters and perhaps even with permission to do so by any means.

He didn't know that, of course. Reynolds had certainly proven capable of devising his own villainy. And Kit had given Michael Haviland his word that nothing of what was in those dispatches would ever be revealed. His word in exchange for Haviland's. An oath sworn on his honor.

He was bound by it still. If Kit asked, he knew his father would not reveal the contents of those papers. He would understand the importance of the vow Kit had made.

"I had nothing to do with your son's death, Sir Roland," Kit said. "He volunteered for a dangerous mission and was killed as a result. I have done no wrong that I *can* admit to."

There was a small relaxation in the watching men, a hint

of movement. Kit realized the others had been waiting a long time for whatever he would say. Frozen, motionless, they had simply awaited his response. It could have been nothing else, of course, but the memories of last night had almost defeated him.

"Put them away," he said to his father. "I gave him my word." The earl's eyes held his, searching as they had not in a very long time. Looking into his soul, it seemed. But Ryde was the one who had taught him the lessons of honor. He had demanded those of Kit all his life. So St. John did not doubt his father's obedience to them now.

Kit turned to Roger and nodded. The rest was only ritual, but it must be played out, of course. They had all come here to insure that this was done as it should be. With honor.

Ten paces. Such a small distance when they had stepped them off and turned to face one another. It seemed to Kit that he could see, in the split second before he fired, every line in the old man's face, put there by grief and by love. Both of those Kit understood, better now than he ever had before.

His ball went where he directed it, as straight and as true as any he had ever fired from his grandfather's pistol. It whispered over the top of the shoulder of the old man's coat.

When they examined it later, Kit believed they might be able to see where it had brushed the fabric. He controlled his urge to smile. Well done, he thought. Exactly as he had intended. No one could ever claim that he had tried to miss.

Now there was nothing to do but wait. Despite the fact that time had seemed to hesitate, he knew it would be a matter of only a heartbeat. Maybe two, even if the old man were very slow.

He watched the muzzle of the long dueling pistol line

up and steady, carefully aimed at his heart. There was no reason for the general to hurry now that Kit had fired. And the distance was so slight that there was also no possibility, given the time to do it right, that Haviland might miss.

Judith, Kit had time to think. One heartbeat, sending the rich heart's blood to his brain to form that word. It was his last thought before the second shot shattered the breathless, waiting silence under the elms.

Judith woke, her mouth dry, parted in a voiceless scream. Her heart was racing, threatening to tear its way out of her chest. But the noise, whatever she thought she heard, had not been in this room. She sat up in the disordered bed, jerked upright by a sound that was not a sound. By a scene that she could not have seen.

She looked around the still, silent bedroom. The fire that had burned on the hearth last night was out. Even the ashes were cold and gray, like the thin light that crept into the room between the folds of the draperies. She fought to control her breathing, holding on to the thought that it had only been a nightmare. Only a dream. And Kit...

Her eyes searched the bed where he had lain beside her. And then the room again. He wasn't here. There was no one here. She was alone, and the sudden desolation that depressed her spirit was as black as the glass had been behind the limp, lifeless curtains last night. She couldn't understand why Kit would leave her.

She looked again at the windows, gauging time by the growing light as she had done so often in Portugal. It was only a little past dawn, she realized. Only a few minutes past sunrise.

The rest of the room was still shadowed. And empty. She shivered and, sitting alone in the bed they had shared, she pulled the sheet around her trembling, naked body to fight its emptiness.

"Kit," she called softly, and then she waited.

Her voice echoed hollowly in the vast room, but he didn't answer her. She lay back in the tangled bed, remembering the dream. That was exactly what would happen tomorrow unless someone stopped it. But the earl had told her there was nothing he could do. And Kit could not, in honor, follow any path other than the one he had been forced to take.

But Michael had already died to protect his father, and now Kit would die also. For that same reason. And it wasn't right. Two deaths to prevent a proud old man from learning the truth about his son. No matter what Kit had told her about her own honor, she knew a second blood sacrifice on the altar of the Haviland family tradition was no more right than it would be for Kit to shoot Sir Roland. And not honorable, no matter what Kit thought.

She would have to tell General Haviland the truth, even if it meant breaking her word, destroying her honor. There were higher laws than the rules men devise to guide their lives. Kit might choose to abide by man's law, but she would not. Not any longer.

It took her only minutes to dress, moving quickly through the cold half-light of dawn. She wondered if any of the servants were awake. The earl's coachman would be surprised at her request, of course, but he would obey it. And she would make Michael's father hear the truth. And make him believe it.

"My lord!"

The shocked exclamation of Haviland's second rang even more loudly than Roger's anguished cry. The surgeon ignored both, rushing past them to the field where the combatants had, only seconds before, solemnly paced off the distance.

"He's not hurt," the earl of Ryde said calmly. "I didn't hit *him.*"

The pistol he held out at arm's length did not waver even now. It was not until the surgeon had reached the general that the earl began to lower his gun. His eyes moved to Kit's and then briefly met the shocked gaze of his elder son. Amusement lurked in their depths as they studied Roger's stunned face.

"This is an outrage, Ryde," the general's second said furiously. "I have *never* seen anything like it. It is against every convention of the code we have come here today to honor."

"Outrage?" Ryde repeated, watching the surgeon pick up the shattered pistol he had shot out of the old man's hand. "It would be outrage if I allowed that obstinate old martinet to put a ball into an innocent man. That, sir, would be outrage."

"But the rules, my lord—"

"The rules be damned," Ryde said, "and you and Haviland be damned with them. My son has done *nothing* wrong. I don't intend to stand by and watch him shot for that fool's mistaken pride."

"How dare you, sir," Haviland said. His voice and face were rigid with anger.

"I *dare* because I'm right. Your son was a coward and a drunkard. These papers prove it, but you wouldn't look at them. You don't *want* to know the truth. But be warned, Haviland, I'll never let you kill my son to protect the reputation of yours."

"There's not a word of truth—"

"Truth is *not* what people believe, sir. Truth is what happened. You can't change this, no matter how much you might wish to make it something else. And I suspect you knew the truth about your son all along. A man seldom reaches manhood without some evidence of his true character revealed. Especially to those…who love him.''

"Whatever is written in those dispatches are lies," Haviland said.

"Smythe lied? St. John lied? Your son's wife lied? And now even Reynolds?" Ryde enumerated mockingly. "All of them lied. Even you aren't that big a fool. And neither, I believe, is the world, despite however foolishly they have thus far behaved in this."

The silence grew again, almost as heavy as that before the second shot. "Your choice," Ryde said finally to break it. "*You* will be the one to admit you were wrong, General Haviland. And you will do it publicly. Or I shall see that these papers are introduced into evidence in the military inquiry of the incident which I will demand. And I assure you I have influence enough with this government to see that investigation carried out."

Sir Roland's features had changed, the lines deepening somehow, his face aging before their eyes. But still he made no answer to the earl's demands.

"I warn you," Ryde said softly. "I've had enough of this. Enough of you and of this scandal. You *know* the truth because in your heart you knew your son. Put an end to this insanity before you also put an end to whatever good name he once had."

"What do you want?" the old man asked.

"A public admission that you and Reynolds were wrong about St. John. You may arrange that however you wish. You may claim to have received a letter from your son, written before his death, verifying exactly what Kit has said from the beginning. That Haviland volunteered for the mission that cost him his life. That his wife was faithful. That *nothing* of what my son did was dishonorable or in any way led to Captain Haviland's death.''

The old man said nothing for a long time. "How do you know that I shall be believed? And that what occurred here today won't simply spawn more gossip."

"I can vouch for my sons." The earl looked at the others in turn, assessing before he spoke. "The rest are bound by their own honor to abide by whatever settlement the two of you reach. And I will personally challenge the man who reveals anything of what happened here. It seems I've not lost my touch," Ryde said.

There was an undeniable note of pride in his father's voice, Kit thought. The earl himself had taught Kit to shoot, endlessly exacting and demanding in those lessons, as he had been in every other. Everything had to be done over and over again until it was right. Until it was perfect. Always perfect.

"You have my word," the general agreed.

"A wise decision," Ryde said. "And your promise that you'll never slander my son's name again? Or his wife's. I want your oath, sir."

"On my honor," Haviland said.

Ryde nodded. His eyes found Kit's finally. "Without honor," the earl quoted softly, "there is nothing. Perhaps that's a lesson I taught *too* well."

"No," Kit denied. There were so many things he should say to his father, he supposed, but he could not think how to word any of them in the face of what Ryde had done for him.

That his father had shot the gun from Haviland's hand went against every precept of honor Kit had ever been taught, and yet it also transcended them. *I won't let you kill my son to protect yours.* And it had been a very long time since he had heard that particular certainty in his father's voice.

"Take the coach," his father suggested. "They're still fresh enough for a run." The dark eyes gleamed again with amusement, but given the earl's next sentence, Kit wasn't sure exactly what had prompted it. "I'll ride back with your brother. I'm sure there are some *things* he wishes to discuss with me."

"Thank you, sir," Kit said. The fact that he was alive and would be allowed to remain alive was beginning to become a reality. How do you thank someone for again giving you life?

"I imagine she's waiting for you," his father said, his eyes strangely soft.

Kit nodded, his throat too thickened with emotion to answer, and then he began to walk toward his father's waiting carriage.

"And Kit," the earl said.

St. John turned back.

"Tell her I did it for *my* sake."

"Sir?" Kit asked.

"She'll understand. It seems she understands a great deal. More than I ever did," the earl said. He cleared the unfamiliar emotion from his voice. "Go on, boy. She was told this duel would take place tomorrow. But by now, of course…"

Again Kit nodded. And, giving in to an impulse he didn't pause to examine, he put his hand on his father's shoulder and squeezed it gently, exactly as he had Sergeant Cochran's.

The earl's eyes met his, and then his arms reached out, enclosing his younger son and holding him tightly against his chest for a moment before he stepped back.

"Go on," he ordered gruffly. "And Kit... Godspeed, my dear son."

It was General Haviland's housekeeper who explained to Judith why she couldn't see him. And when she had been turned away from his door, Judith sat a long time in the countess's phaeton, letting the scope of her error sink in. She had never even asked. Had never bothered to verify what she had been told. She had simply assumed the information Lady Marbury gave her was correct.

Now she knew that it was not. The duel she had come here to prevent had already taken place. This dawn and not tomorrow's. That was, of course, why Kit had left her. Why he had stolen away from the bed they shared last night without waking her.

"Home, my lady?" the coachman turned finally to ask.

Because she could think of nothing else she could do and nowhere she could go besides home, she nodded. Kit had been right last night, and she had been wrong. It had been too late, she thought, as the horses began to move. It had all come far too late.

Judith was not waiting for him as his father had suggested she would be. Kit had bounded up the stairs, taking them two at a time, finally beginning to realize that, thanks to his father, it really was all over. The long nightmare was at an end, and finally he and Judith...

He flung open the door, almost exactly as he had done last night, but she wasn't there. The bed was as he had left it. Shadowed. Disordered. And the letters he had written to his family were still on his desk.

Only one thing was missing. The small, infinitely precious body of his wife. He could not imagine where Judith had gone. It was still early enough that she couldn't have had an engagement. And his father had told him she believed the duel to be tomorrow, so it made no sense that she wasn't here where he had left her sleeping. Where else could she be?

When Judith pushed open the door, she saw him. He was standing by the long windows, and their light enriched the darkness of his hair and made the strong, handsome planes of his face almost luminescent when he turned.

Her eyes widened, but she didn't come into the room. Instead, she hesitated on the threshold trying to decide if the shadowed figure limned against the light was real. Or if he were only a figment of her desire. Her need.

All the way home she had remembered. How his body felt beneath her hands. How it tasted against her tongue. How it moved above hers in the darkness, teaching her things she had never dreamed existed between a man and a woman. Instructing her heart as well as her body.

Remembering it all. And then the image from the dream would intrude, thrusting into her mind with all its horror. She had not begun dealing with that. Her mind was numb, and that was how she wanted it. She had managed to maintain a distance from the agony all the way home, waiting to think again until she reached these rooms. And then...

He had said nothing. Surely if this were really Kit, and not something she had conjured up with her grief, then he would speak to her. One word. Her name. Something, surely, to let her know.

"Judith?" he said softly.

She took a breath. And then another. That had been his voice. There had been nothing extraordinary about it. A little puzzled perhaps. Questioning.

She blinked, because her eyes were burning, and was infinitely relieved to find that he was still there. She took a step into the room and then another. His cloak had been thrown over the chair, and it hadn't been there this morning when she had left. There had been no sign of Kit's presence in this room.

She put her fingers on top of it, moving them against the familiar coarseness of the wool. It was damp. An English morning's dampness. And then she remembered to take another breath. Almost acquiring again the familiar pattern and rhythm of breathing. Her eyes examined his body, tracing over it carefully, and then they returned to his face.

"I dreamed you were dead," she whispered. "And when I woke, you weren't here. I was so afraid, Kit. So I went to tell Michael's father the truth. And they said..." She took a shuddering breath, remembering the shock.

He smiled at her. "I told you there was nothing to be afraid of," he said softly, his voice comforting.

"And Michael's father? The duel, Kit? What about—"

"He's fine, my darling. And it's over, Judith. All of it's finally over."

It took a moment for the assurance to penetrate the sense of dread that had held her since she had awakened, alone, in this cold, dark room. "How can it be over?" she asked, wondering.

"Ryde said to tell you..." Kit hesitated, because he wasn't sure what his father's message was intended to convey, just as he couldn't be sure of what had passed between the earl and his wife.

They were the two people who had never deviated from the path of honor. At least never before. Until this morning. And they had both done what they had done for love of him.

"Ryde stopped the duel by shooting the pistol out of Haviland's hand," Kit explained. "He said to tell you that he did it for *his* sake, and that you would understand what he meant.''

''I had told him that what you intended today was done to protect him. Because you loved him so much that you couldn't bear to dishonor him. You were willing to die—for his sake.''

''Then...'' Again Kit hesitated, trying to understand.

''And today, Ryde also did what he did for *his* sake, Kit. Because he loved you more than his honor. He was willing to do anything, even destroy that cherished honor, to protect you.''

The impact of that realization was evident on the handsome features, and she hesitated to ask about the rest. What Kit had told her, however, didn't begin to explain why he believed the situation had been completely changed by his father's actions.

''What will General Haviland do now?'' she asked. ''Surely he will—''

''It's over, Judith,'' he said again. Simply. That was really all she needed to understand.

''Are you sure?''

''On my honor,'' he said, smiling at her. ''You have my word, my darling. And my father's.''

She shook her head slowly, but her eyes held his and in them began to grow what had not been there since she had left the general's door. Hope. Hope for the future neither of them had believed last night they would be allowed to share.

And now, it seemed, they would. Because a man who had lived his entire life by the rules and narrow conventions that he truly believed in had broken them. *For my sake*, Kit thought, unconsciously repeating his father's words which he hadn't understood.

''Then...'' she said softly.

"It's over," he said again, perhaps because he, too, was finding that hard to believe and to accept what it meant.

She came to him then and gave him her hands, just as she had last night. He took them and brought them both to his lips, pressing a kiss on the tips of her fingers.

My beloved wife Judith. Always. And now, truly, forever.

* * * * *

Please watch for Gayle Wilson's
NEVER LET HER GO,
a November 1998 release
from Harlequin Intrigue,
available in your local bookstore
this October.

Take 2 bestselling love stories FREE

Plus get a FREE surprise gift!

Special Limited-Time Offer

Mail to Harlequin Reader Service®

> P.O. Box 609
> Fort Erie, Ontario
> L2A 5X3

YES! Please send me 2 free Harlequin Historical™ novels and my free surprise gift. Then send me 4 brand-new novels every month, which I will receive before they appear in bookstores. Bill me at the low price of $4.19 each plus 25¢ delivery and GST*. That's the complete price, and a saving of over 10% off the cover prices—quite a bargain! I understand that accepting the books and gift places me under no obligation ever to buy any books. I can always return a shipment and cancel at any time. Even if I never buy another book from Harlequin, the 2 free books and the surprise gift are mine to keep forever.

347 HEN CH7M

Name _____ (PLEASE PRINT) _____

Address _____ Apt. No. _____

City _____ Province _____ Postal Code _____

This offer is limited to one order per household and not valid to present Harlequin Historical™ subscribers. *Terms and prices are subject to change without notice. Canadian residents will be charged applicable provincial taxes and GST.

CHIS-98 ©1990 Harlequin Enterprises Limited

COMING NEXT MONTH FROM
HARLEQUIN HISTORICALS